A SILVER CLASSIC

The Call of the Wild

and Other Stories

JACK LONDON

SILVER BURDETT COMPANY
Morristown, New Jersey
Glenview, Illinois • Palo Alto • Dallas • Atlanta

This edition contains the complete and unabridged 1903 text of *The Call of the Wild.*
The short stories are also complete and unabridged.

Acknowledgment Page G23: Excerpt from *American Fiction: An Historical and Critical Survey* by Arthur Hobson Quinn. Copyright © 1936 by Appleton-Century-Crofts. Reprinted by permission of Prentice-Hall, Inc., Englewood Cliffs, New Jersey.

Illustrations Page iv: Edward Malsberg. Page G2: Map "The Klondike" reprinted with permission of The Bodley Head from *The Bodley Head Jack London.*

Library of Congress Card Number 80-54135

ISBN 0-382-03434-1

THE SILVER CLASSICS

The Adventures of Tom Sawyer
MARK TWAIN

Treasure Island
ROBERT LOUIS STEVENSON

The Call of the Wild and Other Stories
JACK LONDON

Sherlock Holmes, Master Detective
ARTHUR CONAN DOYLE

Tales of Imagination and Suspense
ANTHOLOGY: 16 STORIES

Frankenstein
MARY SHELLEY

Classic Short Stories
ANTHOLOGY: 18 STORIES

Adventures of Huckleberry Finn
MARK TWAIN

The Red Badge of Courage and Other Favorites
STEPHEN CRANE

The Scarlet Letter
NATHANIEL HAWTHORNE

The Turn of the Screw and *Washington Square*
HENRY JAMES

A Tale of Two Cities
CHARLES DICKENS

CONTENTS

THE CALL OF THE WILD

1. Into the Primitive

Old longings nomadic leap,
Chafing at custom's chain;
Again from its brumal sleep
Wakens the ferine strain.

Buck did not read the newspapers, or he would have known that trouble was brewing, not alone for himself, but for every tidewater dog, strong of muscle and with warm, long hair, from Puget Sound to San Diego. Because men, groping in the Arctic darkness, had found a yellow metal, and because steamship and transportation companies were booming the find, thousands of men were rushing into the Northland. These men wanted dogs, and the dogs they wanted were heavy dogs, with strong muscles by which to toil, and furry coats to protect them from the frost.

Buck lived at a big house in the sun-kissed Santa Clara Valley. Judge Miller's place, it was called. It stood back from the road, half hidden among the trees, through which glimpses could be caught of the wide cool veranda that ran around its four sides. The house was approached by gravelled driveways which wound about through wide-spreading lawns and under the interlacing boughs of tall poplars. At the rear things were on even a more spacious scale than at the front. There were great stables, where a dozen grooms and boys held forth, rows of vine-clad servants' cottages, an endless and orderly array of outhouses, long grape arbors, green pastures, orchards, and berry patches. Then there was the pumping plant for the artesian well, and the big cement tank where Judge Miller's boys took their morning plunge and kept cool in the hot afternoon.

And over this great demesne Buck ruled. Here he was born, and here he had lived the four years of his life. It was true, there were other dogs. There could not but be other dogs on so vast a place, but they did not count. They came and went, resided in the populous kennels, or lived obscurely in the recesses of the house after the fashion of Toots, the Japanese pug, or Ysabel, the Mexican hairless—strange creatures that rarely put nose out of doors or set foot to ground. On the other hand, there were the fox terriers, a score of them at least, who yelped fearful promises at Toots and Ysabel looking out of the windows at them and protected by a legion of housemaids armed with brooms and mops.

But Buck was neither house-dog nor kennel dog. The whole realm was his. He plunged into the swimming tank or went hunting with the Judge's sons; he escorted Mollie and Alice, the Judge's daughters, on long twilight or early morning rambles; on wintry nights he lay at the Judge's feet before the roaring library fire; he carried the Judge's grandsons on his back, or rolled them in the grass, and guarded their footsteps through wild adventures down to the fountain in the stable yard, and even beyond, where the paddocks were, and the berry patches. Among the terriers he stalked imperiously, and Toots and Ysabel he utterly ignored, for he was king—king over all creeping, crawling, flying things of Judge Miller's place, humans included.

His father, Elmo, a huge St. Bernard, had been the Judge's inseparable companion, and Buck bid fair to follow in the way of his father. He was not so large—he weighed only one hundred and forty pounds—for his mother, Shep, had been a Scotch shepherd dog. Nevertheless, one hundred and forty pounds, to which was added the dignity that comes of good living and universal respect, enabled him to carry himself in right royal fashion. During the four years since his puppyhood he had lived the life of a sated aristocrat; he had a fine pride in himself, was ever a trifle egotistical, as country gentlemen sometimes become because of their insular situation. But he had saved himself by not becoming a mere pampered house-dog. Hunting and kindred outdoor delights had kept down the fat and hardened his muscles; and to him, as to the cold-tubbing races, the love of water had been a tonic and a health preserver.

And this was the manner of dog Buck was in the fall of 1897, when the Klondike strike dragged men from all the world into the frozen North. But Buck did not read the newspapers, and he did not know that Manuel, one of the gardener's helpers, was an undesirable acquaintance. Manuel had one besetting sin. He loved to play Chinese lottery. Also, in his gambling, he had one besetting weakness—faith in a system; and this made his damnation certain. For to play a system requires money, while the wages of a gardener's helper do not lap over the needs of a wife and numerous progeny.

The Judge was at a meeting of the Raisin Growers' Association, and the boys were busy organizing an athletic club, on the memorable night of Manuel's treachery. No one saw him and Buck go off through the orchard on what Buck imagined was merely a stroll. And with the exception of a solitary man, no one saw them arrive at the little flag station known as College Park. This man talked with Manuel, and money chinked between them.

"You might wrap up the goods before you deliver 'm," the stranger said gruffly, and Manuel doubled a piece of stout rope around Buck's neck under the collar.

"Twist it, an' you'll choke 'm plentee," said Manuel, and the stranger grunted a ready affirmative.

Buck had accepted the rope with quiet dignity. To be sure, it was an unwonted performance: but he had learned to trust in men he knew, and to give them credit for a wisdom that outreached his own. But when the ends of the rope were placed in the stranger's hands, he growled menacingly. He had merely intimated his displeasure, in his pride believing that to intimate was to command. But to his surprise the rope tightened around his neck, shutting off his breath. In quick rage he sprang at the man, who met him halfway, grappled him close by the throat, and with a deft twist threw him over on his back. Then the rope tightened mercilessly, while Buck struggled in a fury, his tongue lolling out of his mouth and his great chest panting futilely. Never in all his life had he been so vilely treated, and never in all his life had he been so angry. But his strength ebbed, his eyes glazed, and he knew nothing when the train was flagged and the two men threw him into the baggage car.

The next he knew, he was dimly aware that his tongue was hurting and that he was being jolted along in some kind of a conveyance. The hoarse shriek of a locomotive whistling a crossing told him where he was. He had travelled too often with the Judge not to know the sensation of riding in a baggage car. He opened his eyes, and into them came the unbridled anger of a kidnapped king. The man sprang for his throat, but Buck was too quick for him. His jaws closed on the hand, nor did they relax till his senses were choked out of him once more.

"Yep, has fits," the man said, hiding his mangled hand from the baggageman, who had been attracted by the sounds of struggle. "I'm takin' 'm up for the boss to 'Frisco. A crack dog-doctor there thinks that he can cure 'm."

Concerning that night's ride, the man spoke most eloquently for himself, in a little shed back of a saloon on the San Francisco water front.

"All I get is fifty for it," he grumbled; "an' I wouldn't do it over for a thousand, cold cash."

His hand was wrapped in a bloody handkerchief, and the right trouser leg was ripped from knee to ankle.

"How much did the other mug get?" the saloon-keeper demanded.

"A hundred," was the reply. "Wouldn't take a sou less, so help me."

"That makes a hundred and fifty," the saloon-keeper calculated; "and he's worth it, or I'm a squarehead."

The kidnapper undid the bloody wrappings and looked at his lacerated hand. "If I don't get the hydrophoby—"

"It'll be because you was born to hang," laughed the saloon-keeper. "Here lend me a hand before you pull your freight," he added.

Dazed, suffering intolerable pain from throat and tongue, with the life half throttled out of him, Buck attempted to face his tormentors. But he was thrown down and choked repeatedly, till they succeeded in filing the heavy brass collar from off his neck. Then the rope was removed, and he was flung into a cagelike crate.

There he lay for the remainder of the weary night, nursing his wrath and wounded pride. He could not understand what it all meant. What did they want with him, these strange men? Why were they keeping him pent up in this narrow crate? He did not know why, but he felt oppressed by the vague sense of impending calamity. Several times during the night he sprang to his feet when the shed door rattled open, expecting to see the Judge, or the boys at least. But each time it was the bulging face of the saloon-keeper that peered in at him by the sickly light of a tallow candle. And each time the joyful bark that trembled in Buck's throat was twisted into a savage growl.

But the saloon-keeper let him alone, and in the morning four men entered and picked up the crate. More tormentors, Buck decided, for they were evil-looking creatures, ragged and unkempt; and he stormed and raged at them through the bars. They only laughed and poked sticks at him, which he promptly assailed with his teeth till he realized that that was what they wanted. Whereupon he lay down sullenly and allowed the crate to be lifted into a wagon. Then he, and the crate in which he was imprisoned, began a passage through many hands. Clerks in the express office took charge of him; he was carted about in another wagon; a truck carried him, with an assortment of boxes and parcels, upon a ferry steamer; he was trucked off the steamer into a great railway depot, and finally he was deposited in an express car.

For two days and nights this express car was dragged along at the tail of shrieking locomotives; and for two days and nights Buck neither ate nor drank. In his anger he had met the first advances of the express messengers with growls, and they had retaliated by teasing him. When he flung himself against the bars, quivering and frothing, they laughed at him and taunted him. They growled and barked like detestable dogs, mewed, and flapped their arms and crowed. It was all very silly, he knew; but therefore the more outrage to his dignity, and his anger waxed and waxed. He did not mind the hunger so much, but the lack of water caused him severe suffering and fanned his wrath to fever pitch. For that matter, high-strung and finely sensitive, the ill treatment had flung him into a fever, which was fed by the inflammation of his parched and swollen throat and tongue.

He was glad for one thing: the rope was off his neck. That had given them an unfair advantage; but now that it was off, he would show them. They would never get another rope around his neck. Upon that he was resolved. For two days and nights he neither ate nor drank, and during those two days and nights of torment, he accumulated a fund of wrath that boded ill for whoever first fell foul of him. His eyes turned bloodshot, and he was metamorphosed into a raging fiend. So changed was he that the Judge himself would not have recognized him; and the express messengers breathed with relief when they bundled him off the train at Seattle.

Four men gingerly carried the crate from the wagon into a small, high-walled back yard. A stout man, with a red sweater that sagged generously at the neck, came out and signed the book for the driver. That was the man,

Buck divined, the next tormentor, and he hurled himself savagely against the bars. The man smiled grimly, and brought a hatchet and a club.

"You aint' going to take him out now?" the driver asked.

"Sure," the man replied, driving the hatchet into the crate for a pry.

There was an instantaneous scattering of the four men who had carried it in, and from safe perches on top the wall they prepared to watch the performance.

Buck rushed at the splintering wood, sinking his teeth into it, surging and wrestling with it. Wherever the hatchet fell on the outside, he was there on the inside, snarling and growling, as furiously anxious to get out as the man in the red sweater was calmly intent on getting him out.

"Now, you red-eyed devil," he said, when he had made an opening sufficient for the passage of Buck's body. At the same time he dropped the hatchet and shifted the club to his right hand.

And Buck was truly a red-eyed devil, as he drew himself together for the spring, hair bristling, mouth foaming, a mad glitter in his blood-shot eyes. Straight at the man he launched his one hundred and forty pounds of fury, surcharged with the pent passion of two days and nights. In mid air, just as his jaws were about to close on the man, he received a shock that checked his body and brought his teeth together with an agonizing clip. He whirled over, fetching the ground on his back and side. He had never been struck by a club in his life, and did not understand. With a snarl that was part bark and more scream he was again on his feet and launched into the air.

And again the shock came and he was brought crushingly to the ground. This time he was aware that it was the club, but his madness knew no caution. A dozen times he charged, and as often the club broke the charge and smashed him down.

After a particularly fierce blow he crawled to his feet, too dazed to rush. He staggered limply about, the blood flowing from nose and mouth and ears, his beautiful coat sprayed and flecked with bloody slaver. Then the man advanced and deliberately dealt him a frightful blow on the nose. All the pain he had endured was as nothing compared with the exquisite agony of this. With a roar that was almost lionlike in its ferocity, he again hurled himself at the man. But the man, shifting the club from right to left, coolly caught him by the under jaw, at the same time wrenching downward and backward. Buck described a complete circle in the air, and half of another, then crashed to the ground on his head and chest.

For the last time he rushed. The man struck the shrewd blow he had purposely withheld for so long, and Buck crumpled up and went down, knocked utterly senseless.

"He's no slouch at dog-breakin', that's wot I say," one of the men on the wall cried enthusiastically.

"Druther break cayuses any day, and twice on Sundays," was the reply of the driver, as he climbed on the wagon and started the horses.

Buck's senses came back to him, but not his strength. He lay where he had fallen, and from there he watched the man in the red sweater.

"'Answers to the name of Buck,'" the man soliloquized, quoting from the saloon-keeper's letter which had announced the consignment of the crate and contents. "Well, Buck, my boy," he went on in a genial voice, "we've had our little ruction, and the best thing we can do is to let it go at that. You've learned your place, and I know mine. Be a good dog and all 'll go well and the goose hang high. Be a bad dog, and I'll whale the stuffin' outa you. Understand?"

As he spoke he fearlessly patted the head he had so mercilessly pounded, and though Buck's hair involuntarily bristled at touch of the hand, he endured it without protest. When the man brought him water he drank eagerly, and later bolted a generous meal of raw meat, chunk by chunk, from the man's hand.

He was beaten (he knew that); but he was not broken. He saw, once for all, that he stood no chance against a man with a club. He had learned the lesson, and in all his after life he never forgot it. That club was a revelation. It was his introduction to the reign of primitive law, and he met the introduction halfway. The facts of life took on a fiercer aspect; and while he faced that aspect uncowed, he faced it with all the latent cunning of his nature aroused. As the days went by, other dogs came, in crates and at the ends of ropes, some docilely, and some raging and roaring as he had come; and, one and all, he watched them pass under the dominion of the man in the red sweater. Again and again, as he looked at each brutal performance, the lesson was driven home to Buck: a man with a club was a law-giver, a master to be obeyed, though not necessarily conciliated. Of this last Buck was never guilty, though he did see beaten dogs that fawned upon the man, and wagged their tails, and licked his hand. Also he saw one dog, that would neither conciliate nor obey, finally killed in the struggle for mastery.

Now and again men came, strangers, who talked excitedly, wheedlingly, and in all kinds of fashions to the man in the red sweater. And at such times that money passed between them the strangers took one or more of the dogs away with them. Buck wondered where they went, for they never came back; but the fear of the future was strong upon him, and he was glad each time when he was not selected.

Yet his time came, in the end, in the form of a little weazened man who spat broken English and many strange and uncouth exclamations which Buck could not understand.

"*Sacredam!*" he cried, when his eyes lit upon Buck. "Dat one dam bully dog! Eh? How moch?"

"Three hundred, and a present at that," was the prompt reply of the man in the red sweater. "And seein' it's government money, you ain't got no kick coming, eh, Perrault?"

Perrault grinned. Considering that the price of dogs had been boomed skyward by the unwonted demand, it was not an unfair sum for so fine an animal. The Canadian Government would be no loser, nor would its dispatches travel the slower. Perrault knew dogs, and when he looked at Buck he knew that he was one in a thousand—"One in ten t'ousand," he commented mentally.

Buck saw money pass between them, and was not surprised when Curly, a good-natured Newfoundland, and he were led away by the little weazened man. That was the last he saw of the man in the red sweater, and as Curly and he looked at receding Seattle from the deck of the *Narwhal*, it was the last he saw of the warm Southland. Curly and he were taken below by Perrault and turned over to a black-faced giant called François. Perrault was a French-Canadian, and swarthy; but François was a French-Canadian half-breed, and twice as swarthy. They were a new kind of men to Buck (of which he was destined to see many more), and while he developed no affection for them, he none the less grew honestly to respect them. He speedily learned that Perrault and François were fair men, calm and impartial in administering justice, and too wise in the way of dogs to be fooled by dogs.

In the 'tween-decks of the *Narwhal*, Buck and Curly joined two other dogs. One of them was a big, snow-white fellow from Spitzbergen who had been brought away by a whaling captain, and who had later accompanied a Geological Survey into the Barrens.

He was friendly, in a treacherous sort of way, smiling into one's face the while he meditated some underhand trick, as, for instance, when he stole from Buck's food at the first meal. As Buck sprang to punish him, the lash of François's whip sang through the air, reaching the culprit first; and nothing remained to Buck but to recover the bone. That was fair of François, he decided, and the half-breed began his rise in Buck's estimation.

The other dog made no advances, nor received any; also, he did not attempt to steal from the newcomers. He was a gloomy, morose fellow, and he showed Curly plainly that all he desired was to be left alone, and further, that there would be trouble if he were not left alone. "Dave" he was called, and he ate and slept, or yawned between times, and took interest in nothing, not even when the *Narwhal* crossed Queen Charlotte Sound and rolled and pitched and bucked like a thing possessed.

When Buck and Curly grew excited, half wild with fear, he raised his head as though annoyed, favored them with an incurious glance, yawned, and went to sleep again. 15

Day and night the ship throbbed to the tireless pulse of the propeller, and though one day was very like another, it was apparent to Buck that the weather was steadily growing colder. At last, one morning, the propeller was quiet, and the *Narwhal* was pervaded with an atmosphere of excitement. He felt it, as did the other dogs, and knew that a change was at hand. François leashed them and brought them on deck. At the first step upon the cold surface, Buck's feet sank into white mushy something very like mud. He sprang back with a snort. More of this white stuff was falling through the air. He shook himself, but more of it fell upon him. He sniffed it curiously, then licked some up on his tongue. It bit like fire, and the next instant was gone. This puzzled him. He tried it again, with the same result. The onlookers laughed uproariously, and he felt ashamed, he knew not why, for it was his first snow.

2. *The Law of Club and Fang*

Buck's first day on the Dyea beach was like a nightmare. Every hour was filled with shock and surprise. He had been suddenly jerked from the heart of civilization and flung into the heart of things primordial. No lazy, sun-kissed life was this, with nothing to do but loaf and be bored. Here was neither peace, nor rest, nor a moment's safety. All was confusion and action, and every moment life and limb were in peril. There was imperative need to be constantly alert; for these dogs and men were not town dogs and men. They were savages, all of them, who knew no law but the law of club and fang.

He had never seen dogs fight as these wolfish creatures fought, and his first experience taught him an unforgettable lesson. It is true, it was a vicarious experience, else he would not have lived to profit by it. Curly was the victim. They were camped near the log store, where she, in her friendly way, made advances to a husky dog the size of a full-grown wolf, though not half so large as she. There was no warning, only a leap in like a flash, a metallic clip of teeth, a leap out equally swift, and Curly's face was ripped open from eye to jaw.

It was the wolf manner of fighting, to strike and leap away; but there was more to it than this. Thirty or forty huskies ran to the spot and surrounded the combatants in an intent and silent circle. Buck did not comprehend that silent intentness, nor the eager way with which they were licking their chops. Curly rushed her antagonist, who struck again and leaped aside. He met her next rush with his chest, in a peculiar fashion that tumbled her off her feet. She never regained them. This was what the onlooking huskies had waited for. They closed in upon her, snarling and yelping, and she was buried, screaming with agony, beneath the bristling mass of bodies.

So sudden was it, and so unexpected, that Buck was taken aback. He saw Spitz run out his scarlet tongue in a way he had of laughing; and he saw François, swinging an axe, spring into the mess of dogs. Three men with clubs were helping him to scatter them. It did not take long. Two minutes from the time Curly went down, the last of her assailants were clubbed off. But she lay there limp and lifeless in the bloody, trampled snow, almost literally torn to pieces, the swart half-breed standing over her and cursing horribly. The scene often came back to Buck to trouble him in his sleep. So that was the way. No fair play. Once down, that was the end of you. Well, he would see to it that he never went down. Spitz ran out his tongue and laughed again, and from that moment Buck hated him with a bitter and deathless hatred.

Before he had recovered from the shock caused by the tragic passing of Curly, he received another shock. François fastened upon him an arrangement of straps and buckles. It was a harness, such as he had seen the grooms put on the horses at home. And as he had seen horses work, so he was set to work, hauling François on a sled to the forest that fringed the valley, and returning with a load of firewood. Though his dignity was sorely hurt by thus being made a draft animal, he was too wise to rebel.

18 He buckled down with a will and did his best, though it was all new and strange. François was stern, demanding instant obedience, and by virtue of his whip receiving instant obedience; while Dave, who was an experienced wheeler, nipped Buck's hind quarters whenever he was in error. Spitz was the leader, likewise experienced, and while he could not always get at Buck, he growled sharp reproof now and again, or cunningly threw his weight in the traces to jerk Buck into the way he should go. Buck learned easily, and under the combined tuition of his two mates and François made remarkable progress. Ere they returned to camp he knew enough to stop at "ho," to go ahead at "mush," to swing wide on the bends, and to keep clear of the wheeler when the loaded sled shot downhill at their heels.

"T'ree vair' good dogs," François told Perrault. "Dat Buck, heem pool lak hell. I tich heem queek as anyt'ing."

By afternoon, Perrault, who was in a hurry to be on the trail with his dispatches, returned with two more dogs. "Billee" and "Joe," he called them, two brothers, and true huskies both. Sons of the one mother though they were, they were as different as day and night. Billee's one fault was his excessive good nature, while Joe was the very opposite, sour and introspective, with a perpetual snarl and a malignant eye. Buck received them in comradely fashion, Dave ignored them, while Spitz proceeded to thrash first one and then the other. Billee wagged his tail appeasingly, turned to run when he saw that appeasement was of no avail, and cried (still appeasingly) when Spitz's sharp teeth scored his flank. But no matter how Spitz circled, Joe whirled around on his heels to face him, mane bristling, ears laid back, lips writhing and snarling, jaws clipping together as fast as he could snap, and eyes diabolically gleaming—the incarnation of belligerent fear. So terrible was his appearance that Spitz was forced to forego disciplining him; but to cover his own discomfiture he turned upon the inoffensive and wailing Billee and drove him to the confines of the camp.

By evening Perrault secured another dog, an old husky, long and lean and gaunt, with a battle-scarred face and a single eye which flashed a warning of prowess that commanded respect. He was called Sol-leks, which means the Angry One. Like Dave, he asked nothing, gave nothing, expected nothing; and when he marched slowly and deliberately into their midst, even Spitz left him alone. He had one peculiarity which Buck was unlucky enough to discover. He did not like to be approached on his blind side. Of this offence Buck was unwittingly guilty, and the first knowledge he had of his indiscretion was when Sol-leks, whirled upon him and slashed his shoulder to the bone for three inches up and down. Forever after Buck avoided his blind side, and to the last of their comradeship had no more trouble. His only apparent ambition, like Dave's, was to be left alone, though, as Buck was afterward to learn, each of them possessed one other and even more vital ambition.

That night Buck faced the great problem of sleeping. The tent, illuminated by a candle, glowed warmly in the midst of the white plain; and when he, as a matter of course, entered it, both Perrault and François bombarded him with curses and cooking utensils, till he recovered from his consternation and fled ignominiously into the outer cold. A chill wind was blowing that nipped him sharply and bit with especial venom into his wounded shoulder. He lay down on the snow and attempted to sleep, but the frost soon drove him shivering to his feet. Miserable and disconsolate, he wandered about among the many tents, only to find that one place was as cold as another. Here and there savage dogs rushed upon him, but he bristled his neck hair and snarled (for he was learning fast), and they let him go his way unmolested.

Finally an idea came to him. He would return and see how his own team mates were making out. To his astonishment, they had disappeared. Again he wandered about through the great camp, looking for them, and again he returned. Were they in the tent? No, that could not be, else he would not have been driven out. Then where could they possibly be? With drooping tail and shivering body, very forlorn indeed, he aimlessly circled the tent. Suddenly the snow gave way beneath his fore legs and he sank down. Something wriggled under his feet. He sprang back, bristling and snarling, fearful of the unseen and unknown. But a friendly little yelp reassured him, and he went back to investigate. A whiff of warm air ascended to his nostrils, and there, curled up under the snow in a snug ball, lay Billee. He whined placatingly, squirmed and wriggled to show his good will and intentions, and even ventured, as a bribe for peace, to lick Buck's face with his warm wet tongue.

Another lesson. So that was the way they did it, eh? Buck confidently selected a spot, and with much fuss and waste effort proceeded to dig a hole for himself. In a trice the heat from his body filled the confined space and he was asleep. The day had been long and arduous, and he slept soundly and comfortably, though he growled and barked and wrestled with bad dreams.

Nor did he open his eyes till roused by the noises of the waking camp. At first he did not know where he was. It had snowed during the night and he was completely buried. The snow walls pressed him on every side, and a great surge of fear swept through him—the fear of the wild thing for the trap. It was a token that he was harking back through his own life to the lives of his forebears, for he was a civilized dog, an unduly civilized dog and of his own experience knew no trap and so could not of himself fear it. The muscles of his whole body contracted spasmodically and instinctively, the hair on his neck and shoulders stood on end, and with a ferocious snarl he bounded straight up into the blinding day, the snow flying about him in a flashing cloud. Ere he landed on his feet, he saw the white camp spread out before him and knew where he was and remembered all that had passed from the time he went for a stroll with Manuel to the hole he had dug for himself the night before.

A shout from François hailed his appearance. "Wot I say?" the dog driver cried to Perrault. "Dat Buck for sure learn queek as anyt'ing."

Perrault nodded gravely. As courier for the Canadian Government, bearing important dispatches, he was anxious to secure the best dogs, and he was particularly gladdened by the possession of Buck.

Three more huskies were added to the team inside an hour, making a total of nine, and before another quarter of an hour had passed they were in harness and swinging up the trail toward the Dyea Cañon. Buck was glad to be gone, and though the work was hard he found he did not particularly despise it. He was surprised at the eagerness

22 which animated the whole team and which was communicated to him; but still more surprising was the change wrought in Dave and Sol-leks. They were new dogs, utterly transformed by the harness. All passiveness and unconcern had dropped from them. They were alert and active, anxious that the work should go well, and fiercely irritable with whatever, by delay or confusion, retarded that work. The toil of the traces seemed the supreme expression of their being, and all that they lived for and the only thing in which they took delight.

Dave was wheeler or sled dog, pulling in front of him was Buck, then came Sol-leks; the rest of the team was strung out ahead, single file, to the leader, which position was filled by Spitz.

Buck had been purposely placed between Dave and Sol-leks so that he might receive instruction. Apt scholar that he was, they were equally apt teachers, never allowing him to linger long in error, and enforcing their teaching with their sharp teeth. Dave was fair and very wise. He never nipped Buck without cause, and he never failed to nip him when he stood in need of it. As François's whip backed him up, Buck found it to be cheaper to mend his ways than to retaliate. Once, during a brief halt, when he got tangled in the traces and delayed the start, both Dave and Sol-leks flew at him and administered a sound trouncing. The resulting tangle was even worse, but Buck took good care to keep the traces clear thereafter; and ere the day was done, so well had he mastered his work, his mates about ceased nagging him. François's whip snapped less frequently, and Perrault even honored Buck by lifting up his feet and carefully examining them.

It was a hard day's run, up the cañon, through Sheep

Camp, past the Scales and the timber line, across glaciers and snowdrifts hundreds of feet deep, and over the great Chilkoot Divide, which stands between the salt water and the fresh and guards forbiddingly the sad and lonely North. They made good time down the chain of lakes which fills the craters of extinct volcanoes, and late that night pulled into the huge camp at the head of Lake Bennett, where thousands of goldseekers were building boats against the breakup of the ice in the spring. Buck made his hole in the snow and slept the sleep of the exhausted just, but all too early was routed out in the cold darkness and harnessed with his mates to the sled.

That day they made forty miles, the trail being packed; but the next day, and for many days to follow, they broke their own trail, worked harder, and made poorer time. As a rule, Perrault travelled ahead of the team, packing the snow with webbed shoes to make it easier for them. François, guiding the sled at the gee-pole, sometimes exchanged places with him but not often. Perrault was in a hurry, and he prided himself on his knowledge of ice, which knowledge was indispensable, for the fall ice was very thin, and where there was swift water, there was no ice at all.

Day after day, for days unending, Buck toiled in the traces. Always, they broke camp in the dark, and the first gray of dawn found them hitting the trail with fresh miles reeled off behind them. And always they pitched camp after dark, eating their bit of fish, and crawling to sleep into the snow. Buck was ravenous. The pound and a half of sun-dried salmon, which was his ration for each day, seemed to go nowhere. He never had enough, and suffered from perpetual hunger pangs. Yet the other dogs, because they weighed less and were born to the life, received a pound only of the fish and managed to keep in good condition.

He swiftly lost the fastidiousness which had characterized his old life. A dainty eater, he found that his mates, finishing first, robbed him of his unfinished ration. There was no defending it. While he was fighting off two or three, it was disappearing down the throats of the others. To remedy this, he ate as fast as they; and, so greatly did hunger compel him, he was not above taking what did not belong to him. He watched and learned. When he saw Pike, one of the new dogs, a clever malingerer and thief, slyly steal a slice of bacon when Perrault's back was turned, he duplicated the performance the following day, getting away with the whole chunk. A great uproar was raised, but he was unsuspected, while Dub, an awkward blunderer who was always getting caught, was punished for Buck's misdeed.

This first theft marked Buck as fit to survive in the hostile Northland environment. It marked his adaptability, his capacity to adjust himself to changing conditions, the lack of which would have meant swift and terrible death. It marked, further, the decay or going to pieces of his moral nature, a vain thing and a handicap in the ruthless struggle for existence. It was all well enough in the Southland, under the law of love and fellowship, to respect private property and personal feelings; but in the Northland, under the law of club and fang, whoso took such things into account was a fool, and in so far as he observed them he would fail to prosper.

Not that Buck reasoned it out. He was fit, that was all,

and unconsciously he accommodated himself to the new mode of life. All his days, no matter what the odds, he had never run from a fight. But the club of the man in the red sweater had beaten into him a more fundamental and primitive code. Civilized, he could have died for a moral consideration, say the defense of Judge Miller's riding whip; but the completeness of his decivilization was now evidenced by his ability to flee from the defense of a moral consideration and so save his hide. He did not steal for joy of it, but because of the clamor of his stomach. He did not rob openly, but stole secretly and cunningly, out of respect for club and fang. In short, the things he did were done because it was easier to do them than not to do them.

His development (or retrogression) was rapid. His muscles became hard as iron and he grew callous to all ordinary pain. He achieved an internal as well as external economy. He could eat anything, no matter how loathsome or indigestible; and, once eaten, the juices of his stomach extracted the last least particle of nutriment; and his blood carried it to the farthest reaches of his body, building it into the toughest and stoutest of tissues. Sight and scent became remarkably keen, while his hearing developed such acuteness that in his sleep he heard the faintest sound and knew whether it heralded peace or peril. He learned to bite the ice out with his teeth when it collected between his toes; and when he was thirsty and there was a thick scum of ice over the water hole, he would break it by rearing and striking it with stiff fore legs. His most conspicuous trait was an ability to scent the wind and forecast it a night in advance. No matter how breathless the air when he dug his nest by tree or bank, the wind that later blew inevitably found him to leeward, sheltered and snug.

And not only did he learn by experience, but instincts long dead became alive again. The domesticated generations fell from him. In vague ways he remembered back to the youth of the breed, to the time the wild dogs ranged in packs through the primeval forest, and killed their meat as they ran it down. It was no task for him to learn to fight with cut and slash and the quick wolf snap. In this manner had fought forgotten ancestors. They quickened the old life within him, and the old tricks which they had stamped into the heredity of the breed were his tricks. They came to him without effort or discovery, as though they had been his always. And when, on the still cold nights, he pointed his nose at a star and howled long and wolflike, it was his ancestors, dead and dust, pointing nose at star and howling down through the centuries and through him. And his cadences were their cadences, the cadences which voiced their woe and what to them was the meaning of the stillness, and the cold, and dark.

Thus, as token of what a puppet thing life is, the ancient song surged through him and he came into his own again; and he came because men had found a yellow metal in the North, and because Manuel was a gardener's helper whose wages did not lap over the needs of his wife and divers small copies of himself.

3. *The Dominant Primordial Beast*

The dominant primordial beast was strong in Buck, and under the fierce conditions of trail life it grew and grew. Yet it was a secret growth. His new-born cunning gave him poise and control. He was too busy adjusting himself to the new life to feel at ease, and not only did he not pick fights, but he avoided them whenever possible. A certain deliberateness characterized his attitude. He was not prone to rashness and precipitate action; and in the bitter hatred between him and Spitz he betrayed no impatience, shunned all offensive acts.

On the other hand, possibly because he divined in Buck a dangerous rival, Spitz never lost an opportunity of showing his teeth. He even went out of his way to bully Buck, striving constantly to start the fight which could end only in the death of one or the other.

Early in the trip this might have taken place had it not been for an unwonted accident. At the end of this day they made a bleak and miserable camp on the shore of Lake Laberge. Driving snow, a wind that cut like a white-hot knife, and darkness, had forced them to grope for a camping place. They could hardly have fared worse. At their backs rose a perpendicular wall of rock, and Perrault and François were compelled to make their fire and spread their sleeping robes on the ice of the lake itself. The tent they had discarded at Dyea in order to travel light. A few sticks of driftwood furnished them with a fire that thawed down through the ice and left them to eat supper in the dark.

Close in under the sheltering rock Buck made his nest. So snug and warm was it, that he was loath to leave it when François distributed the fish which he had first thawed over the fire. But when Buck finished his ration and returned, he found his nest occupied. A warning snarl told him that the trespasser was Spitz. Till now Buck had avoided trouble with his enemy, but this was too much. The beast in him roared. He sprang upon Spitz with a fury which surprised them both, and Spitz particularly, for his whole experience with Buck had gone to teach him that his rival was an unusually timid dog, who managed to hold his own only because of his great weight and size.

François was surprised, too, when they shot out in a tangle from the disrupted nest and he divined the cause of the trouble. "A-a-ah!" he cried to Buck. "Gif it to heem, by Gar! Gif it to heem, the dirty t'eef!"

Spitz was equally willing. He was crying with sheer rage and eagerness as he circled back and forth for a chance to spring in. Buck was no less eager, and no less cautious, as he likewise circled back and forth for the advantage. But it was then that the unexpected happened, the thing which projected their struggle for supremacy far into the future, past many a weary mile of trail and toil.

An oath from Perrault, the resounding impact of a club upon a bony frame, and a shrill yelp of pain, heralded the breaking forth of pandemonium. The camp was suddenly discovered to be alive with skulking furry forms,—starving huskies, four or five score of them, who had scented the camp from some Indian village. They had crept in while Buck and Spitz were fighting, and when the two men sprang among them with stout clubs they showed their teeth and fought back. They were crazed by the smell of the food. Perrault found one with head buried in the grub-box. His club landed heavily on the gaunt ribs, and the grub-box was capsized on the ground. On the instant a score of the famished brutes were scrambling for the bread and bacon. The clubs fell upon them unheeded. They yelped and howled under the rain of blows, but struggled none the less madly till the last crumb had been devoured.

In the meantime the astonished team-dogs had burst out of their nests only to be set upon by the fierce invaders. Never had Buck seen such dogs. It seemed as though their bones would burst through their skins. They were mere skeletons, draped loosely in draggled hides, with blazing eyes and slavered fangs. But the hunger-madness made them terrifying, irresistible. There was no opposing them. The team-dogs were swept back against the cliff at the first onset. Buck was beset by three huskies, and in a trice his head and shoulders were ripped and slashed. The din was frightful. Billee was crying as usual. Dave and Sol-leks, dripping blood from a score of wounds, were fighting bravely side by side. Joe was snapping like a demon. Once, his teeth closed on the fore leg of a husky, and he crunched down through the bone. Pike, the malingerer, leaped upon the crippled animal, breaking its neck with a quick dash of teeth and a jerk. Buck got a frothing adversary by the throat, and was sprayed with blood when his teeth sank through the jugular. The warm taste of it in his mouth goaded him to greater fierceness. He flung himself upon another, and at the same time felt teeth sink into his own throat. It was Spitz treacherously attacking from the side.

Perrault and François, having cleaned out their part of the camp, hurried to save their sled dogs. The wild wave of famished beasts rolled back before them, and Buck shook himself free. But it was only for a moment. The two men were compelled to run back to save the grub, upon which the huskies returned to the attack on the team. Billee, terrified into bravery, sprang through the savage circle and fled away over the ice. Pike and Dub followed on his heels, with the rest of the team behind. As Buck drew himself together to spring after them, out of the tail of his eye he saw Spitz rush upon him with the evident intention of overthrowing him. Once off his feet and under that mass of huskies, there was no hope for him. But he braced himself to the shock of Spitz's charge, then joined the flight out on the lake.

Later, the nine team-dogs gathered together and sought shelter in the forest. Though unpursued, they were in a sorry plight. There was not one who was not wounded in four or five places, while some were wounded grievously. Dub was badly injured in a hind leg; Dolly, the last husky added to the team at Dyea, had a badly torn throat; Joe had lost an eye; while Billee, the good-natured, with an ear chewed and rent to ribbons, cried and whimpered throughout the night. At daybreak they limped warily back to camp, to find the marauders gone and the two men in bad tempers. Fully half their grub supply was gone. The huskies had chewed through the sled lashings and canvas coverings. In fact, nothing, no matter how remotely eatable, had escaped them. They had eaten a pair of Perrault's moose-hide moccasins, chunks out of the leather traces, and even two feet of lash from the end of François's whip. He broke from a mournful contemplation of it to look over his wounded dogs.

"Ah, my frien's," he said softly, "mebbe it mek you mad dog, dose many bites. Mebbe all mad dog, *sacredam!* Wot you t'ink, eh, Perrault?"

The courier shook his head dubiously. With four hundred miles of trail still between him and Dawson, he could ill afford to have madness break out among his dogs. Two hours of cursing and exertion got the harnesses into shape, and the wound-stiffened team was under way, struggling painfully over the hardest part of the trail they had yet encountered, and for that matter, the hardest between them and Dawson.

The Thirtymile River was wide open. Its wild water defied the frost, and it was in the eddies only and in the quiet places that the ice held at all. Six days of exhausting toil were required to cover those thirty terrible miles. And terrible they were, for every foot of them was accomplished at the risk of life to dog and man. A dozen times, Perrault, nosing the way, broke through the ice bridges, being saved by the long pole he carried, which he so held that it fell each time across the hole made by his body. But a cold snap was on, the thermometer registering fifty below zero, and each time he broke through he was compelled for very life to build a fire and dry his garments.

Nothing daunted him. It was because nothing daunted him that he had been chosen for government courier. He took all manner of risks, resolutely thrusting his little weazened face into the frost and struggling on from dim dawn to dark. He skirted the frowning shores on rim ice that bent and crackled under foot and on which they dared not halt. Once, the sled broke through, with Dave and Buck, and they were half-frozen and all but drowned by the time they were dragged out. The usual fire was necessary to save them. They were coated solidly with ice, and the two men kept them on the run around the fire, sweating and thawing, so close that they were singed by the flames.

At another time Spitz went through, dragging the whole team after him up to Buck, who strained backward with all his strength, his fore paws on the slippery edge and the ice quivering and snapping all around. But behind him was Dave, likewise straining backward, and behind the sled was François, pulling till his tendons cracked.

Again, the rim ice broke away before and behind, and there was no escape except up the cliff. Perrault scaled it by a miracle, while François prayed for just that miracle; and with every thong and sledlashing and the last bit of harness rove into a long rope, the dogs were hoisted, one by one, to the cliff crest. François came up last, after the sled and load. Then came the search for a place to descend, which decent was ultimately made by the aid of the rope, and night found them back on the river with a quarter of a mile to the day's credit.

By the time they made the Hootalinqua and good ice, Buck was played out. The rest of the dogs were in like condition; but Perrault, to make up lost time, pushed them late and early. The first day they covered thirty-five miles to the Big Salmon; the next day thirty-five more to the Little Salmon; the third day forty miles, which brought them well up toward the Five Fingers.

Buck's feet were not so compact and hard as the feet of the huskies. His had softened during the many generations since the day his last wild ancestor was tamed by a cave dweller or river man. All day long he limped in agony, and camp once made, lay down like a dead dog. Hungry as he was, he would not move to receive his ration of fish, which François had to bring to him. Also, the dog-driver rubbed Buck's feet for half an hour each night after supper, and sacrificed the tops of his own moccasins to make four moccasins for Buck. This was a great relief, and Buck caused even the weazened face of Perrault to twist itself into a grin one morning, when François forgot the moccasins and Buck lay on his back, his four feet waving appealingly in the air, and refused to budge without them. Later his feet grew hard to the trail, and the worn-out foot-gear was thrown away.

At the Pelly one morning, as they were harnessing up, Dolly, who had never been conspicuous for anything, went suddenly mad. She announced her condition by a long, heartbreaking wolf howl that sent every dog bristling with fear, then sprang straight for Buck. He had never seen a dog go mad, nor did he have any reason to fear madness; yet he knew that here was horror, and fled away from it in panic. Straight away he raced, with Dolly, panting and frothing, one leap behind; nor could she gain on him, so great was his terror, nor could he leave her, so great was her madness. He plunged through the wooded breast of the island, flew down to the lower end, crossed a back channel filled with rough ice to another island, gained a third island, curved back to the main river, and in desperation started to cross it. And all the time, though he did not look, he could hear her snarling just one leap behind. François called to him a quarter of a mile away and he doubled back, still one leap ahead, gasping painfully for air and putting all his faith in that François would save him. The dog-driver held the axe poised in his hand, and as Buck shot past him the axe crashed down upon mad Dolly's head.

Buck staggered over against the sled, exhausted, sobbing for breath, helpless. This was Spitz's opportunity. He sprang upon Buck, and twice his teeth sank into his unresisting foe and ripped and tore the flesh to the bone. Then François's lash descended, and Buck had the satisfaction of watching Spitz receive the worst whipping as yet administered to any of the team.

"One devil, dat Spitz," remarked Perrault. "Some dam day heem keel dat Buck."

"Dat Buck two devils," was François's rejoinder. "All de tam I watch dat Buck I know for sure. Lissen: some dam fine day heem get mad lak hell an' den heem chew dat Spitz all up an' spit heem out on de snow. Sure. I know."

From then on it was war between them. Spitz, as lead dog and acknowledged master of the team, felt his supremacy threatened by this strange Southland dog. And strange Buck was to him, for of the many Southland dogs he had known, not one had shown up worthily in camp and on the trail. They were all too soft, dying under the toil, the frost, and starvation. Buck was the exception. He alone endured and prospered, matching the husky in strength, savagery, and cunning. Then he was a masterful dog, and what made him dangerous was the fact that the club of the man in the red sweater had knocked all blind pluck and rashness out of his desire for mastery. He was preeminently cunning, and could bide his time with a patience that was nothing less than primitive.

It was inevitable that the clash for leadership should come. Buck wanted it. He wanted it because it was his nature, because he had been gripped tight by that nameless, incomprehensible pride of the trail and trace—that pride which holds dogs in the toil to the last gasp, which lures them to die joyfully in the harness, and breaks their hearts if they are cut out of the harness. This was the pride of Dave as wheeldog, of Sol-leks as he pulled with all his strength; the pride that laid hold of them at break of camp, transforming them from sour and sullen brutes into straining, eager, ambitious creatures; the pride that spurred them on all day and dropped them at pitch of camp at night, letting them fall into gloomy unrest and uncontent. This was the pride that bore up Spitz and made him thrash the sled dogs who blundered and shirked in the traces or hid away at harness-up time in the morning. Likewise it was this pride that made him fear Buck as a possible lead-dog. And this was Buck's pride, too.

He openly threatened the other's leadership. He came between him and the shirks he should have punished. And he did it deliberately. One night there was a heavy snowfall, and in the morning Pike, the malingerer, did not appear. He was securely hidden in his nest under a foot of snow. François called him and sought him in vain. Spitz was wild with wrath. He raged through the camp, smelling and digging in every likely place, snarling so frightfully that Pike heard and shivered in his hiding-place.

But when he was at last unearthed, and Spitz flew at him to punish him, Buck flew, with equal rage, in between. So unexpected was it, and so shrewdly managed, that Spitz was hurled backward and off his feet. Pike, who had been trembling abjectly, took heart at this open mutiny, and sprang upon his overthrown leader. Buck, to whom fair play was a forgotten code, likewise sprang upon Spitz. But François, chuckling at the incident while unswerving in the administration of justice, brought his lash down upon Buck with all his might. This failed to drive Buck from his prostrate rival, and the butt of the whip was brought into play. Half-stunned by the blow, Buck was knocked backward and the lash laid upon him again and again, while Spitz soundly punished the many times offending Pike.

In the days that followed, as Dawson grew closer and closer, Buck still continued to interfere between Spitz and the culprits; but he did it craftily, when François was not around. With the covert mutiny of Buck, a general insubordination sprang up and increased. Dave and Solleks were unaffected, but the rest of the team went from bad to worse. Things no longer went right. There was continual bickering and jangling. Trouble was always afoot, and at the bottom of it was Buck. He kept François busy, for the dog-driver was in constant apprehension of the life-and-death struggle between the two which he knew must take place sooner or later; and on more than one night the sounds of quarrelling and strife among the other dogs turned him out of his sleeping robe, fearful that Buck and Spitz were at it.

But the opportunity did not present itself, and they pulled into Dawson one dreary afternoon with the great fight still to come. Here were many men, and countless dogs, and Buck found them all at work. It seemed the ordained order of things that dogs should work. All day they swung up and down the main street in long teams, and in the night their jingling bells still went by. They hauled cabin logs and firewood, freighted up to the mines, and did all manner of work that horses did in the Santa Clara Valley. Here and there Buck met Southland dogs, but in the main they were the wild wolf husky breed. Every night, regularly, at nine, at twelve, at three, they lifted a nocturnal song, a weird and eerie chant, in which it was Buck's delight to join.

With the aurora borealis flaming coldly overhead, or the stars leaping in the frost dance, and the land numb and frozen under its pall of snow, this song of the huskies might have been the defiance of life, only it was pitched in minor key, with long-drawn wailings and half-sobs, and was more the pleading of life, the articulate travail of existence. It was an old song, old as the breed itself—one of the first songs of the younger world in a day when songs were sad. It was invested with the woe of unnumbered generations, this plaint by which Buck was so strangely stirred. When he moaned and sobbed, it was with the pain of living that was of old the pain of his wild fathers, and the fear and mystery of the cold and dark that was to them fear and mystery. And that he should be stirred by it marked the completeness with which he harked back through the ages of fire and roof to the raw beginnings of life in the howling ages.

Seven days from the time they pulled into Dawson, they dropped down the steep bank by the Barracks to the Yukon Trail, and pulled for Dyea and Salt Water. Perrault was carrying dispatches if anything more urgent than those he had brought in; also, the travel pride had gripped him, and he purposed to make the record trip of the year. Several things favored him in this. The week's rest had recuperated the dogs and put them in thorough trim. The trail they had broken into the country was packed hard by later journeyers. And further, the police had arranged in two or three places deposits of grub for dog and man, and he was travelling light.

They made Sixtymile, which is a fifty-mile run, on the first day; and the second day saw them booming up the Yukon well on their way to Pelly. But such splendid running was achieved not without great trouble and vexation on the part of François. The insidious revolt led by Buck had destroyed the solidarity of the team. It no longer was as one dog leaping in the traces. The encouragement Buck gave the rebels led them into all kinds of petty misdemeanors. No more was Spitz a leader greatly to be feared. The old awe departed, and they grew equal to challenging his authority. Pike robbed him of half a fish one night, and gulped it down under the protection of Buck. Another night Dub and Joe fought Spitz and made him forego the punishment they deserved. And even Billee, the good-natured, was less good-natured, and whined not half so placatingly as in former days. Buck never came near Spitz without snarling and bristling menacingly. In fact, his conduct approached that of a bully, and he was given to swaggering up and down before Spitz's very nose.

The breaking down of discipline likewise affected the dogs in their relations with one another. They quarrelled and bickered more than ever among themselves, till at times the camp was a howling bedlam. Dave and Sol-leks alone were unaltered, though they were made irritable by the unending squabbling. François swore strange barbarous oaths, and stamped the snow in futile rage, and tore his hair. His lash was always singing among the dogs, but it was of small avail. Directly his back was turned they were at it again. He backed up Spitz with his whip, while Buck backed up the remainder of the team. François knew he was behind all the trouble, and Buck knew he knew; but Buck was too clever ever again to be caught red-handed. He worked faithfully in the harness, for the toil had become a delight to him; yet it was a greater delight slyly to precipitate a fight amongst his mates and tangle the traces.

At the mouth of the Takhini, one night after supper, Dub turned up a snowshoe rabbit, blundered it, and missed. In a second the whole team was in full cry. A hundred yards away was a camp of the Northwest Police, with fifty dogs, huskies all, who joined the chase. The rabbit sped down the river, turned off into a small creek, up the frozen bed of which it held steadily. It ran lightly on the surface of the snow, while the dogs ploughed through by main strength. Buck led the pack, sixty strong, around bend after bend, but he could not gain. He lay down low to the race, whining eagerly, his splendid body flashing forward, leap by leap, in the wan white moonlight. And leap by leap, like some pale frost wraith, the snowshoe rabbit flashed on ahead.

All that stirring of old instincts which at stated periods drives men out from the sounding cities to forest and plain to kill things by chemically propelled leaden pellets, the blood lust, the joy to kill—all this was Buck's, only it was infinitely more intimate. He was ranging at the head of the pack, running the wild thing down, the living meat, to kill with his own teeth and wash his muzzle to the eyes in warm blood.

There is an ecstasy that marks the summit of life, and beyond which life cannot rise. And such is the paradox of living, this ecstasy comes when one is most alive, and it comes as a complete forgetfulness that one is alive. This ecstasy, this forgetfulness of living, comes to the artist, caught up and out of himself in a sheet of flame; it comes to the soldier, war-mad on a stricken field and refusing quarter; and it came to Buck, leading the pack, sounding the old wolf cry, straining after the food that was alive and that fled swiftly before him through the moonlight. He was sounding the deeps of his nature, and of the parts of his nature that were deeper than he, going back into the womb of Time. He was mastered by the sheer surging of life, the tidal wave of being, the perfect joy of each separate muscle, joint, and sinew and that it was everything that was not death, that it was aglow and rampant, expressing itself in movement, flying exultantly under the stars and over the face of dead matter that did not move.

But Spitz, cold and calculating even in his supreme moods, left the pack and cut across a narrow neck of land where the creek made a long bend around. Buck did not know of this, and as he rounded the bend, the frost wraith of a rabbit still flitting before him, he saw another and larger frost wraith leap from the overhanging bank into the immediate path of the rabbit. It was Spitz. The rabbit could not turn, and as the white teeth broke its back in mid air it shrieked as loudly as a stricken man may shriek. At sound of this, the cry of Life plunging down from Life's apex in the grip of Death, the full pack at Buck's heels raised a hell's chorus of delight.

Buck did not cry out. He did not check himself, but drove in upon Spitz, shoulder to shoulder, so hard that he missed the throat. They rolled over and over in the powdery snow. Spitz gained his feet almost as though he had not been overthrown, slashing Buck down the shoulder and leaping clear. Twice his teeth clipped together, like the steel jaws of a trap, as he backed away for better footing, with lean and lifting lips that writhed and snarled.

In a flash Buck knew it. The time had come. It was to the death. As they circled about, snarling, ears laid back, keenly watchful for the advantage, the scene came to Buck with a sense of familiarity. He seemed to remember it all—the white woods, and earth, and moonlight, and the thrill of battle. Over the whiteness and silence brooded a ghostly calm. There was not the faintest whisper of air—nothing moved, not a leaf quivered, the visible breaths of the dogs rising slowly and lingering in the frosty air. They had made short work of the snowshoe rabbit, these dogs that were ill-tamed wolves; and they were now drawn up in an expectant circle. They, too, were silent, their eyes only gleaming and their breaths drifting slowly upward. To Buck it was nothing new or strange, this scene of old time. It was as though it had always been, the wonted way of things.

Spitz was a practised fighter. From Spitzbergen through the Arctic, and across Canada and the Barrens, he had held his own with all manner of dogs and achieved to mastery over them. Bitter rage was his, but never blind rage. In passion to rend and destroy, he never forgot that his enemy was in like passion to rend and destroy. He never rushed till he was prepared to receive a rush; never attacked till he had first defended that attack.

In vain Buck strove to sink his teeth in the neck of the big white dog. Wherever his fangs struck for the softer flesh, they were countered by the fangs of Spitz. Fang clashed fang, and lips were cut and bleeding, but Buck could not penetrate his enemy's guard. Then he warmed up and enveloped Spitz in a whirlwind of rushes. Time and time again he tried for the snow-white throat, where life bubbled near to the surface, and each time and every time Spitz slashed him and got away. Then Buck took to rushing, as though for the throat, when, suddenly drawing back his head and curving in from the side, he would drive his shoulder at the shoulder of Spitz, as a ram by which to overthrow him. But instead, Buck's shoulder was slashed down each time as Spitz leaped lightly away.

Spitz was untouched, while Buck was streaming with blood and panting hard. The fight was growing desperate. And all the while the silent and wolfish circle waited to finish off whichever dog went down. As Buck grew winded, Spitz took to rushing, and he kept him staggering for footing. Once Buck went over, and the whole circle of sixty dogs started up; but he recovered himself, almost in mid air, and the circle sank down again and waited.

But Buck possessed a quality that made for greatness—imagination. He fought by instinct, but he could fight by head as well. He rushed, as though attempting the old shoulder trick, but at the last instant swept low to the snow and in. His teeth closed on Spitz's left fore leg. There was a crunch of breaking bone, and the white dog faced him on three legs. Thrice he tried to knock him over, then repeated the trick and broke the right fore leg. Despite the pain and helplessness, Spitz struggled madly to keep up. He saw the silent circle, with gleaming eyes, lolling tongues, and silvery breaths drifting upward, closing in upon him as he had seen similar circles close in upon beaten antagonists in the past. Only this time he was the one who was beaten.

There was no hope for him. Buck was inexorable. Mercy was a thing reserved for gentler climes. He maneuvered for the final rush. The circle had tightened till he could feel the breaths of the huskies on his flanks. He could see them, beyond Spitz and to either side, half crouching for the spring, their eyes fixed upon him. A pause seemed to fall. Every animal was motionless as though turned to stone. Only Spitz quivered and bristled as he staggered back and forth, snarling with horrible menace, as though to frighten off impending death. Then Buck sprang in and out, but while he was in, shoulder had at last squarely met shoulder. The dark circle became a dot on the moon-flooded snow as Spitz disappeared from view. Buck stood and looked on, the successful champion, the dominant primordial beast who had made his kill and found it good.

4. *Who Has Won to Mastership*

"Eh? wot I say? I spik true w'en I say dat Buck two devils."

This was François's speech next morning when he discovered Spitz missing and Buck covered with wounds. He drew him to the fire and by its light pointed them out.

"Dat Spitz fight lak hell," said Perrault, as he surveyed the gaping rips and cuts.

"An' dat Buck fight lak two hells," was François's answer. "An' now we make good time. No more Spitz, no more trouble, sure."

While Perrault packed the camp outfit and loaded the sled, the dog driver proceeded to harness the dogs. Buck trotted up to the place Spitz would have occupied as leader; but François, not noticing him, brought Sol-leks to the coveted position. In his judgment, Sol-leks was the best lead dog left. Buck sprang upon Sol-leks in a fury, driving him back and standing in his place.

"Eh? eh?" François cried, slapping his thighs gleefully. "Look at dat Buck. Heem keel dat Spitz, heem t'ink to take de job."

"Go 'way, Chook!" he cried, but Buck refused to budge.

He took Buck by the scruff of the neck, and though the dog growled threateningly, dragged him to one side and replaced Sol-leks. The old dog did not like it, and showed plainly that he was afraid of Buck. François was obdurate, but when he turned his back Buck again displaced Sol-leks, who was not at all unwilling to go.

François was angry. "Now, by Gar, I feex you!" he cried, coming back with a heavy club in his hand.

Buck remembered the man in the red sweater, and retreated slowly; nor did he attempt to charge in when Solleks was once more brought forward. But he circled just beyond the range of the club, snarling with bitterness and rage; and while he circle he watched the club so as to dodge it if thrown by François, for he was become wise in the way of clubs.

The driver went about his work, and he called to Buck when he was ready to put him in his old place in front of Dave. Buck retreated two or three steps. François followed him up, whereupon he again retreated. After some time of this, François threw down the club, thinking that Buck feared a thrashing. But Buck was in open revolt. He wanted, not to escape a clubbing, but to have the leadership. It was his by right. He had earned it, and he would not be content with less.

Perrault took a hand. Between them they ran him about for the better part of an hour. They threw clubs at him. He dodged. They cursed him, and his fathers and mothers before him, and all his seed to come after him down to the remotest generation, and every hair on his body and drop of blood in his veins; and he answered curse with snarl and kept out of their reach. He did not try to run away, but retreated around and around the camp, advertising plainly that when his desire was met, he would come in and be good.

François sat down and scratched his head. Perrault

 looked at his watch and swore. Time was flying, and they should have been on the trail an hour gone. François scratched his head again. He shook it and grinned sheepishly at the courier, who shrugged his shoulders in sign that they were beaten. Then François went up to where Sol-leks stood and called to Buck. Buck laughed, as dogs laugh, yet kept his distance. François unfastened Sol-lek's traces and put him back in his old place. The team stood harnessed to the sled in an unbroken line, ready for the trail. There was no place for Buck save at the front. Once more François called, and once more Buck laughed and kept away.

"T'row down de club," Perrault commanded.

François complied, whereupon Buck trotted in, laughing triumphantly, and swung around into position at the head of the team. His traces were fastened, the sled broken out, and with both men running they dashed out on to the river trail.

Highly as the dog driver had forevalued Buck, with his two devils, he found, while the day was yet young, that he had undervalued. At a bound Buck took up the duties of leadership; and where judgment was required, and quick thinking and quick acting, he showed himself the superior even of Spitz, of whom François had never seen an equal.

But it was in giving the law and making his mates live up to it, that Buck excelled. Dave and Sol-leks did not mind the change in leadership. It was none of their business. Their business was to toil, and toil mightily, in the traces. So long as that were not interfered with, they did not care what happened. Billee, the good-natured, could lead for all they cared so long as he kept order. The rest

of them, however, had grown unruly during the last days
of Spitz, and their surprise was great now that Buck proceeded to lick them into shape.

Pike, who pulled at Buck's heels, and who never put an ounce more of his weight against the breast band than he was compelled to do, was swiftly and repeatedly shaken for loafing, and ere the first day was done he was pulling more than ever before in his life. The first night in camp, Joe, the sour one, was punished roundly—a thing that Spitz had never succeeded in doing. Buck simply smothered him by virtue of superior weight, and cut him up till he ceased snapping and began to whine for mercy.

The general tone of the team picked up immediately. It recovered its old-time solidarity, and once more the dogs leaped as one dog in the traces. At the Rink Rapids two native huskies, Teek and Koona, were added; and the celerity with which Buck broke them in took away François's breath.

"Nevaire such a dog as dat Buck!" he cried. "No, nevaire! Heem worth one t'ousan' dollair, by Gar! Eh? Wot you say, Perrault?"

And Perrault nodded. He was ahead of the record then, and gaining day by day. The trail was in excellent condition, well packed and hard, and there was no new-fallen snow with which to contend. It was not too cold. The temperature dropped to fifty below zero and remained there the whole trip. The men rode and ran by turn, and the dogs were kept on the jump, with but infrequent stoppages.

The Thirtymile River was comparatively coated with ice, and they covered in one day going out what had taken them ten days coming in. In one run they made a sixty-mile dash from the foot of Lake Laberge to the Whitehorse Rapids. Across Marsh, Tagish, and Bennett (seventy miles of lakes), they flew so fast that the man whose turn it was to run towed behind the sled at the end of a rope. And on the last night of the second week they topped White Pass and dropped down the sea slope with the lights of Skagway and of the shipping at their feet.

It was a record run. Each day for fourteen days they had averaged forty miles. For three days Perrault and François threw chests up and down the main street of Skagway and were deluged with invitations to drink, while the team was the constant center of a worshipful crowd of dog busters and mushers. Then three or four Western bad men aspired to clean out the town, were riddled like timber boxes for their pains, and public interest turned to other idols. Next came official orders. François called Buck to him, threw his arms around him, wept over him. And that was the last of François and Perrault. Like other men, they passed out of Buck's life for good.

A Scotch half-breed took charge of him and his mates, and in company with a dozen other dog teams he started back over the weary trail to Dawson. It was no light running now, nor record time, but heavy toil each day, with a heavy load behind; for this was the mail train, carrying word from the world to the men who sought gold under the shadow of the Pole.

Buck did not like it, but he bore up well to the work, taking pride in it after the manner of Dave and Sol-leks, and seeing that his mates, whether they prided in it or not, did their fair share. It was a monotonous life, operating with machinelike regularity. One day was very like another. At a certain time each morning the cooks turned out, fires were built, and breakfast was eaten. Then while some broke camp, others harnessed the dogs, and they were under way an hour or so before the darkness which gave warning of dawn. At night, camp was made. Some pitched the flies, others cut firewood and pine boughs for the beds, and still others carried water or ice for the cooks. Also, the dogs were fed. To them, this was the one feature of the day, though it was good to loaf around, after the fish was eaten, for an hour or so with the other dogs, of which there were fivescore and odd. There were fierce fighters among them, but three battles with the fiercest brought Buck to mastery, so that when he bristled and showed his teeth they got out of his way.

Best of all, perhaps, he loved to lie near the fire, hind legs crouched under him, fore legs stretched out in front, head raised, and eyes blinking dreamily at the flames. Sometimes he thought of Judge Miller's big house in the sun-kissed Santa Clara Valley, and of the cement swimming tank, and Ysabel, the Mexican hairless, and Toots, the Japanese pug; but oftener he remembered the man in the red sweater, the death of Curly, the great fight with Spitz, and the good things he had eaten or would like to eat. He was not homesick. The Sunland was very dim and distant, and such memories had no power over him. Far more potent were the memories of his heredity that gave things he had never seen before a seeming familiarity; the instincts (which were but the memories of his ancestors become habits) which had lapsed in later days, and still later, in him, quickened and became alive again.

Sometimes as he crouched there, blinking dreamily at the flames, it seemed that the flames were of another fire, and that as he crouched by this other fire he saw another and different man from the half-breed cook before him. This other man was shorter of leg and longer of arm, with muscles that were stringy and knotty rather than rounded and swelling. The hair of this man was long and matted, and his head slanted back under it from the eyes. He uttered strange sounds, and seemed very much afraid of the darkness, into which he peered continually, clutching in his hand, which hung midway between knee and foot, a stick with a heavy stone made fast to the end. He was all but naked, a ragged and fire-scorched skin hanging part way down his back, but on his body there was much hair. In some places, across the chest and shoulders and down the outside of the arms and thighs, it was matted into almost a thick fur. He did not stand erect, but with trunk inclined forward from the hips, on legs that bent at the knees. About his body there was a peculiar springiness, or resiliency, almost catlike, and a quick alertness as of one who lived in perpetual fear of things seen and unseen.

At other times this hairy man squatted by the fire with head between his legs and slept. On such occasions his elbows were on his knees, his hands clasped above his head as though to shed rain by the hairy arms. And beyond that fire, in the circling darkness, Buck could see many gleaming coals, two by two, always two by two, which he knew to be the eyes of great beasts of prey. And he could hear the crashing of their bodies though the undergrowth, and the noises they made in the night. And dreaming there by the Yukon bank, with lazy eyes blinking at the fire, these sounds and sights of another world would make the hair to rise along his back and stand on end across his shoulders and up his neck, till he whimpered low and suppressedly, or growled softly, and the half-breed cook shouted at him, "Hey, you Buck, wake up!'" Whereupon the other world would vanish and the real world come into his eyes, and he would get up and yawn and stretch as though he had been asleep.

It was a hard trip, with the mail behind them, and the heavy work wore them down. They were short of weight and in poor condition when they made Dawson, and should have had a ten days' or a week's rest at least. But in two days' time they dropped down the Yukon bank from the Barracks, loaded with letters for the outside. The dogs were tired, the drivers grumbling, and to make matters worse, it snowed every day. This meant a soft trail, greater friction on the runners, and heavier pulling for the dogs; yet the drivers were fair through it all, and did their best for the animals.

Each night the dogs were attended to first. They ate before the drivers ate, and no man sought his sleeping robe till he had seen to the feet of the dogs he drove. Still, their strength went down. Since the beginning of the winter they had travelled eighteen hundred miles, dragging sleds the whole weary distance; and eighteen hundred miles will tell upon life of the toughest. Buck stood it, keeping his mates up to their work and maintaining discipline, though he too was very tired. Billee cried and whimpered regularly in his sleep each night. Joe was sourer than ever, and Sol-leks was unapproachable, blind side or other side.

But it was Dave who suffered most of all. Something had gone wrong with him. He became more morose and irritable, and when camp was pitched at once made his nest, where his driver fed him. Once out of the harness and down, he did not get on his feet again till harness-up time in the morning. Sometimes, in the traces, when jerked by a sudden stoppage of the sled, or by straining to start it, he would cry out with pain. The driver examined him, but could find nothing. All the drivers became interested in his case. They talked it over at meal time, and over their last pipes before going to bed, and one night they held a consultation. He was brought from his nest to the fire and was pressed and prodded till he cried out many times. Something was wrong inside, but they could locate no broken bones, could not make it out.

By the time Cassiar Bar was reached, he was so weak that he was falling repeatedly in the traces. The Scotch half-breed called a halt and took him out of the team, making the next dog, Sol-leks, fast to the sled. His intention was to rest Dave, letting him run free behind the sled. Sick as he was, Dave resented being taken out, grunting and growling while the traces were unfastened, and whimpering broken-heartedly when he saw Sol-leks in the position he had held and served so long. For the pride of trace and trail was his, and sick unto death, he could not bear that another dog should do his work.

When the sled started, he floundered in the soft snow alongside the beaten trail, attacking Sol-leks with his teeth, rushing against him and trying to thrust him off into the soft snow on the other side, striving to leap inside his traces and get between him and the sled, and all the while whining and yelping and crying with grief and pain. The half-breed tried to drive him away with the whip; but he paid no heed to the stinging lash, and the man had not the heart to strike harder. Dave refused to run quietly on the trail behind the sled, where the going was easy, but continued to flounder alongside in the soft snow, where the going was most difficult, till exhausted, then he fell, and lay where he fell, howling lugubriously as the long train of sleds churned by.

With the last remnant of his strength he managed to stagger along behind till the train made another stop, when he floundered past the sleds to his own, where he stood alongside Sol-leks. His driver lingered a moment to get a light for his pipe from the man behind. Then he returned and started his dogs. They swung out on the trail with remarkable lack of exertion, turned their heads uneasily, and stopped in surprise. The driver was surprised, too; the sled had not moved. He called his comrades to witness the sight. Dave had bitten through both of Sol-leks's traces, and was standing directly in front of the sled in his proper place.

He pleaded with his eyes to remain there. The driver was perplexed. His comrades talked of how a dog could break its heart through being denied the work that killed it, and recalled instances they had known, where dogs, too old for the toil, or injured, had died because they were cut out of the traces. Also, they held it a mercy, since Dave was to die anyway, that he should die in the traces, heart-easy and content. So he was harnessed in again, and proudly he pulled as of old, though more than once he cried out involuntarily from the bite of his inward hurt. Several times he fell down and was dragged in the traces, and once the sled ran upon him so that he limped thereafter on one of his hind legs.

But he held out till camp was reached, when his driver made a place for him by the fire. Morning found him too weak to travel. At harness-up time he tried to crawl to his driver. By convulsive efforts he got on his feet, staggered, and fell. Then he wormed his way forward slowly toward where the harnesses were being put on his mates. He would advance his fore legs and drag up his body with a sort of hitching movement, when he would advance his fore legs and hitch ahead again for a few more inches. His strength left him, and the last his mates saw of him he lay gasping in the snow and yearning toward them. But they could hear him mournfully howling till they passed out of sight behind a belt of river timber.

Here the train was halted. The Scotch half-breed slowly retraced his steps to the camp they had left. The men ceased talking. A revolver shot rang out. The man came back hurriedly. The whips snapped, the bells tinkled merrily, the sleds churned along the trail; but Buck knew, and every dog knew, what had taken place behind the belt of river trees.

5. The Toil of Trace and Trail

Thirty days from the time it left Dawson, the Salt Water Mail, with Buck and his mates at the fore, arrived at Skagway. They were in a wretched state, worn out and worn down. Buck's one hundred and forty pounds had dwindled to one hundred and fifteen. The rest of his mates, though lighter dogs, had relatively lost more weight than he. Pike, the malingerer, who, in his lifetime of deceit, had often successfully feigned a hurt leg, was now limping in earnest. Sol-leks was limping, and Dub was suffering from a wrenched shoulder blade.

They were all terribly footsore. No spring or rebound was left in them. Their feet fell heavily on the trail, jarring their bodies and doubling the fatigue of a day's travel. There was nothing the matter with them except that they were dead tired. It was not the dead tiredness that comes through brief and and excessive effort, from which recovery is a matter of hours; but it was the dead tiredness that comes through the slow and prolonged strength drainage of months of toil. There was no power of recuperation left, no reserve strength to call upon. It had been all used, the last least bit of it. Every muscle, every fibre, every cell, was tired, dead tired. And there was reason for it. In less than five months they had travelled twenty-five hundred miles, during the last eighteen hundred of which they had had but five day's rest. When they arrived at Skagway they were apparently on their last legs. They could barely keep the traces taut, and on the down grades just managed to keep out of the way of the sled.

"Mush on, poor sore feets," the driver encouraged them as they tottered down the main street of Skagway. "Dis is de las'. Den we get one long res'. Eh? For sure. One bully long res'."

The drivers confidently expected a long stopover. Themselves, they had covered twelve hundred miles with two days' rest, and in the nature of reason and common justice they deserved an interval of loafing. But so many were the men who had rushed into the Klondike, and so many were the sweethearts, wives, and kin that had not rushed in, that the congested mail was taking on Alpine proportions; also, there were official orders. Fresh batches of Hudson Bay dogs were to take the places of those worthless for the trail. The worthless ones were to be got rid of, and, since dogs count for little against dollars, they were to be sold.

Three days passed, by which time Buck and his mates found how really tired and weak they were. Then, on the morning of the fourth day, two men from the States came along and bought them, harness and all, for a song. The men addressed each other as "Hal" and "Charles." Charles was a middle-aged, lightish-colored man, with weak and watery eyes and a mustache that twisted fiercely and vigorously up, giving the lie to the limply drooping lip it concealed. Hal was a youngster of nineteen or twenty, with a big Colt's revolver and a hunting knife strapped about him on a belt that fairly bristled with cartridges. This belt was the most salient thing about him. It advertised his callowness—a callowness sheer and unutterable. Both men were manifestly out of place, and why such as they should adventure the North is part of the mystery of things that passes understanding.

Buck heard the chaffering, saw the money pass between the man and the Government agent, and knew that the Scotch half-breed and the mail-train drivers were passing out of his life on the heels of Perrault and François and the others who had gone before. When driven with his mates to the new owners' camp, Buck saw a slipshod and slovenly affair, tent half stretched, dishes unwashed, everything in disorder; also, he saw a woman. "Mercedes" the men called her. She was Charles's wife and Hal's sister—a nice family party.

Buck watched them apprehensively as they proceeded to take down the tent and load the sled. There was a great deal of effort about their manner, but no businesslike method. The tent was rolled into an awkward bundle three times as large as it should have been. The tin dishes were packed away unwashed. Mercedes continually fluttered in the way of her men and kept up an unbroken chattering of remonstrance and advice. When they put a clothes sack on the front of the sled, she suggested it should go on the back; and when they had it put on the back, and covered it over with a couple of other bundles, she discovered overlooked articles which could abide nowhere else but in that very sack, and they unloaded again.

Three men from a neighboring tent came out and looked on, grinning and winking at one another.

"You've got a right smart load as it is," said one of them; "and it's not me should tell you your business, but I wouldn't tote that tent along if I was you."

"Undreamed of!" cried Mercedes, throwing up her hands in dainty dismay. "However in the world could I manage without a tent?"

"It's springtime, and you won't get any more cold weather," the man replied.

She shook her head decidedly, and Charles and Hal put the last odds and ends on top the mountainous load.

"Think it'll ride?" one of the men asked.

"Why shouldn't it?" Charles demanded rather shortly.

"Oh, that's all right, that's all right," the man hastened meekly to say. "I was just a-wonderin', that is all. It seemed a mite top-heavy."

Charles turned his back and drew the lashings down as well as he could, which was not in the least well.

"An' of course the dogs can hike along all day with that contraption behind them," affirmed a second of the men.

"Certainly," said Hal, with freezing politeness, taking hold of the gee-pole with one hand and swinging his whip from the other. "Mush!" he shouted. "Mush on there!"

The dogs sprang against the breastbands, strained hard for a few moments, then relaxed. They were unable to move the sled.

"The lazy brutes, I'll show them," he cried, preparing to lash out at them with the whip.

But Mercedes interfered, crying, "Oh, Hal, you mustn't," as she caught hold of the whip and wrenched it from him. "The poor dears! Now you must promise you won't be harsh with them for the rest of the trip, or I won't go a step."

"Precious lot you know about dogs," her brother

sneered; "and I wish you'd leave me alone. They're lazy, I tell you, and you've got to whip them to get anything out of them. That's their way. You ask any one. Ask one of those men."

Mercedes looked at them imploringly, untold repugnance at sight of pain written in her pretty face.

"They're weak as water, if you want to know," came the reply from one of the men. "Plumb tuckered out, that's what's the matter. They need a rest."

"Rest be blanked," said Hal, with his beardless lips; and Mercedes said, "Oh!" in pain and sorrow at the oath.

But she was a clannish creature, and rushed at once to the defense of her brother. "Never mind that man," she said pointedly. "You're driving our dogs and you do what you think best with them."

Again Hal's whip fell upon the dogs. They threw themselves against the breastbands, dug their feet into the packed snow, got down low to it, and put forth all their strength. The sled held as though it were an anchor. After two efforts, they stood still, panting. The whip was whistling savagely, when once more Mercedes interfered. She dropped on her knees before Buck, with tears in her eyes, and put her arms around his neck.

"You poor, poor dears," she cried sympathetically, "why don't you pull hard?—then you wouldn't be whipped." Buck did not like her, but he was feeling too miserable to resist her, taking it as part of the day's miserable work.

One of the onlookers, who had been clenching his teeth to suppress hot speech, now spoke up:

"It's not that I care a whoop what becomes of you, but for the dogs' sakes I just want to tell you, you can help them a mighty lot by breaking out that sled. The runners are froze fast. Throw your weight against the gee-pole, right and left, and break it out."

A third time the attempt was made, but this time, following the advice, Hal broke out the runners which had been frozen to the snow. The overloaded and unwieldy sled forged ahead, Buck and his mates struggling frantically under the rain of blows. A hundred yards ahead the path turned and sloped steeply into the main street. It would have required an experienced man to keep the top-heavy sled upright, and Hal was not such a man. As they swung on the turn the sled went over, spilling half its load through the loose lashings. The dogs never stopped. The lightened sled bounded on its side behind them. They were angry because of the ill treatment they had received and the unjust load. Buck was raging. He broke into a run, the team following his lead. Hal cried, "Whoa! whoa!" but they gave no heed. He tripped and was pulled off his feet. The capsized sled ground over him, and the dogs dashed on up the street, adding to the gayety of Skagway as they scattered the remainder of the outfit along its chief thoroughfare.

Kindhearted citizens caught the dogs and gathered up the scattered belongings. Also, they gave advice. Half the load and twice the dogs, if they ever expected to reach Dawson, was what was said. Hal and his sister and brother-in-law listened unwillingly, pitched tent, and over-hauled the outfit, canned goods were turned out that made men laugh, for canned goods on the Long Trail is a thing to dream about. "Blankets for a hotel," quoth one of the men who laughed and helped. "Half as many is too much; get rid of them. Throw away that tent, and all those dishes—who's going to wash them anyway? Good Lord, do you think you're travelling on a Pullman?" 61

And so it went, the inexorable elimination of the superfluous. Mercedes cried when her clothes bags were dumped on the ground and article after article was thrown out. She cried in general, and she cried in particular over each discarded thing. She clasped hands about knees, rocking back and forth broken heartedly. She averred she would not go an inch, not for a dozen Charleses. She appealed to everybody and to everything, finally wiping her eyes and proceeding to cast out even articles of apparel that were imperative necessaries. And in her zeal, when she had finished with her own, she attacked the belongings of her men and went through them like a tornado.

This accomplished, the outfit, though cut in half, was still a formidable bulk. Charles and Hal went out in the evening and bought six Outside dogs. These, added to the six of the original team, and Teek and Koona, the huskies obtained at the Rink Rapids on the record trip, brought the team up to fourteen. But the Outside dogs, though practically broken in since their landing, did not amount to much. Three were short-haired pointers, one was a Newfoundland, and the other two were mongrels of indeterminate breed. They did not seem to know anything, these newcomers. Buck and his comrades looked upon them with disgust, and though he speedily taught them their places and what not to do, he could not reach them what to do. They did not take kindly to trace and trail. With the exception of the two mongrels, they were bewildered and spirit-broken by the strange savage environment in which they found themselves and by ill treat-

62 ment they had received. The two mongrels were without spirit at all; bones were only things breakable about them.

With the newcomers hopeless and forlorn, and the old team worn out by twenty-five hundred miles of continuous trail, the outlook was anything but bright. The two men, however, were quite cheerful. And they were proud, too. They were doing the thing in style, with fourteen dogs. They had seen other sleds depart over the pass for Dawson or come in from Dawson, but never had they seen a sled with so many as fourteen dogs. In the nature of Arctic travel there was a reason why fourteen dogs should not drag one sled, and that was that one sled could not carry the food for fourteen dogs. But Charles and Hal did not know this. They had worked the trip out with a pencil, so much to a dog, so many dogs, and so many days, Q. E. D. Mercedes looked over their shoulders and nodded comprehensively, it was all so very simple.

Late next morning Buck led the long team up the street. There was nothing lively about it, no snap or go in him and his fellows. They were starting dead weary. Four times he had covered the distance between Salt Water and Dawson, and the knowledge that, jaded and tired, he was facing the same trail once more, made him bitter. His heart was not in the work, nor was the heart of any dog. The Outsides were timid and frightened, the Insides without confidence in their masters.

Buck felt vaguely that there was no depending upon these two men and the woman. They did not know how to do anything, and as the days went by it became apparent that they could not learn. They were slack in all things, without order or discipline. It took them half the night to pitch a slovenly camp, and half the morning to break that camp and get the sled loaded in fashion so slovenly that for the rest of the day they were occupied in stopping and rearranging the load. Some days they did not make ten miles. On other days they were unable to get started at all. And on no day did they succeed in making more than half the distance used by the men as a basis in their dog food computation.

It was inevitable that they should go short on dog food. But they hastened it by overfeeding, bringing the day nearer when underfeeding would commence. The Outside dogs, whose digestions had not been trained by chronic famine to make the most of little, had voracious appetites. And when, in addition to this, the worn-out huskies pulled weakly, Hal decided that the orthodox ration was too small. He doubled it. And to cap it all, when Mercedes, with tears in her pretty eyes and a quaver in her throat, could not cajole him into giving the dogs still more, she stole from the fish sacks and fed them slyly. But it was not food that Buck and the huskies needed, but rest. And though they were making poor time, the heavy load they dragged sapped their strength severely.

Then came the underfeeding. Hal awoke one day to the fact that his dog food was half gone and the distance only quarter covered; further, that for love or money no additional dog food was to be obtained. So he cut down even the orthodox ration and tried to increase the day's travel. His sister and brother-in-law seconded him; but they were frustrated by their heavy outfit and their own incompetence. It was a simple matter to give the dogs

64 less food; but it was impossible to make the dogs travel faster, while their own inability to get under way earlier in the morning prevented them from travelling longer hours. Not only did they not know how to work dogs, but they did not know how to work themselves.

The first to go with Dub. Poor blundering thief that he was, always getting caught and punished, he had none the less been a faithful worker. His wrenched shoulder blade, untreated and unrested, went from bad to worse, till finally Hal shot him with the big Colt's revolver. It is a saying of the country that an Outside dog starves to death on the ration of the husky, so the six Outside dogs under Buck could do no less than die on half the ration of the husky. The Newfoundland went first, followed by the three short-haired pointers, the two mongrels hanging more grittily on to life, but going in the end.

By this time all the amenities and gentlenesses of the Southland had fallen away from the three people. Shorn of its glamour and romance, Arctic travel became to them a reality too harsh for their manhood and womanhood. Mercedes ceased weeping over the dogs, being too occupied with weeping over herself and with quarrelling with her husband and brother. To quarrel was the one thing they were never too weary to do. Their irritability arose out of their misery, increased with it, doubled upon it, outdistanced it. The wonderful patience of the trail which comes to men who toil hard and suffer sore, and remain sweet of speech and kindly, did not come to these two men and the woman. They had no inkling of such a patience. They were stiff and in pain; their muscles ached, their bones ached, their very hearts ached; and because of this they became sharp of speech, and hard words were first on their lips in the morning and last at night.

Charles and Hal wrangled whenever Mercedes gave them a chance. It was the cherished belief of each that he did more than his share of the work, and neither forbore to speak this belief at every opportunity. Sometimes Mercedes sided with her husband, sometimes with her brother. The result was a beautiful and unending family quarrel. Starting from a dispute as to which should chop a few sticks for the fire (a dispute which concerned only Charles and Hal), presently would be lugged in the rest of the family, fathers, mothers, uncles, cousins, people thousands of miles away, and some of them dead. That Hal's views on art, or the sort of society plays his mother's brother wrote, should have anything to do with the chopping of a few sticks of firewood, passes comprehension; nevertheless the quarrel was as likely to tend in that direction as in the direction of Charles's political prejudices. And that Charles's sister's tale-bearing tongue should be relevant to the building of a Yukon fire, was apparent only to Mercedes, who disburdened herself of copious opinions upon that topic, and incidentally upon a few other traits unpleasantly peculiar to her husband's family. In the meantime the fire remained unbuilt, the camp half pitched, and the dogs unfed.

Mercedes nursed a special grievance—the grievance of sex. She was pretty and soft, and had been chivalrously treated all her days. But the present treatment by her husband and brother was everything save chivalrous. It was her custom to be helpless. They complained. Upon which impeachment of what to her was her most essential sex prerogative, she made their lives unendurable. She no longer considered the dogs, and because she was sore and tired, she persisted in riding on the sled. She was pretty and soft, but she weighed one hundred and twenty pounds—a lusty last straw to the load dragged by the weak and starving animals. She rode for days, till they fell in the traces and the sled stood still. Charles and Hal begged her to get off and walk, pleaded with her, entreated, the while she wept and importuned Heaven with a recital of their brutality.

On one occasion they took her off the sled by main strength. They never did it again. She let her legs go limp like a spoiled child, and sat down on the trail. They went on their way, but she did not move. After they had travelled three miles they unloaded the sled, came back for her, and by main strength put her on the sled again.

In the excess of their own misery they were callous to the suffering of their animals. Hal's theory, which he practised on others, was that one must get hardened. He had started out preaching it to his sister and brother-in-law. Failing there, he hammered it into the dogs with a club. At the Five Fingers the dog food gave out, and a toothless old squaw offered to trade them a few pounds of frozen horsehide for the Colt's revolver that kept the big hunting knife company at Hal's hip. A poor substitute for food was this hide, just as it had been stripped from the starved horses of the cattlemen six months back. In its frozen state it was more like strips of galvanized iron, and when a dog wrestled it into his stomach it thawed into thin and innutritious leathery strings and into a mass of short hair, irritating and indigestible.

And through it all Buck staggered along at the head of the team as in a nightmare. He pulled when he could; when he could no longer pull, he fell down and remained down till blows from whip or club drove him to his feet again. All the stiffness and gloss had gone out of his beautiful furry coat. The hair hung down, limp and draggled, or matted with dried blood where Hal's club had bruised him. His muscles had wasted away to knotty strings, and the flesh pads had disappeared, so that each rib and every bone in his frame were outlined cleanly through the loose hide that was wrinkled in folds of emptiness. It was heartbreaking, only Buck's heart was unbreakable. The man in the red sweater had proved that.

As it was with Buck, so was it with his mates. They were perambulating skeletons. There were seven all together, including him. In their very great misery they had become insensible to the bite of the lash or the bruise of the club. The pain of the beating was dull and distant, just as the things their eyes saw and their ears heard seemed dull and distant. They were not half living, or quarter living. They were simply so many bags of bones in which sparks of life fluttered faintly. When a halt was made, they dropped down in the traces like dead dogs, and the spark dimmed and paled and seemed to go out. And when the club or whip fell upon them, the spark fluttered feebly up, and they tottered to their feet and staggered on.

There came a day when Billee, the good-natured, fell and could not rise. Hal had traded off his revolver, so he took the axe and knocked Billee on the head as he lay in the traces, then cut the carcass out of the harness and dragged it to one side. Buck saw, and his mates saw, and they knew that this thing was very close to them. In the next day Koona went, and but five of them remained: Joe, too far gone to be malignant; Pike, crippled and limping, only half conscious and not conscious enough longer to malinger; Sol-leks, the one-eyed, still faithful to be toil of the trace and trail, and mournful in that he had so little strength with which to pull; Teek, who had not travelled so far that winter and who was now beaten more than the others because he was fresher; and Buck, still at the head of the team, but no longer enforcing discipline or striving to enfore it, blind with weakness half the time and keeping the trail by the loom of it and by the dim feel of his feet.

It was beautiful spring weather, but neither dogs nor humans were aware of it. Each day the sun rose earlier and set later. It was dawn by three in the morning, and twilight lingered till nine at night. The whole long day was a blaze of sunshine. The ghostly winter silence had given way to the great spring murmur of awakening life. This murmur arose from all the land, fraught with the joy of living. It came from the things that lived and moved again, things which had been as dead and which had not moved during the long months of frost. The sap was rising in the pines. The willows and aspens were bursting out in young buds. Shrubs and vines were putting on fresh garbs of green. Crickets sang in the nights, and in the days all manner of creeping, crawling things rustled forth into the sun. Partridges and woodpeckers were booming and knocking in the forest. Squirrels were chattering, birds singing, and overhead honked the wild fowl driving up from the South in cunning wedges that split the air.

From every hill slope came the trickle of running water, the music of unseen fountains. All things were thawing, bending, snapping. The Yukon was straining to break loose the ice that bound it down. It ate away from beneath; the sun ate from above. Air holes formed, fissures sprang and spread apart, while thin sections of ice fell through bodily into the river. And amid all this bursting, rending, throbbing of awakening life, under the blazing sun and through the soft-sighing breezes, like wayfarers to death, staggered the two men, the woman, and the huskies. 69

With the dogs falling, Mercedes weeping and riding, Hal swearing innocuously, and Charles's eyes wistfully watering, they staggered into John Thornton's camp at the mouth of White River. When they halted, the dogs dropped down as though they had all been struck dead. Mercedes dried her eyes and looked at John Thornton. Charles sat down on a log to rest. He sat down very slowly and painstakingly what of his great stiffness. Hal did the talking. John Thornton was whittling the last touches on an axe-handle he had made from a stick of birch. He whittled and listened, gave monosyllabic replies, and, when it was asked, terse advice. He knew the breed, and he gave his advice in the certainty that it would not be followed.

"They told us up above that the bottom was dropping out of the trail and that the best thing for us to do was to lay over," Hal said in response to Thornton's warning to take no more chances on the rotten ice. "They told us we couldn't make White River, and here we are." This last with a sneering ring of triumph in it.

"And they told you true," John Thornton answered.

"The bottom's likely to drop out at any moment. Only fools, with the blind luck of fools, could have made it. I tell you straight, I wouldn't risk my carcass on that ice for all the gold in Alaska."

"That's because you're not a fool, I suppose," said Hal. "All the same, we'll go on to Dawson." He uncoiled his whip. "Get up there, Buck! Hi! Get up there! Mush on!"

Thornton went on whittling. It was idle, he knew, to get between a fool and his folly; while two or three fools more or less would not alter the scheme of things.

But the team did not get up at the command. It had long since passed into the stage where blows were required to rouse it. The whip flashed out, here and there, on its merciless errands. John Thornton compressed his lips. Sol-leks was the first to crawl to his feet. Teek followed. Joe came next, yelping with pain. Pike made painful efforts. Twice he fell over, when half up, and on the third attempt managed to rise. Buck made no effort. He lay quietly where he had fallen. The lash bit into him again and again, but he neither whined nor struggled. Several times Thornton started, as though to speak, but changed his mind. A moisture came into his eyes, and, as the whipping continued, he arose and walked irresolutely up and down.

This was the first time Buck had failed, in itself a sufficient reason to drive Hal into a rage. He exchanged the whip for the customary club. Buck refused to move under the rain of heavier blows which now fell upon him. Like his mates, he was barely able to get up, but, unlike them, he had made up his mind not to get up. He had a vague feeling of impending doom. This had been strong upon him when he pulled into the bank, and it had not departed from him. What of the thin and rotten ice he had felt under his feet all day, it seemed that he sensed disaster close at hand, out there ahead on the ice where his master was trying to drive him. He refused to stir. So greatly had he suffered, and so far gone was he, that the blows did not hurt much. And as they continued to fall upon him, the spark of life within flickered and went down. It was nearly out. He felt strangely numb. As though from a great distance, he was aware that he was being beaten. The last sensations of pain left him. He no longer felt anything, though very faintly he could hear the impact of the club upon his body. But it was no longer his body, it seemed so far away.

And then, suddenly, without warning, uttering a cry that was inarticulate and more like the cry of an animal, John Thornton sprang upon the man who wielded the club. Hal was hurled backward, as though struck by a falling tree. Mercedes screamed. Charles looked on wistfully, wiped his watery eyes, but did not get up because of his stiffness.

John Thornton stood over Buck, struggling to control himself, too convulsed with rage to speak.

"If you strike that dog again, I'll kill you," he at last managed to say in a choking voice.

"It's my dog," Hal replied, wiping the blood from his mouth as he came back. "Get out of my way, or I'll fix you. I'm going to Dawson."

Thornton stood between him and Buck and evinced no intention of getting out of the way. Hal drew his long hunting knife. Mercedes screamed, cried, laughed, and manifested the chaotic abandonment of hysteria. Thornton rapped Hal's knuckles with the axe handle, knocking the knife to the ground. He rapped his knuckles again as he tried to pick it up. Then he stooped, picked it up himself, and with two strokes cut Buck's traces.

Hal had no fight left in him. Besides, his hands were full with his sister, or his arms, rather; while Buck was too near dead to be of further use in hauling the sled. A few minutes later they pulled out from the bank and down the river. Buck heard them go and raised his head to see. Pike was leading, Sol-leks was at the wheel, and between were Joe and Teek. They were limping and staggering. Mercedes was riding the loaded sled. Hal guided at the gee-pole, and Charles stumbled along in the rear.

As Buck watched them, Thornton knelt beside him and with rough, kindly hands searched for broken bones. By the time his search had disclosed nothing more than many bruises and a state of terrible starvation, the sled was a quarter of a mile away. Dog and man watched it crawling along the ice. Suddenly, they saw its back end drop down, as into a rut, and the gee-pole, with Hal clinging to it, jerk into the air. Mercedes's scream came to their ears. They saw Charles turn and make one step to run back, and then a whole section of ice give way and dogs and humans disappear. A yawning hole was all that was to be seen. The bottom had dropped out of the trail.

John Thornton and Buck looked at each other.

"You poor devil," said John Thornton and Buck licked his hand.

6. For the Love of a Man

When John Thornton froze his feet in the previous December, his partners had made him comfortable and left him to get well, going on themselves up the river to get out a raft of sawlogs for Dawson. He was still limping slightly at the time he rescued Buck, but with the continued warm weather even the slight limp left him. And here, lying by the river bank through the long spring days, watching the running water, listening lazily to the songs of birds and the hum of nature, Buck slowly won back his strength.

A rest comes very good after one has travelled three thousand miles, and it must be confessed that Buck waxed lazy as his wounds healed, his muscles swelled out, and the flesh came back to cover his bones. For that matter, they were all loafing—Buck, John Thornton, and Skeet and Nig—waiting for the raft to come that was to carry them down to Dawson. Skeet was a little Irish setter who early made friends with Buck, who in a dying condition, was unable to resent her first advances. She had the doctor trait which some dogs possess, and as a mother cat washes her kittens, so she washed and cleansed Buck's wounds. Regularly, each morning after he had finished his breakfast, she performed her self-appointed task, till he came to look for her ministrations as much as he did for Thornton's. Nig, equally friendly though less demonstra-

74 tive, was a huge black dog, half bloodhound and half deerhound, with eyes that laughed and a boundless good nature.

To Buck's surprise these dogs manifested no jealousy toward him. They seemed to share the kindliness and largeness of John Thornton. As Buck grew stronger they enticed him into all sorts of ridiculous games, in which Thornton himself could not forbear to join, and in this fashion Buck romped through his convalescence and into a new existence. Love, genuine passionate love, was his for the first time. This he had never experienced at Judge Miller's down in the sun-kissed Santa Clara Valley. With the Judge's sons, hunting and tramping, it had been a working partnership; with the Judge's grandsons, a sort of pompous guardianship; and with the Judge himself, a stately and dignified friendship. But love that was feverish and burning, that was adoration, that was madness, it had taken John Thornton to arouse.

This man had saved his life, which was something; but, further, he was the ideal master. Other men saw to the welfare of their dogs from a sense of duty and business expediency; he saw to the welfare of his as if they were his own children, because he could not help it. And he saw further. He never forgot a kindly greeting or a cheering word, and to sit down for a long talk with them ("gas" he called it) was as much his delight as theirs. He had a way of taking Buck's head roughly between his hands, and resting his own head upon Buck's, of shaking him back and forth, the while calling him ill names that to Buck were love names. Buck knew no greater joy than that rough embrace and the sound of murmured oaths, and at each jerk back and forth it seemed that his heart would be shaken out of his body so great was its ecstasy. And when, released, he sprang to his feet, his mouth laughing, his eyes eloquent, his throat vibrant with unuttered sound, and in that fashion remained without movement, John Thornton would reverently exclaim, "God! you can all but speak!"

Buck had a trick of love expression that was akin to hurt. He would often seize Thornton's hand in his mouth and close so fiercely that the flesh bore the impress of his teeth for some time afterward. And as Buck understood the oaths to be love words, so the man understood this feigned bite for a caress.

For the most part, however, Buck's love was expressed in adoration. While he went wild with happiness when Thornton touched him or spoke to him, he did not seek these tokens. Unlike Skeet, who was wont to shove her nose under Thornton's hand and nudge and nudge till petted, or Nig, who would stalk up and rest his great head on Thornton's knee, Buck was content to adore at a distance. He would lie by the hour, eager, alert, at Thornton's feet, looking up into his face, dwelling upon it, studying it, following with keenest interest each fleeting expression, every movement or change of feature. Or, as chance might have it, he would lie farther away, to the side or rear, watching the outlines of the man and the occasional movements of his body. And often, such was the communion in which they lived, the strength of Buck's gaze would draw John Thornton's head around, and he would return the gaze, without speech, his heart shining out of his eyes as Buck's heart shone out.

For a long time after his rescue, Buck did not like Thornton to get out of his sight. From the moment he left the tent to when he entered it again, Buck would follow at his heels. His transient masters since he had come into the Northland had bred in him a fear that no master could be permanent. He was afraid that Thornton would pass out of his life as Perrault and François and the Scotch half-breed had passed out. Even in the night, in his dreams, he was haunted by this fear. At such times he would shake off sleep and creep through the chill to the flap of the tent, where he would stand and listen to the sound of his master's breathing.

But in spite of this great love he bore John Thornton, which seemed to bespeak the soft civilizing influence, the strain of the primitive, which the Northland had aroused in him, remained alive and active. Faithfulness and devotion, things born of fire and roof, were his; yet he retained his wildness and wiliness. He was a thing of the wild, come in from the wild to sit by John Thornton's fire, rather than a dog of the soft Southland stamped with the marks of generations of civilization. Because of his very great love, he could not steal from this man, but from any other man, in any other camp, he did not hesitate an instant, while the cunning with which he stole enabled him to escape detection.

His face and body were scored by the teeth of many dogs, and he fought as fiercely as ever and more shrewdly. Skeet and Nig were too good-natured for quarrelling—besides, they belonged to John Thornton; but the strange dog, no matter what the breed or valor, swiftly acknowledged Buck's supremacy or found himself struggling for life with a terrible antagonist. And Buck was merciless. He had learned well the law of club and fang, and he never forwent an advantage or drew back from a foe he had started on the way to Death. He had lessoned from Spitz, and from the chief fighting dogs of the police and mail, and knew there was no middle course. He must master or be mastered; while to show mercy was a weakness. Mercy did not exist in the primordial life. It was misunderstood for fear, and such misunderstandings made for death. Kill or be killed, eat or be eaten, was the law; and this mandate, down out of the depths of Time, he obeyed.

He was older than the days he had seen and the breaths he had drawn. He linked the past with the present, and the eternity behind him throbbed through him in a mighty rhythm to which he swayed as the tides and seasons swayed. He sat by John Thornton's fire, a broad-breasted dog, white-fanged and long-furred; but behind him were the shades of all manner of dogs, half wolves and wild wolves, urgent and prompting, tasting the savor of the meat he ate, thirsting for the water he drank, scenting the wind with him, listening with him and telling him the sounds made by the wild life in the forest, dictating his moods, directing his actions, lying down to sleep with him when he lay down, and dreaming with him and beyond him and becoming themselves the stuff of his dreams.

So peremptorily did these shades beckon him, that each day mankind and the claims of mankind slipped farther from him. Deep in the forest a call was sounding, and as often as he heard this call, mysteriously thrilling and luring, he felt compelled to turn his back upon the fire and the beaten earth around it, and to plunge into the forest, and on and on, he knew not where or why; nor did he wonder where or why, the call sounding imperiously, deep in the forest. But as often as he gained the soft unbroken earth and the green shade, the love for John Thornton drew him back to the fire again.

Thornton alone held him. The rest of mankind was as nothing. Chance travellers might praise or pet him; but he was cold under it all, and from a too demonstrative man he would get up and walk away. When Thornton's partners, Hans and Pete, arrived on the long-expected raft, Buck refused to notice them till he learned they were close to Thornton; after that he tolerated them in a passive sort of way, accepting favors from them as though he favored them by accepting. They were of the same large type as Thornton, living close to the earth, thinking simply and seeing clearly; and ere they swung the raft into the big eddy by the sawmill at Dawson, they understood Buck and his ways, and did not insist upon an intimacy such as obtained with Skeet and Nig.

For Thornton, however, his love seemed to grow and grow. He alone among men could put a pack upon Buck's back in the summer travelling. Nothing was too great for Buck to do, when Thornton commanded. One day (they had grub-staked themselves from the proceeds of the raft and left Dawson for the headwaters of the Tanana) the men and dogs were sitting on the crest of a cliff which fell away, straight down, to naked bedrock three hundred feet below. John Thornton was sitting near the edge, Buck at his shoulder. A thoughtless whim seized Thornton, and he drew the attention of Hans and Pete to the experiment he had in mind. "Jump, Buck!" he commanded, sweeping his arm out and over the chasm. The next instant he was grappling with Buck on the extreme edge, while Hans and Pete were dragging them back into safety.

"It's uncanny," Pete said, after it was over and they had caught their speech.

Thornton shook his head. "No, it is splendid, and it is terrible, too. Do you know, it sometimes makes me afraid."

"I'm not hankering to be the man that lays hands on you while he's around," Pete announced conclusively, nodding his head toward Buck.

"Py Jingo!" was Han's contribution. "Not mineself either."

It was at Circle City, ere the year was out, that Pete's apprehensions were realized. "Black" Burton, a man evil-tempered and malicious, had been picking a quarrel with a tenderfoot at the bar, when Thornton stepped good-naturedly between. Buck, as was his custom, was lying in a corner, head on paws, watching his master's every action. Burton struck out, without warning, straight from the shoulder. Thornton was sent spinning, and saved himself from falling only by clutching the rail of the bar.

Those who were looking on heard what was neither bark nor yelp, but a something which is best described as a roar, and they saw Buck's body rise up in the air as he left the floor for Burton's throat. The man saved his life by instinctively throwing out his arm, but was hurled backward to the floor with Buck on top of him. Buck loosed his teeth from the flesh of the arm and drove in again for the throat. This time the man succeeded only in partly blocking, and his throat was torn open. Then the crowd was upon Buck, and he was driven off; but while a surgeon checked the bleeding, he prowled up and down, growling furiously, attempting to rush in, and being forced back by an array of hostile clubs. A "miners' meeting," called on the spot, decided that the dog had sufficient provocation, and Buck was discharged. But his reputation was made, and from that day his name spread through every camp in Alaska.

Later on, in the fall of the year, he saved John Thornton's life in quite another fashion. The three partners were lining a long and narrow poling boat down a bad stretch of rapids on the Fortymile Creek. Hans and Pete moved along the bank, snubbing with a thin manila rope from tree to tree, while Thornton remained in the boat, helping its descent by means of a pole, and shouting directions to the shore. Buck, on the bank, worried and anxious, kept abreast of the boat, his eyes never off his master.

At a particularly bad spot, where a ledge of barely submerged rocks jutted out into the river, Hans cast off the rope, and, while Thornton poled the boat out into the stream, ran down the bank with the end in his hand to snub the boat when it had cleared the ledge. This it did and was flying downstream in a current as swift as a millrace, when Hans checked it with the rope and checked too suddenly. The boat flirted over and snubbed in to the bank bottom up, while Thornton, flung sheer out of it, was carried downstream toward the worse part of the rapids, a stretch of wild water in which no swimmer could live.

Buck had sprung in on the instant; and at the end of three hundred yards, amid a mad swirl of water, he overhauled Thornton. When he felt him grasp his tail, Buck headed for the bank, swimming with all his splendid strength. But the progress shoreward was slow; the progress downstream amazingly rapid. From below came the fatal roaring where the wild current went wilder and was rent in shreds and spray by the rocks which thrust through like the teeth of an enormous comb. The suck of the water as it took the beginning of the last steep pitch was frightful, and Thornton knew that the shore was impossible. He scraped furiously over a rock, bruised across a second, and struck a third with crushing force. He clutched its slippery top with both hands, releasing Buck, and above the roar of the churning water shouted: "Go, Buck! Go!"

Buck could not hold his own, and swept on downstream, struggling desperately, but unable to win back. When he heard Thornton's command repeated, he partly reared out of the water, throwing his head high, as though for a last look, then turned obediently toward the bank. He swam powerfully and was dragged ashore by Pete and Hans at the very point where swimming ceased to be possible and destruction began.

They knew that the time a man could cling to a slippery rock in the face of that driving current was a matter of minutes, and they ran as fast as they could up the bank to a point far above where Thornton was hanging on. They attached the line with which they had been snubbing the boat to Buck's neck and shoulders, being careful that it should neither strangle him nor impede his swimming, and launched him into the stream. He struck out boldly, but not straight enough into the stream. He discovered the mistake too late, when Thornton was abreast of him and a bare half-dozen strokes away while he was being carried helplessly past.

Hans promptly snubbed with the rope, as though Buck were a boat. The rope thus tightening on him in the sweep of the current, he was jerked under the surface, and under the surface he remained til his body struck against the bank and he was hauled out. He was half drowned, and Hans and Pete threw themselves upon him, pounding the breath into him and the water out of him. He staggered to his feet and fell down. The faint sound of Thornton's voice came to them, and though they could not make out the words of it, they knew that he was in his extremity. His master's voice acted on Buck like an electric shock. He sprang to his feet and ran up the bank ahead of the men to the point of his previous departure.

Again the rope was attached and he was launched, and again he struck out, but this time straight into the stream. He had miscalculated once, but he would not be guilty of it a second time. Hans paid out the rope, permitting no slack, while Pete kept it clear of coils. Buck held on till he was on a line straight above Thornton; then he turned, and with the speed of an express train headed down upon him. Thornton saw him coming, and, as Buck struck him like a battering ram, with the whole force of the current behind him, he reached up and closed with both arms around the shaggy neck. Hans snubbed the rope around the tree, and Buck and Thornton were jerked under the water. Strangling, suffocating, sometimes one uppermost and sometimes the other, dragging over the jagged bottom, smashing against rocks and snags, they veered in to the bank.

Thornton came to, belly downward and being violently propelled back and forth across a drift log by

Hans and Pete. His first glance was for Buck, over whose limp and apparently lifeless body Nig was setting up a howl, while Skeet was licking the wet face and closed eyes. Thornton was himself bruised and battered, and he went carefully over Buck's body, when he had been brought around, finding three broken ribs.

"That settles it," he announced. "We camp right here." And camp they did, till Buck's ribs knitted and he was able to travel.

That winter, at Dawson, Buck performed another exploit, not so heroic, perhaps, but one that put his name many notches higher on the totem pole of Alaskan fame. This exploit was particularly gratifying to the three men; for they stood in need of the outfit which it furnished, and were enabled to make a long-desired trip into the virgin East, where miners had not yet appeared. It was brought about by a conversation in the Eldorado Saloon, in which men waxed boastful of their favorite dogs. Buck, because of his record, was the target for these men, and Thornton was driven stoutly to defend him. At the end of half an hour one man stated that his dog could start a sled with five hundred pounds and walk off with it; a second bragged six hundred for his dog; and a third, seven hundred.

"Pooh! Pooh!" said John Thornton, "Buck can start a thousand pounds."

"And break it out? and walk off with it for a hundred yards?" demanded Matthewson, a Bonanza king, he of the seven hundred vaunt.

"And break it out, and walk off with it for a hundred yards," John Thornton said coolly.

"Well," Matthewson said, slowly and deliberately, so

 that all could hear, "I've got a thousand dollars that says he can't. And there it is." So saying, he slammed a sack of gold dust of the size of a bologna sausage down upon the bar.

Nobody spoke. Thornton's bluff, if bluff it was, had been called. He could feel a flush of warm blood creeping up his face. His tongue had tricked him. He did not know whether Buck could start a thousarid pounds. Half a ton! The enormousness of it appalled him. He had great faith in Buck's strength and had often thought him capable of starting such a load; but never, as now, had he faced the possibility of it, the eyes of a dozen men fixed upon him, silent and waiting. Further, he had no thousand dollars; nor had Hans or Pete.

"I've got a sled standing outside now, with twenty fifty-pound sacks of flour on it," Matthewson went on with brutal directness, "so don't let that hinder you."

Thornton did not reply. He did not know what to say. He glanced from face to face in the absent way of a man who has lost the power of thought and is seeking somewhere to find the thing that will start it going again. The face of Jim O'Brien, a Mastodon king and old-time comrade, caught his eyes. It was a cue to him, seeming to rouse him to do what he would never have dreamed of doing.

"Can you lend me a thousand?" he asked, almost in a whisper.

"Sure," answered O'Brien, thumping down a plethoric sack by the side of Matthewson's. "Though it's little faith I'm having, John, that the beast can do the trick."

The Eldorado emptied its occupants into the street to

see the test. The tables were deserted, and the dealers and gamekeepers came forth to see the outcome of the wager and to lay odds. Several hundred men, furred and mittened, banked around the sled within easy distance. Matthewson's sled, loaded with a thousand pounds of flour, had been standing for a couple of hours, and in the intense cold (it was sixty below zero) the runners had frozen fast to the hard-packed snow. Men offered odds of two to one that Buck could not budge the sled. A quibble arose concerning the phrase "break out." O'Brien contended it was Thornton's privilege to knock the runners loose, leaving Buck to "break it out" from a dead standstill. Matthewson insisted that the phrase included breaking the runners from the frozen grip of the snow. A majority of the men who had witnessed the making of the bet decided in his favor, whereat the odds went up to three to one against Buck. There were no takers. Not a man believed him capable of the feat. Thornton had been hurried into the wager, heavy with doubt; and now that he looked at the sled itself, the concrete fact, with the regular team of ten dogs curled up in the snow before it, the more impossible the task appeared. Matthewson waxed jubilant.

"Three to one!" he proclaimed. "I'll lay you another thousand at that figure, Thornton. What d'ye say?"

Thornton's doubt was strong in his face, but his fighting spirit was aroused—the fighting spirit that soars above odds, fails to recognize the impossible, and is deaf to all save the clamor for battle. He called Hans and Pete to him. Their sacks were slim, and with his own the three partners could rake together only two hundred dollars. In the ebb of their fortunes, this sum was their total capital; yet they laid it unhesitatingly against Matthewson's six hundred.

The team of ten dogs was unhitched, and Buck, with his own harness, was put into the sled. He had caught the contagion of the excitement, and he felt that in some way he must do a great thing for John Thornton. Murmurs of admiration at his splendid appearance went up. He was in perfect condition, without an ounce of superfluous flesh, and the one hundred and fifty pounds that he weighed were so many pounds of grit and virility. His furry coat shone with the sheen of silk. Down the neck and across the shoulders, his mane, in repose as it was, half bristled and seemed to lift with every movement, as though excess of vigor made each particular hair alive and active. The great breast and heavy legs were no more than in proportion with the rest of the body where the muscles showed in tight rolls underneath the skin. Men felt these muscles and proclaimed them hard as iron, and the odds went down to two to one.

"Gad, sir! Gad, sir!" stuttered a member of the latest dynasty, a king of the Skookum Benches. "I offer you eight hundred for him, sir, before the test, sir; eight hundred just as he stands."

Thornton shook his head and stepped to Buck's side.

"You must stand off from him," Matthewson protested. "Free play and plenty of room."

The crowd fell silent; only could be heard the voices of the gamblers vainly offering two to one. Everybody acknowledged Buck a magnificent animal, but twenty fifty-pound sacks of flour bulked too large in their eyes for them to loosen their pouch strings.

Thornton knelt down by Buck's side. He took his head in his two hands and rested cheek on cheek. He did not playfully shake him, as was his wont, or murmur soft love curses; but he whispered in his ear. "As you love me, Buck. As you love me," was what he whispered. Buck whined with suppressed eagerness.

The crowd was watching curiously. The affair was growing mysterious. It seemed like a conjuration. As Thornton got to his feet, Buck seized his mittened hand between his jaws, pressing in with his teeth and releasing slowly, half-reluctantly. It was the answer, in terms, not of speech, but of love. Thornton stepped well back.

"Now, Buck," he said.

Buck tightened the traces, then slacked them for a matter of several inches. It was the way he had learned.

"Gee!" Thornton's voice rang out, sharp in the tense silence.

Buck swung to the right, ending the movement in a plunge that took up the slack and with a sudden jerk arrested his one hundred and fifty pounds. The load quivered, and from under the runners arose a crisp crackling.

"Haw!" Thornton commanded.

Buck duplicated the maneuver this time to the left. The crackling turned into a snapping, the sled pivoting and the runners slipping and grating several inches to the side. The sled was broken out. Men were holding their breaths, intensely unconscious of the fact.

"Now, MUSH!"

Thornton's command cracked out like a pistol shot. Buck threw himself forward, tightening the traces with a jarring lunge. His whole body was gathered compactly together in the tremendous effort, the muscles writhing and knotting like live things under the silky fur. His great chest was low to the ground, his head forward and down, while his feet were flying like mad, the claws scarring the hard-packed snow in parallel grooves. The sled swayed and trembled, half-started forward. One of his feet slipped, and one man groaned aloud. Then the sled lurched ahead in what appeared a rapid succession of jerks, though it never really came to a dead stop again . . . half an inch . . . an inch . . . two inches. . . . The jerks perceptibly diminished; as the sled gained momentum, he caught them up, till it was moving steadily along.

Men gasped and began to breathe again, unaware that for a moment they had ceased to breathe. Thornton was running behind, encouraging Buck with short, cheery words. The distance had been measured off, and as he neared the pile of firewood which marked the end of the hundred yards, a cheer began to grow and grow, which burst into a roar as he passed the firewood and halted at command. Every man was tearing himself loose, even Matthewson. Hats and mittens were flying in the air. Men were shaking hands, it did not matter with whom, and bubbling over in a general incoherent babel.

But Thornton fell on his knees beside Buck. Head was against head, and he was shaking him back and forth. Those who hurried up heard him cursing Buck, and he cursed him long and fervently, and softly and lovingly.

"Gad, sir! Gad, sir!" spluttered the Skookum Bench king. "I'll give you a thousand for him, sir, a thousand, sir—twelve hundred, sir."

Thornton rose to his feet. His eyes were wet. The tears were streaming frankly down his cheeks. "Sir," he said to

the Skookum Bench king, "no, sir. You can go to hell, sir. 89
It's the best I can do for you, sir."

Buck seized Thornton's hand in his teeth. Thornton shook him back and forth. As though animated by a common impulse, the onlookers drew back to a respectful distance, nor were they again indiscreet enough to interrupt.

7. *The Sounding of the Call*

When Buck earned sixteen hundred dollars in five minutes for John Thornton, he made it possible for his master to pay off certain debts and to journey with his partners into the East after a fabled lost mine, the history of which was as old as the history of the country. Many men had sought it; few had found it; and more than a few there were who had never returned from the quest. This lost mine was steeped in tragedy and shrouded in mystery. No one knew of the first man. The oldest tradition stopped before it got back to him. From the beginning there had been an ancient and ramshackle cabin. Dying men had sworn to it, and to the mine the site of which it marked, clinching their testimony with nuggets that were unlike any known grade of gold in the Northland.

But no living man had looted this treasure house, and the dead were dead; wherefore John Thornton and Pete and Hans, with Buck and half a dozen other dogs, faced into the East on an unknown trail to achieve where men and dogs as good as themselves had failed. They sledded seventy miles up the Yukon, swung to the left into the Stewart River, passed the Mayo and the McQuesten, and held on until the Stewart itself became a streamlet, threading the upstanding peaks which marked the backbone of the continent.

John Thornton asked little of man or nature. He was

unafraid of the wild. With a handful of salt and a rifle he could plunge into the wilderness and fare wherever he pleased and as long as he pleased. Being in no haste, Indian fashion, he hunted his dinner in the course of the day's travel; and if he failed to find it, like the Indian, he kept on travelling, secure in the knowledge that sooner or later he would come to it. So, on this great journey into the East, straight meat was the bill of fare, ammunition and tools principally made up the load on the sled, and the time-card was drawn upon the limitless future.

To Buck it was boundless delight, this hunting, fishing, and indefinite wandering through strange places. For weeks at a time they would hold on steadily, day after day; and for weeks upon end they would camp, here and there, the dogs loafing and the men burning holes through frozen muck and gravel and washing countless pans of dirt by the heat of the fire. Sometimes they went hungry, sometimes they feasted riotously, all according to the abundance of game and the fortune of hunting. Summer arrived, and dogs and men packed on their backs, rafted across blue mountain lakes, and descended or ascended unknown rivers in slender boats whipsawed from the standing forest.

The months came and went, and back and forth they twisted through the uncharted vastness, where no men were and yet where men had been if the Lost Cabin were true. They went across divides in summer blizzards, shivered under the midnight sun on naked mountains between the timber line and the eternal snows, dropped into summer valleys amid swarming gnats and flies, and in the shadows of glaciers picked strawberries and flowers as ripe and fair as any the Southland could boast. In the fall of the year they penetrated a weird lake country, sad and silent, where wild-fowl had been, but where then there was no life nor sign of life—only the blowing of chill winds, the forming of ice in sheltered places, and the melancholy rippling of waves on lonely beaches.

And through another winter they wandered on the obliterated trails of men who had gone before. Once, they came upon a path blazed through the forest, an ancient path, and the Lost Cabin seemed very near. But the path began nowhere and ended nowhere, and it remained mystery, as the man who made it and the reason he made it remained mystery. Another time they chanced upon the time-graven wreckage of a hunting lodge, and amid the shreds of rotted blankets John Thornton found a long-barrelled flintlock. He knew it for a Hudson Bay Company gun of the young days in the Northwest, when such a gun was worth its height in beaver skins packed flat. And that was all—no hint as to the man who in an early day had reared the lodge and left the gun among the blankets.

Spring came on once more, and at the end of all their wandering they found, not the Lost Cabin, but a shallow placer in a broad valley where the gold showed like yellow butter across the bottom of the washing pan. They sought no farther. Each day they worked earned them thousands of dollars in clean dust and nuggets, and they worked every day. The gold was sacked in moose-hide bags, fifty pounds to the bag, and piled like so much firewood outside the spruce-bough lodge. Like giants they toiled, days flashing on the heels of days like dreams as they heaped the treasure up.

There was nothing for the dogs to do save the hauling

in of meat now and again that Thornton killed, and Buck spent long hours musing by the fire. The vision of the short-legged hairy man came to him more frequently, now that there was little work to be done; and often, blinking by the fire, Buck wandered with him in that other world which he remembered.

The salient thing of this other world seemed fear. When he watched the hairy man sleeping by the fire, head between his knees and hands clasped above, Buck saw that he slept restlessly, with many starts and awakenings, at which times he would peer fearfully into the darkness and fling more wood upon the fire. Did they walk by the beach of a sea, where the hairy man gathered shellfish and ate them as he gathered, it was with eyes that roved everywhere for hidden danger and with legs prepared to run like the wind at its first appearance. Through the forest they crept noiselessly, Buck at the hairy man's heels; and they were alert and vigilant, the pair of them, ears twitching and moving and nostrils quivering, for the man heard and smelled as keenly as Buck. The hairy man could spring up into the trees and travel ahead as fast as on the ground, swinging by the arms from limb to limb, sometimes a dozen feet apart, letting go and catching, never falling, never missing his grip. In fact, he seemed as much at home among the trees as on the ground; and Buck had memories of nights of vigil spent beneath trees wherein the hairy man roosted, holding on tightly as he slept.

And closely akin to the visions of the hairy man was the call still sounding in the depths of the forest. It filled him with a great unrest and strange desires. It caused him to feel a vague, sweet gladness, and he was aware of wild yearnings and stirrings for he knew not what. Sometimes he pursued the call into the forest, looking for it as though it were a tangible thing, barking softly or defiantly, as the mood might dictate. He would thrust his nose into the cool wood moss, or into the black soil where long grasses grew, and snort with joy at the fat earth smells; or he would crouch for hours, as if in concealment, behind fungus-covered trunks of fallen trees, wide-eyed and wide-eared to all that moved and sounded about him. It might be, lying thus, that he hoped to surprise this call he could not understand. But he did not know why he did these various things. He was impelled to do them, and did not reason about them at all.

Irresistible impulses seized him. He would be lying in camp, dozing lazily in the heat of the day, when suddenly his head would lift and his ears cock up, intent and listening, and he would spring to his feet and dash away, and on and on, for hours, through the forest aisles and across the open spaces. He loved to run down dry watercourses, and to creep and spy upon the bird life in the woods. For a day at a time he would lie in the underbrush where he could watch the partridges drumming and strutting up and down. But especially he loved to run in the dim twilight of the summer midnights, listening to the subdued and sleepy murmurs of the forest, reading signs and sounds as man may read a book, and seeking for the mysterious something that called—called, waking or sleeping, at all times, for him to come.

One night he sprang from sleep with a start, eager-eyed, nostrils quivering and scenting, his mane bristling in recurrent waves. From the forest came the call (or one note of it, for the call was many-noted), distinct and definite as never before—a long-drawn howl, like, yet unlike, any noise made by husky dog. And he knew it, in the old familiar way, as a sound heard before. He sprang through the sleeping camp and in swift silence dashed through the woods. As he drew closer to the cry he went more slowly, with caution in every movement, till he came to an open place among the trees, and looking out saw, erect on haunches, with nose pointed to the sky, a long, lean, timber wolf.

He had made no noise, yet it ceased from its howling and tried to sense his presence. Buck stalked into the open, half crouching, body gathered compactly together, tail straight and stiff, feet falling with unwonted care. Every movement advertised commingled threatening and overture of friendliness. It was the menacing truce that marks the meeting of wild beasts that prey. But the wolf fled at sight of him. He followed, with wild leapings, in a frenzy to overtake. He ran him into a blind channel, in the bed of the creek, where a timber jam barred the way. The wolf whirled about, pivoting on his hind legs after the fashion of Joe and of all cornered husky dogs, snarling and bristling, clipping his teeth together in a continuous and rapid succession of snaps.

Buck did not attack, but circled him about and hedged him in with friendly advances. The wolf was suspicious and afraid; for Buck made three of him in weight, while his head barely reached Buck's shoulder. Watching his chance, he darted away, and the chase was resumed. Time and again he was cornered and the thing repeated, though he was in poor condition or Buck could not so easily have overtaken him. He would run till Buck's head was even with his flank, when he would whirl around at bay, only to dash away again at the first opportunity.

But in the end Buck's pertinacity was rewarded; for the wolf, finding that no harm was intended, finally sniffed noses with him. Then they became friendly, and played about in the nervous, half-coy way with which fierce beasts belie their fierceness. After some time of this the wolf started off at an easy lope in a manner that plainly showed he was going somewhere. He made it clear to Buck that he was to come, and they ran side by side through the somber twilight, straight up the creek bed, into the gorge from which it issued, and across the bleak divide where it took its rise.

On the opposite slope of the watershed they came down into a level country where were great stretches of forest and many streams, and through these great stretches they ran steadily, hour after hour, the sun rising higher and the day growing warmer. Buck was wildly glad. He knew he was at last answering the call, running by the side of his wood brother toward the place from where the call surely came. Old memories were coming upon him fast, and he was stirring to them as of old he stirred to the realities of which they were the shadows. He had done this thing before, somewhere in that other and dimly remembered world, and he was doing it again now, running free in the open, the unpacked earth underfoot, the wide sky overhead.

They stopped by a running stream to drink, and, stopping, Buck remembered John Thornton. He sat down. The wolf started on toward the place from where the call surely came, then returned to him, sniffing noses and making actions as though to encourage him. But Buck turned about and started slowly on the back track. For the better part of an hour the wild brother ran by his side, whining softly. Then he sat down, pointed his nose upward, and howled. It was a mournful howl, and as Buck held steadily on his way he heard it grow faint and fainter until it was lost in the distance.

John Thornton was eating dinner when Buck dashed into camp and sprang upon him, in a frenzy of affection, overturning him, scrambling upon him, licking his face, biting his hand—"playing the general tomfool," as John Thornton characterized it, the while he shook Buck back and forth and cursed him lovingly.

For two days and nights Buck never left camp, never let Thornton out of his sight. He followed him about at his work, watched him while he ate, saw him into his blankets at night and out of them in the morning. But after two days the call in the forest began to sound more imperiously than ever. Buck's restlessness came back on him, and he was haunted by recollections of the wild brother, and of the smiling land beyond the divide and the run side by side through the wide forest stretches. Once again he took to wandering in the woods, but the wild brother came no more; and though he listened through long vigils, the mournful howl was never raised.

He began to sleep out at night, staying away from camp for days at a time; and once he crossed the divide at the head of the creek and went down into the land of timber and streams. There he wandered for a week, seeking vainly for fresh sign of the wild brother, killing his meat as he travelled and travelling with the long, easy lope that seems never to tire. He fished for salmon in a broad stream that emptied somewhere into the sea, and by this stream he killed a large black bear, blinded by the mosquitoes while likewise fishing, and raging through the forest helpless and terrible. Even so, it was a hard fight, and it aroused the last latent remnants of Buck's ferocity. And two days later, when he returned to his kill and found a dozen wolverenes quarrelling over the spoil, he scattered them like chaff; and those that fled left two behind who would quarrel no more.

The blood-longing became stronger than ever before. He was a killer, a thing that preyed, living on the things that lived, unaided, alone, by virtue of his own strength and prowess, surviving triumphantly in a hostile environment where only the strong survive. Because of all this he became possessed of a great pride in himself, which communicated itself like a contagion to his physical being. It advertised itself in all his movements, was apparent in the play of every muscle, spoke plainly as speech in the way he carried himself, and made his glorious furry coat if anything more glorious. But for the stray brown on his muzzle and above his eyes, and for the splash of white hair that ran midmost down his chest, he might well have been mistaken for a gigantic wolf, larger than the largest of the breed. From his St. Bernard father he had inherited size and weight, but it was his shepherd mother who had given shape to that size and weight. His muzzle was the long wolf muzzle, save that it was larger than the muzzle of any wolf; and his head, somewhat broader, was the wolf head on a massive scale.

His cunning was wolf cunning, and wild cunning; his intelligence, shepherd intelligence and St. Bernard intelligence; and all this, plus an experience gained in the fiercest of schools, made him as formidable a creature as any that roamed the wild. A carnivorous animal, living on a straight meat diet, he was in full flower, at the high tide of his life, overspilling with vigor and virility. When Thornton passed a caressing hand along his back, a snapping and crackling followed the hand, each hair discharging its pent magnetism at the contact. Every part, brain and body, nerve tissue and fibre, was keyed to the most exquisite pitch; and between all the parts there was a perfect equilibrium or adjustment. To sights and sounds and events which required action, he responded with lightning-like rapidity. Quickly as a husky dog could leap to defend from attack or to attack, he could leap twice as quickly. He saw the movement, or heard sound, and responded in less time than another dog required to compass the mere seeing or hearing. He perceived and determined and responded in the same instant. In point of fact the three actions of perceiving, determining, and responding were sequential; but so infinitesimal were the intervals of time between them that they appeared simultaneous. His muscles were surcharged with vitality, and snapped into play sharply, like steel springs. Life streamed through him in splendid flood, glad and rampant, until it seemed that it would burst him asunder in sheer ecstasy and pour forth generously over the world.

"Never was there such a dog," said John Thornton one day, as the partners watched Buck marching out of camp.

"When he was made, the mould was broke," said Pete.

"Py jingo! I t'ink so mineself," Hans affirmed.

They saw him marching out of camp, but they did not see the instant and terrible transformation which took place as soon as he was within the secrecy of the forest. He no longer marched. At once he became a thing of the wild, stealing along softly, cat-footed, a passing shadow that appeared and disappeared among the shadows. He knew how to take advantage of every cover, to crawl on his belly like a snake, and like a snake to leap and strike. He could take a ptarmigan from its nest, kill a rabbit as it slept, and snap in mid air the little chipmunks fleeing a second too late for the trees. Fish, in open pools, were not too quick for him; nor were beaver, mending their dams, too wary. He killed to eat, not from wantonness; but he preferred to eat what he killed himself. So a lurking humor ran through his deeds, and it was his delight to steal upon the squirrels, and, when he all but had them, to let them go, chattering in mortal fear to the treetops.

As the fall of the year came on, the moose appeared in greater abundance, moving slowly down to meet the winter in the lower and less rigorous valleys. Buck had already dragged down a stray part-grown calf; but he wished strongly for larger and more formidable quarry, and he came upon it one day on the divide at the head of the creek. A band of twenty moose had crossed over from the land of streams and timber, and chief among them was a great bull. He was in a savage temper, and, standing over six feet from the ground, was as formidable an antagonist as ever Buck could desire. Back and forth the bull tossed his great palmated antlers, branching to fourteen points and embracing seven feet within the tips. His small eyes burned with a vicious and bitter light, while he roared with fury at sight of Buck.

From the bull's side, just forward of the flank, protruded a feathered arrowend, which accounted for his savageness. Guided by that instinct which came from the old hunting days of the primordial world, Buck proceeded to cut the bull out from the herd. It was no slight task. He would bark and dance about in front of the bull, just out of reach of the great antlers and of the terrible splay hoofs which could have stamped his life out with a single blow. Unable to turn his back on the fanged danger and go on, the bull would be driven into paroxysms of rage. At such moments he charged Buck, who retreated craftily, luring him on by a simulated inability to escape. But when he was thus separated from his fellows, two or three of the younger bulls would charge back upon Buck and enable the wounded bull to rejoin the herd.

There is a patience of the wild—dogged, tireless, persistent as life itself—that holds motionless for endless hours the spider in its web, the snake in its coils, the panther in its ambuscade; this patience belongs peculiarly to life when it hunts its living food; and it belonged to Buck as he clung to the flank of the herd, retarding its march, irritating the young bulls, worrying the cows with their half-grown calves, and driving the wounded bull mad with helpless rage. For half a day this continued. Buck multiplied himself, attacking from all sides, enveloping the herd in a whirlwind of menace, cutting out his victim as fast as it could rejoin its mates, wearing out the patience of creatures preyed upon, which is a lesser patience than that of creatures preying.

As the day wore along and the sun dropped to its bed in the northwest (the darkness had come back and the fall nights were six hours long), the young bulls retraced their steps more and more reluctantly to the aid of their beset leader. The down-coming winter was harrying them on to the lower levels, and it seemed they could never shake off this tireless creature that held them back. Besides, it was not the life of the herd, or of the young bulls, that was threatened. The life of only one member was demanded, which was a remoter interest than their lives, and in the end they were content to pay the toll.

As twilight fell the old bull stood with lowered head, watching his mates—the cows he had known, the calves he had fathered, the bulls he had mastered—as they shambled on at a rapid pace through the fading light. He could not follow, for before his nose leaped the merciless fanged terror that would not let him go. Three hundredweight more than half a ton he weighed; he had lived a long, strong life, full of fight and struggle, and at the end he faced death at the teeth of a creature whose head did not reach beyond his great knuckled knees.

From then on, night and day, Buck never left his prey, never gave it a moment's rest, never permitted it to browse the leaves of trees or the shoots of young birch and willow. Nor did he give the wounded bull opportunity to slake his burning thirst in the slender trickling streams they crossed. Often, in desperation, he burst into long stretches of flight. At such times Buck did not attempt to stay him, but loped easily at his heels, satisfied with the way the game was played, lying down when the moose stood still, attacking him fiercely when he strove to eat or drink.

The great head drooped more and more under its tree of horns, and the shambling trot grew weaker and weaker. He took to standing for long periods, with nose to the ground and dejected ears dropped limply; and Buck found more time in which to get water for himself and in which to rest. At such moments, panting with red lolling tongue and with eyes fixed upon the big bull, it appeared to Buck that a change was coming over the face of things. He could feel a new stir in the land. As the moose were coming into the land, other kinds of life were coming in. Forest and stream and air seemed palpitant with their presence. The news of it was borne in upon him, not by sight or sound, or smell, but by some other and subtler sense. He heard nothing, saw nothing, yet knew that the land was somehow different; that through it strange things were afoot and ranging; and he resolved to investigate after he had finished the business in hand.

At last, at the end of the fourth day, he pulled the great moose down. For a day and a night he remained by the kill, eating and sleeping, turn and turn about. Then, rested, refreshed and strong, he turned his face toward camp and John Thornton. He broke into the long easy lope, and went on, hour after hour, never at loss for the tangled way, heading straight home through strange country with a certitude of direction that put man and his magnetic needle to shame.

As he held on he became more and more conscious of the new stir in the land. There was life abroad in it different from the life which had been there throughout the summer. No longer was this fact borne in upon him in some subtle, mysterious way. The birds talked of it, the squirrels chattered about it, the very breeze whispered of it. Several times he stopped and drew in the fresh morning air in great sniffs, reading a message which made him leap on with greater speed. He was oppressed with a sense of calamity happening, if it were not calamity already happened; and as he crossed the last watershed and dropped down into the valley toward camp, he proceeded with greater caution.

Three miles away he came upon a fresh trail that sent

 his neck hair rippling and bristling. It led straight toward camp and John Thornton. Buck hurried on, swiftly and stealthily, every nerve straining and tense, alert to the multitudinous details which told a story—all but the end. His nose gave him a varying description of the passage of the life on the heels of which he was travelling. He remarked the pregnant silence of the forest. The bird life had flitted. The squirrels were in hiding. One only he saw—a sleek gray fellow, flattened against a gray dead limb so that he seemed a part of it, a woody excrescence upon the wood itself.

As Buck slid along with the obscureness of a gliding shadow, his nose was jerked suddenly to the side as though a positive force had gripped and pulled it. He followed the new scent into a thicket and found Nig. He was lying on his side, dead where he had dragged himself, an arrow protruding, head and feathers, from either side of his body.

A hundred yards farther on, Buck came upon one of the sled dogs Thornton had bought in Dawson. This dog was thrashing about in a death struggle, directly on the trail, and Buck passed around him without stopping. From the camp came the faint sound of many voices, rising and falling in a singsong chant. Bellying forward to the edge of the clearing, he found Hans, lying on his face, feathered with arrows like a porcupine. At the same instant Buck peered out where the spruce-bough lodge had been and saw what made his hair leap straight up on his neck and shoulders. A gust of overpowering rage swept over him. He did not know that he growled, but he growled aloud with a terrible ferocity. For the last time in his life he allowed passion to usurp cunning and reason, and it was because of his great love for John Thornton that he lost his head.

The Yeehats were dancing about the wreckage of the spruce-bough lodge when they heard a fearful roaring and saw rushing upon them an animal the like of which they had never seen before. It was Buck, a live hurricane of fury, hurling himself upon them in a frenzy to destroy. He sprang at the foremost man (it was the chief of the Yeehats), ripping the throat wide open till the rent jugular spouted a fountain of blood. He did not pause to worry the victim, but ripped in passing, with the next bound tearing wide the throat of a second man. There was no withstanding him. He plunged about in their very midst, tearing, rending, destroying, in constant and terrific motion which defied the arrows they discharged at him. In fact, so inconceivably rapid were his movements, and so closely were the Indians tangled together, that they shot one another with the arrows; and one young hunter, hurling a spear at Buck in mid air, drove it through the chest of another hunter with such force that the point broke through the skin of the back and stood out beyond. Then a panic seized the Yeehats, and they fled in terror to the woods, proclaiming as they fled the advent of the Evil Spirit.

And truly Buck was the Fiend incarnate, raging at their heels and dragging them down like deer as they raced through the trees. It was a fateful day for the Yeehats. They scattered far and wide over the country, and it was not till a week later that the last of the survivors gathered together in a lower valley and counted their

106 losses. As for Buck, wearying of the pursuit, he returned to the desolated camp. He found Pete where he had been killed in his blankets in the first moment of surprise. Thornton's desperate struggle was fresh-written on the earth, and Buck scented every detail of it down to the edge of a deep pool. By the edge, head and fore feet in the water, lay Skeet, faithful to the last. The pool itself, muddy and discolored from the sluice boxes, effectually hid what it contained, and it contained John Thornton; for Buck followed his trace into the water, from which no trace led away.

All day Buck brooded by the pool or roamed restlessly above the camp. Death, as a cessation of movement, as a passing out and away from the lives of the living, he knew, and he knew John Thornton was dead. It left a great void in him, somewhat akin to hunger, but a void which ached and ached, and which food could not fill. At times, when he paused to contemplate the carcasses of the Yeehats, he forgot the pain of it; and at such times he was aware of a great pride in himself—a pride greater than any he had yet experienced. He had killed man, the noblest game of all, and he had killed in the face of the law of club and fang. He sniffed the bodies curiously. They had died so easily. It was harder to kill a husky dog than them. They were no match at all, were it not for their arrows and spears and clubs. Thenceforward he would be unafraid of them except when they bore in their hands their arrows, spears, and clubs.

Night came on, and a full moon rose high over the trees into the sky, lighting the land till it lay bathed in ghostly day. And with the coming of the night, brooding and mourning by the pool, Buck became alive to a stirring of the new life in the forest other than that which the Yeehats had made. He stood up, listening and scenting. From far away drifted a faint, sharp yelp, followed by a chorus of similar sharp yelps. As the moments passed the yelps grew closer and louder. Again Buck knew them as things heard in that other world which persisted in his memory. He walked to the center of the open space and listened. It was the call, the many-noted call, sounding more luringly and compelling than ever before. And as never before, he was ready to obey. John Thornton was dead. The last tie was broken. Man and the claims of man no longer bound him.

Hunting their living meat, as the Yeehats were hunting it, on the flanks of the migrating moose, the wolf pack had at last crossed over from the land of streams and timber and invaded Buck's valley. Into the clearing where the moonlight streamed, they poured in a silvery flood; and in the center of the clearing stood Buck, motionless as a statue, waiting their coming. They were awed, so still and large he stood, and a moment's pause fell, till the boldest one leaped straight for him. Like a flash Buck struck, breaking the neck. Then he stood, without movement, as before, the stricken wolf rolling in agony behind him. Three others tried it in sharp succession; and one after the other they drew back, streaming blood from slashed throats or shoulders.

This was sufficient to fling the whole pack forward, pell-mell, crowded together, blocked and confused by its eagerness to pull down the prey. Buck's marvellous quickness and agility stood him in good stead. Pivoting on his hind legs, and snapping and gashing, he was everywhere at once, presenting a front which was apparently unbroken so swiftly did he whirl and guard from side to side. But to prevent them from getting behind him, he was forced back, down past the pool and into a creek bed, till he brought up against a high gravel bank. He worked along to a right angle in the bank which the men had made in the course of mining, and in this angle he came to bay, protected on three sides and with nothing to do but face the front.

And so well did he face it, that at the end of half an hour the wolves drew back discomfited. The tongues of all were out and lolling, the white fangs showing cruelly white in the moonlight. Some were lying down with heads raised and ears pricked forward; others stood on their feet, watching him; and still others were lapping water from the pool. One wolf, long and lean and gray, advanced cautiously, in a friendly manner, and Buck recognized the wild brother with whom he had run for a night and a day. He was whining softly, and, as Buck whined, they touched noses.

Then an old wolf, gaunt and battle-scarred, came forward. Buck writhed his lips into the preliminary of a snarl, but sniffed noses with him. Whereupon the old wolf sat down, pointed nose at the moon, and broke out the long wolf howl. The others sat down and howled. And now the call came to Buck in unmistakable accents. He, too, sat down and howled. This over, he came out of his angle and the pack crowded around him, sniffing in half-friendly, half-savage manner. The leaders lifted the yelp of the pack and sprang away into the woods. The wolves swung in behind, yelping in chorus. And Buck ran with them, side by side with the wild brother, yelping as he ran.

And here may well end the story of Buck. The years were not many when the Yeehats noted a change in the breed of timber wolves; for some were seen with splashes of brown on head and muzzle, and with a rift of white centering down the chest. But more remarkable than this, the Yeehats tell of a Ghost Dog that runs at the head of the pack. They are afraid of this Ghost Dog, for it has cunning greater than they, stealing from their camps in fierce winters, robbing their traps, slaying their dogs, and defying their bravest hunters.

Nay, the tale grows worse. Hunters there are who fail to return to the camp, and hunters there have been whom their tribesmen found with throats slashed cruelly open and with wolf prints about them in the snow greater than the prints of any wolf. Each fall, when the Yeehats follow the movement of the moose, there is a certain valley which they never enter. And women there are who become sad when the word goes over the fire of how the Evil Spirit came to select that valley for an abiding place.

In the summers there is one visitor, however, to that valley, of which the Yeehats do not know. It is a great, gloriously coated wolf, like, and yet unlike, all other wolves. He crosses along from the smiling timber land and comes down into an open space among the trees. Here a yellow stream flows from rotted moose-hide sacks and sinks into the ground, with long grasses growing through it and vegetable mould overruning it and hiding its yellow from the sun; and here he muses for a time, howling once, long and mournfully, ere he departs.

But he is not always alone. When the long winter nights come on and the wolves follow their meat into the lower valleys, he may be seen running at the head of the pack through the pale moonlight or glimmering borealis, leaping gigantic above his fellows, his great throat a-bellow as he sings a song of the younger world, which is the song of the pack.

THAT SPOT

I don't think much of Stephen Mackaye any more, though I used to swear by him. I know that in those days I loved him more than my own brother. If ever I meet Stephen Mackaye again, I shall not be responsible for my actions. It passes beyond me that a man with whom I shared food and blanket, and with whom I mushed over the Chilkoot Trail, should turn out the way he did. I always sized Steve up as a square man, a kindly comrade, without an iota of anything vindictive or malicious in his nature. I shall never trust my judgment in men again. Why, I nursed that man through typhoid fever; we starved together on the headwaters of the Stewart; and he saved my life on the Little Salmon. And now, after the years we were together, all I can say of Stephen Mackaye is that he is the meanest man I ever knew.

We started for the Klondike in the fall rush of 1897, and we started too late to get over Chilkoot Pass before the freeze-up. We packed our outfit on our backs part way over, when the snow began to fly, and then we had to buy dogs in order to sled it the rest of the way. That was how we came to get that Spot. Dogs were high, and we paid one hundred and ten dollars for him. He looked worth it. I say *looked*, because he was one of the finest-appearing dogs I ever saw. He weighed sixty pounds, and he had all the lines of a good sled animal. We never could make out his breed. He wasn't husky, nor Malemute, nor Hudson Bay; he looked like all of them and he didn't look like any of them; and on top of it all he had some of the white man's dog in him, for on one side, in the thick of the mixed yellow-brown-red-and-dirty-white that was his prevailing color, there was a spot of coal black as big as a water bucket. That was why we called him Spot.

He was a good looker all right. When he was in condition his muscles stood out in bunches all over him. And he was the strongest-looking brute I ever saw in Alaska, also the most intelligent-looking. To run your eyes over him, you'd think he could outpull three dogs of his own weight. Maybe he could, but I never saw it. His intelligence didn't run that way. He could steal and forage to perfection; he had an instinct that was positively grewsome for divining when work was to be done and for making a sneak accordingly; and for getting lost and not staying lost he was nothing short of inspired. But when it came to work, the way that intelligence dribbled out of him and left him a mere clot of wobbling, stupid jelly would make your heart bleed.

There are times when I think it wasn't stupidity. Maybe, like some men I know, he was too wise to work. I shouldn't wonder if he put it all over us with that intelligence of his. Maybe he figured it all out and decided that a licking now and again and no work was a whole lot better than work all the time and no licking. He was intelligent enough for such a computation. I tell you, I've sat and looked into that dog's eyes till the shivers ran up and down my spine and the marrow crawled like yeast, what of the intelligence I saw shining out. I can't express myself about that intelligence. It is beyond mere words. I saw it, that's all. At times it was like gazing into a human soul, to look into his eyes; and what I saw there frightened me and started all sorts of ideas in my own mind of reincarnation and all the rest. I tell you I sensed something big in that brute's eyes; there was a message there, but I wasn't big enough myself to catch it. Whatever it was (I know I'm making a fool of myself)—whatever it was, it baffled me. I can't give an inkling of what I saw in that brute's eyes; it wasn't light, it wasn't color; it was something that moved, away back, when the eyes themselves weren't moving. And I guess I didn't see it move, either; I only sensed that it moved. It was an expression—that's what it was—and I got an impression of it. No; it was different from a mere expression; it was more than that. I don't know what it was, but it gave me a feeling of kinship just the same. Oh, no, not sentimental kinship. It was, rather, a kinship of equality. Thoses eyes never pleaded like a deer's eyes. They challenged. No, it wasn't defiance. It was just a calm assumption of equality. And I don't think it was deliberate. My belief is that it was unconscious on his part. It was there because it was there, and it couldn't help shining out. No, I don't mean shine. It didn't shine; it *moved.* I know I'm talking rot, but if you'd looked into that animal's eyes the way I have, you'd understand. Steve was affected the same way I was. Why, I tried to kill that Spot once—he was no good for anything; and I fell down on it. I led him out into the brush, and he came along slow and unwilling. He knew what was going on. I stopped in a likely place, put my foot on the rope, and pulled my big Colt's. And that dog sat down and looked at me. I tell you he didn't plead. He just looked. And I saw all kinds of incomprehensible things moving, yes, *moving*, in those eyes of his. I didn't really see them move; I thought I saw them, for, as I said before, I guess I only sensed them. And I want to tell you right now that it got beyond me. It was like killing a man, a conscious, brave man who looked calmly into your gun as much as to say, "Who's afraid?" Then, too, the message seemed so near that, instead of pulling the trigger quick, I stopped to see if I could catch the message. There it was, right before me, glimmering all around in those eyes of his. And then it was too late. I got scared. I was trembly all over, and my stomach generated a nervous palpitation that made me seasick. I just sat down and looked at that dog, and he looked at me, till I thought I was going crazy. Do you want to know what I did? I threw down the gun and ran back to camp with the fear of God in my heart. Steve laughed at me. But I notice that Steve led Spot into the woods, a week later, for the same purpose, and that Steve came back alone, and a little later Spot drifted back, too.

At any rate, Spot wouldn't work. We paid a hundred and ten dollars for him from the bottom of our sack, and he wouldn't work. He wouldn't even tighten the traces. Steve spoke to him the first time we put him in harness, and he sort of shivered, that was all. Not an ounce on the traces. He just stood still and wobbled, like so much jelly. Steve touched him with the whip. He yelped, but not an ounce. Steve touched him again, a bit harder, and he howled—the regular long wolf howl. Then Steve got mad and gave him half a dozen, and I came on the run from the tent.

I told Steve he was brutal with the animal, and we had some words—the first we'd ever had. He threw the whip down in the snow and walked away mad. I picked it up and went to it. That Spot trembled and wobbled and cowered before ever I swung the lash, and with first bite of it he howled like a lost soul. Next he lay down in the snow. I started the rest of the dogs, and they dragged him along while I threw the whip into him. He rolled over on his back and bumped along, his four legs waving in the air, himself howling as though he was going through a sausage machine. Steve came back and laughed at me, and I apologized for what I'd said.

There was no getting any work out of that Spot; and to make up for it, he was the biggest pig-glutton of a dog I ever saw. On top of that, he was the cleverest thief. There was no circumventing him. Many a breakfast we went without our bacon because Spot had been there first. And it was because of him that we nearly starved to death up the Stewart. He figured out the way to break into our meat-cache, and what he didn't eat, the rest of the team did. But he was impartial. He stole from everybody. He was a restless dog, always very busy snooping around or going somewhere. And there was never a camp within five miles that he didn't raid. The worst of it was that they always came back on us to pay his board bill, which was just, being the law of the land; but it was mighty hard on us, especially that first winter on the Chilkoot, when we were busted, paying for whole hams and sides of bacon that we never ate. He could fight, too, that Spot. He could do everything but work. He never pulled a pound, but he was the boss of the whole team. The way he made those dogs stand around was an education. He bullied them, and there was always one or more of them fresh-marked with his fangs. But he was more than a bully. He wasn't afraid of anything that walked on four legs; and I've seen him march, single-handed, into a strange team, without any provocation whatever, and put the *kibosh* on the whole outfit. Did I say he could eat? I caught him eating the whip once. That's straight. He started in at the lash, and when I caught him he was down to the handle, and still going.

But he was a good looker. At the end of the first week we sold him for seventy-five dollars to the Mounted Police. They had experienced dog drivers, and we knew that by the time he'd covered the six hundred miles to Dawson he'd be a good sled dog. I say we *knew,* for we were just getting acquainted with that Spot. A little later we were not brash enough to know anything where he was concerned. A week later we woke up in the morning to the dangdest dog fight we'd ever heard. It was that Spot come back and knocking the team into shape. We ate a pretty depressing breakfast, I can tell you; but cheered up two hours afterward when we sold him to an official courier, bound in to Dawson with government dispatches. That Spot was only three days in coming back, and, as usual, celebrated his arrival with a rough-house.

We spent the winter and spring, after our own outfit was across the pass, freighting other people's outfits; and we made a fat stake. Also, we made money out of Spot. If we sold him once, we sold him twenty times. He always came back, and no one asked for their money. We didn't want the money. We'd have paid handsomely for any one to take him off our hands for keeps. We had to get rid of him, and we couldn't give him away, for that would have been suspicious. But he was such a fine looker that we never had any difficulty in selling him. "Unbroke," we'd say, and they'd pay any old price for him. We sold him as low as twenty-five dollars, and once we got a hundred and fifty for him. That particular party returned him in person, refused to take his money back, and the way he abused us was something awful. He said it was cheap at the price to tell us what he thought of us; and we felt he was so justified that we never talked back. But to this day I've never quite regained all the old self-respect that was mine before that man talked to me.

When the ice cleared out of the lakes and river, we put our outfit in a Lake Bennett boat and started for Dawson. We had a good team of dogs, and of course we piled them on top the outfit. That Spot was along—there was no losing him; and a dozen times, the first day, he knocked one or another of the dogs overboard in the course of fighting with them. It was close quarters, and he didn't like being crowded.

"What that dog needs is space." Steve said the second day. "Let's maroon him."

We did, running the boat in a Caribou Crossing for him to jump ashore. Two of the other dogs, good dogs, followed him; and we lost two whole days trying to find them. We never saw those two dogs again; but the quietness and relief we enjoyed made us decide, like the man who refused his hundred and fifty, that it was cheap at the price. For the first time in months Steve and I laughed and whistled and sang. We were as happy as clams. The dark days were over. The nightmare had been lifted. That Spot was gone.

Three weeks later, one morning, Steve and I were standing on the river bank at Dawson. A small boat was just arriving from Lake Bennett. I saw Steve give a start, and heard him say something that was not nice and that was not under his breath. Then I looked; and there, in the bow of the boat, with ears pricked up, sat Spot. Steve and I sneaked immediately, like beaten curs, like cowards, like absconders from justice. It was this last that the lieutenant of police thought when he saw us sneaking. He surmised that there were law-officers in the boat who were after us. He didn't wait to find out, but kept us in sight, and in the M. & M. saloon got us in a corner. We had a merry time explaining, for we refused to go back to the boat and meet Spot; and finally he held us under guard of another policeman while he went to the boat. After we got clear of him, we started for the cabin, and when we arrived, there was that Spot sitting on the stoop waiting for us. Now how did he know we lived there? There were forty thousand people in Dawson that summer, and how did he *savve* our cabin out of all the cabins? How did he know we were in Dawson, anyway? I leave it to you. But don't forget what I have said about his intelligence and that immortal something I have seen glimmering in his eyes.

There was no getting rid of him any more. There were too many people in Dawson who had bought him up on Chilkoot, and the story got around. Half a dozen times we put him on board steamboats going down the Yukon; but he merely went ashore at the first landing and trotted back up the bank. We couldn't sell him, we couldn't kill him (both Steve and I had tried), and nobody else was able to kill him. He bore a charmed life. I've seen him go down in a dog fight on the main street with fifty dogs on top of him, and when they were separated, he'd appear on all his four legs, unharmed, while two of the dogs that had been on top of him would be lying dead.

I saw him steal a chunk of moose meat from Major Dinwiddie's cache so heavy that he could just keep one jump ahead of Mrs. Dinwiddie's squaw cook, who was after him with an axe. As he went up the hill, after the squaw gave up, Major Dinwiddie himself came out and pumped his Winchester into the landscape. He emptied his magazine twice, and never touched that Spot. Then a policeman came along and arrested him for discharging firearms inside the city limits. Major Dinwiddie paid his fine, and Steve and I paid him for the moose meat at the rate of a dollar a pound, bones and all. That was what he paid for it. Meat was high that year.

I am only telling what I saw with my own eyes. And now I'll tell you something, also. I saw that Spot fall through a water hole. The ice was three and a half feet thick, and the current sucked him under like a straw. Three hundred yards below was the big water hole used by the hospital. Spot crawled out of the hospital water hole, licked off the water, bit out the ice that had formed between his toes, trotted up the bank, and whipped a big Newfoundland belonging to the Gold Commissioner.

In the fall of 1898, Steve and I poled up the Yukon on the last water, bound for Stewart River. We took the dogs along, all except Spot. We figured we'd been feeding him long enough. He'd cost us more time and trouble and money and grub than we'd got by selling him on the Chilkoot—especially grub. So Steve and I tied him down in the cabin and pulled our freight. We camped that night at the mouth of Indian River, and Steve and I were pretty facetious over having shaken him. Steve was a funny cuss, and I was just sitting up in the blankets and laughing when a tornado hit camp. The way that Spot walked into those dogs and gave them what-for was hair-raising. Now how did he get loose? It's up to you. I haven't any theory. And how did he get across the Klondike River? That's another facer. And anyway, how did he know we had gone up the Yukon? You see, we went by water, and he couldn't smell our tracks. Steve and I began to get superstitious about that dog. He got on our nerves, too; and, between you and me, we were just a mite afraid of him.

The freeze-up came on when we were at the mouth of Henderson Creek, and we traded him off for two sacks of flour to an outfit that was bound up White River after copper. Now that whole outfit was lost. Never trace nor hide nor hair of men, dogs, sleds, or anything was ever found. They dropped clean out of sight. It became one of the mysteries of the country. Steve and I plugged away up the Stewart, and six weeks afterward that Spot crawled into camp. He was a perambulating skeleton, and could just drag along; but he got there. And what I want to know is who told him we were up the Stewart? We could have gone a thousand other places. How did he know? You tell me, and I'll tell you.

No losing him. At the Mayo he started a row with an Indian dog. The buck who owned the dog took a swing at Spot with an axe, missed him, and killed his own dog.

 Talk about magic and turning bullets aside—I, for one, consider it blamed sight harder to turn an axe aside with a big buck at the other end of it. And I saw him do it with my own eyes. That buck didn't want to kill his own dog. You've got to show me.

I told you about Spot breaking into our meat cache. It was nearly the death of us. There wasn't any more meat to be killed, and meat was all we had to live on. The moose had gone back several hundred miles and the Indians with them. There we were. Spring was on, and we had to wait for the river to break. We got pretty thin before we decided to eat the dogs, and we decided to eat Spot first. Do you know what that dog did? He sneaked. Now how did he know our minds were made up to eat him? We sat up nights laying for him, but he never came back, and we ate the other dogs. We ate the whole team.

And now for the sequel. You know what it is when a big river breaks up and few billion tons of ice go out, jamming and milling and grinding. Just in the thick of it, when the Stewart went out, rumbling and roaring, we sighted Spot out in the middle. He'd got caught as he was trying to cross up above somewhere. Steve and I yelled and shouted and ran up and down the bank, tossing our hats in the air. Sometimes we'd stop and hug each other, we were that boisterous, for we saw Spot's finish. He didn't have a chance in a million. He didn't have any chance at all. After the ice run, we got into a canoe and paddled down to the Yukon, and down the Yukon to Dawson, stopping to feed up for a week at the cabins at the mouth of Henderson Creek. And as we came in to the bank at Dawson, there sat that Spot, waiting for us, his ears pricked up, his tail wagging, his mouth smiling, extending a hearty welcome to us. Now how did he get out of that ice? How did he know we were coming to Dawson, to the very hour and minute, to be out there on the bank waiting for us?

The more I think of that Spot, the more I am convinced that there are things in this world that go beyond science. On no scientific grounds can that Spot be explained. It's psychic phenomena, or mysticism, or something of that sort, I guess, with a lot of theosophy thrown in. The Klondike is a good country. I might have been there yet, and become a millionaire, if it hadn't been for Spot. He got on my nerves. I stood him for two years all together, and then I guess my stamina broke. It was the summer of 1899 when I pulled out. I didn't say anything to Steve. I just sneaked. But I fixed it up all right. I wrote Steve a note, and enclosed a package of "rough-on-rats," telling him what to do with it. I was worn down to skin and bone by that Spot, and I was that nervous that I'd jump and look around when there wasn't anybody within hailing distance. But it was astonishing the way I recuperated when I got quit of him. I got back twenty pounds before I arrived in San Francisco, and by the time I'd crossed the ferry to Oakland I was my old self again, so that even my wife looked in vain for any change in me.

Steve wrote to me once, and his letter seemed irritated. He took it kind of hard because I'd left him with Spot. Also, he said he'd used the "rough-on-rats," per directions, and that there was nothing doing. A year went by. I was back in the office and prospering in all ways—even getting a bit fat. And then Steve arrived. He didn't look me up. I read his name in the steamer list, and wondered why. But I didn't wonder long. I got up one morning and found that Spot chained to the gatepost and holding up the milkman. Steve went north to Seattle, I learned, that very morning. I didn't put on any more weight. My wife made be buy him a collar and tag, and within an hour he showed his gratitude by killing her pet Persian cat. There is no getting rid of that Spot. He will be with me until I die, for he'll never die. My appetite is not so good since he arrived, and my wife says I am looking peaked. Last night that Spot got into Mr. Harvey's hen-house (Harvey is my next door neighbor) and killed nineteen of his fancy-bred chickens. I shall have to pay for them. My neighbor on the other side quarrelled with my wife and then moved out. Spot was the cause of it. And that is why I am disappointed in Stephen Mackaye. I had no idea he was so mean a man.

IN YEDDO BAY

Somewhere along Theater Street he had lost it. He remembered being hustled somewhat roughly on the bridge over one of the canals that cross that busy thoroughfare. Possibly some slant-eyed, light-fingered pickpocket was even then enjoying the fifty-odd yen his purse had contained. And then again, he thought, me might have lost it himself, just lost it carelessly.

Hopelessly, and for the twentieth time, he searched in all his pockets for the missing purse. It was not there. His hand lingered in his empty hip pocket, and he woefully regarded the voluble and vociferous restaurant keeper, who insanely clamored: "Twenty-five sen! You pay now! Twenty-five sen!"

"But my purse!" the boy said. "I tell you I've lost it somewhere."

Whereupon the restaurant keeper lifted his arms indignantly and shrieked: "Twenty-five sen! Twenty-five sen! You pay now!"

Quite a crowd had collected, and it was growing embarrassing for Alf Davis.

It was so ridiculous and petty, Alf thought. Such a disturbance about nothing! And, decidedly, he must be doing something. Thoughts of diving wildly through that forest of legs, and of striking out at whomsoever opposed him, flashed through his mind; but, as though divining his purpose, one of the waiters, a short and chunky chap with an evil-looking cast in one eye, seized him by the arm.

"You pay now! You pay now! Twenty-five sen!" yelled the proprietor, hoarse with rage.

Alf was red in the face, too, from mortification; but he resolutely set out on another exploration. He had given up the purse, pinning his last hope on stray coins. In the little change-pocket of his coat he found a ten-sen piece and five-copper sen; and remembering having recently missed a ten-sen piece, he cut the seam of the pocket and resurrected the coin from the depths of the lining. Twenty-five sen he held in his hand, the sum required to pay for the supper he had eaten. He turned them over to the proprietor, who counted them, grew suddenly calm, and bowed obsequiously—in fact, the whole crowd bowed obsequiously and melted away.

Alf Davis was a young sailor, just turned sixteen, on board the *Annie Mine*, an American sailing schooner, which had run into Yokohama to ship its season's catch of skins to London. And in this, his second trip ashore, he was beginning to snatch his first puzzling glimpses of the Oriental mind. He laughed when the bowing and kotowing was over, and turned on his heel to confront another problem. How was he to get aboard ship? It was eleven o'clock at night, and there would be no ship's boats ashore, while the outlook for hiring a native boatman, with nothing but empty pockets to draw upon, was not particularly inviting.

Keeping a sharp lookout for shipmates, he went down to the pier. At Yokohama there are no long lines of wharves. The shipping lies out at anchor, enabling a few hundred of the short-legged people to make a livelihood by carrying passengers to and from the shore.

A dozen sampan men and boys hailed Alf and offered their services. He selected the most favorable-looking one, an old and beneficent-appearing man with a withered leg. Alf stepped into his sampan and sat down. It was quite dark and he could not see what the old fellow was doing, though he evidently was doing nothing about shoving off and getting under way. At last he limped over and peered into Alf's face.

"Ten sen," he said.

"Yes, I know, ten sen," Alf answered carelessly. "But hurry up. American schooner."

"Ten sen. You pay now," the old fellow insisted.

Alf felt himself grow hot all over at the hateful words "pay now." "You take me to American schooner; then I pay," he said.

But the man stood up patiently before him, held out his hand, and said, "Ten sen. You pay now."

Alf tried to explain. He had no money. He had lost his purse. But he would pay. As soon as he got aboard the American schooner, then he would pay. No; he would not even go aboard the American schooner. He would call to his shipmates, and they would give the sampan man the ten sen first. After than he would go aboard. So it was all right, of course.

To all of which the beneficent-appearing old man replied: "You pay now. Ten sen." And, to make matters worse, the other sampan men squatted on the pier steps, listening.

Alf, chagrined and angry, stood up to step ashore. But the old fellow laid a detaining hand on his sleeve. "You give shirt now. I take you 'Merican schooner," he proposed.

Then it was that all of Alf's American independence flamed up in his breast. The Anglo-Saxon has a born dislike of being imposed upon, and to Alf this was sheer robbery! Ten sen was equivalent to six American cents, while his shirt, which was of good quality and was new, had cost him two dollars.

He turned his back on the man without a word, and went out to the end of the pier, the crowd, laughing with great gusto, following at his heels. The majority of them were heavy set, muscular fellows, and the July night being one of sweltering heat, they were clad in the least possible raiment. The water people of any race are rough and turbulent, and it struck Alf that to be out at midnight on a pier end with such a crowd of wharfmen, in a big Japanese city, was not as safe as it might be.

One burly fellow, with a shock of black hair and ferocious eyes, came up. The rest shoved in after him to take part in the discussion.

"Give me shoes," the man said. "Give me shoes now. I take you 'Merican schooner."

Alf shook his head, whereat the crowd clamored that he accept the proposal. Now the Anglo-Saxon is so constituted that to browbeat or bully him is the last way under the sun of getting him to do any certain thing. He will dare willingly, but he will not permit himself to be driven. So this attempt of the boatmen to force Alf only aroused all the dogged stubbornness of his race. The same qualities were in him that are in men who lead forlorn hopes; and there, under the stars, on the lonely pier, encircled by the jostling and shouldering gang, he resolved that he would die rather than submit to the indignity of being robbed of a single stitch of clothing. Not value, but principle, was at stake.

Then somebody thrust roughly against him from behind. He whirled about with flashing eyes, and the circle involuntarily gave ground. But the crowd was growing more boisterous. Each and every article of clothing he had on was demanded by one or another, and these demands were shouted simultaneously at the tops of very healthy lungs.

Alf had long since ceased to say anything, but he knew that the situation was getting dangerous, and that the only thing left to him was to get away. His face was set doggedly, his eyes glinted like points of steel, and his body was firmly and confidently poised. This air of determination sufficiently impressed the boatmen to make them give way before him when he started to walk toward the shore end of the pier. But they trooped along beside him and behind him, shouting and laughing more noisily than ever. One of the youngsters, about Alf's size and build, impudently snatched his cap from his head; but before he could put it on his own head, Alf struck out from the shoulder, and sent the fellow rolling on the stones.

The cap flew out of his hand and disappeared among the many legs. Alf did some quick thinking; his sailor pride would not permit him to leave the cap in their hands. He followed in the direction it had sped, and soon found it under the bare foot of a stalwart fellow, who kept his weight stolidly upon it. Alf tried to get the cap out by a sudden jerk, but failed. He shoved against the man's leg, but the man only grunted. It was challenge direct, and Alf accepted it. Like a flash one leg was behind the man and Alf had thrust strongly with his shoulder against the fellow's chest. Nothing could save the man from the fierce vigorousness of the trick, and he was hurled over and backward.

Next, the cap was on Alf's head and his fists were up before him. Then he whirled about to prevent attack from behind, and all those in that quarter fled precipitately. This was what he wanted. None remained between him and the shore end. The pier was narrow. Facing them and threatening with his fist those who attempted to pass him on either side, he continued his retreat. It was exciting work, walking backward and at the same time checking that surging mass of men. But the dark-skinned peoples, the world over, have learned to respect the white man's fist; and it was the battles fought by many sailors, more than his own warlike front, that gave Alf the victory.

Where the pier adjoins the shore was the station of the harbor police, and Alf backed into the electric-lighted office, very much to the amusement of the dapper lieutenant in charge. The sampan men, grown quiet and orderly, clustered like flies by the open door, through which they could see and hear what passed.

Alf explained his difficulty in few words, and demanded, as the privilege of a stranger in a strange land, that the lieutenant put him aboard in the police boat. The lieutenant, in turn, who knew all the "rules and regulations" by heart, explained that the harbor police were not ferrymen, and that the police boats had other functions to perform than that of transporting belated and penniless sailormen to their ships. He also said he knew the sampan men to be natural-born robbers, but that so long as they robbed within the law he was powerless. It was their right to collect fares in advance, and who was he to command them to take a passenger and collect fare at the journey's end? Alf acknowledged the justice of his remarks, but suggested that while he could not command he might persuade. The lieutenant was willing to oblige, and went to the door, from where he delivered a speech to the crowd. But they, too, knew their rights, and, when the officer had finished, shouted in chorus their abominable "Ten sen! You pay now! You pay now!"

"You see, I can do nothing," said the lieutenant, who, by the way, spoke perfect English. "But I have warned them not to harm or molest you, so you will be safe, at least. The night is warm and half over. Lie down somewhere and go to sleep. I would permit you to sleep here in the office, were it not against the rules and regulations."

Alf thanked him for his kindness and courtesy; but the sampan men had aroused all his pride of race and doggedness, and the problem could not be solved that way. To sleep out the night on the stones was an acknowledgment of defeat.

"The sampan men refuse to take me out!"

The lieutenant nodded.

"And you refuse to take me out?"

Again the lieutenant nodded.

"Well, then, it's not in the rules and regulations that you can prevent my taking myself out?"

The lieutenant was perplexed. "There is no boat," he said.

"That's not the question," Alf proclaimed hotly. "If I take myself out, everybody's satisfied and no harm done?"

"Yes; what you say is true," persisted the puzzled lieutenant. "But you cannot take yourself out."

"You just watch me," was the retort.

Down went Alf's cap on the office floor. Right and left he kicked off his low-cut shoes. Trousers and shirt followed.

"Remember," he said in ringing tones, "I, as a citizen of the United States, shall hold you, the city of Yokohama, and the government of Japan responsible for those clothes. Good night."

He plunged through the doorway, scattering the astounded boatmen to either side, and ran out on the pier. But they quickly recovered and ran after him, shouting with glee at the new phase the situation had taken on. It was a night long remembered among the water folk of Yokohama town. Straight to the end Alf ran, and, without pause, dived off cleanly and neatly into the water. He struck out with a lusty, single overhand stroke till curiosity prompted him to halt for a moment. Out of the darkness, from where the pier should be, voices were calling to him.

He turned on his back, floated, and listened.

 "All right! All right!" he could distinguish from the babel. "No pay now; pay bime by! Come back! Come back now; pay bime by!"

"No, thank you," he called back. "No pay at all. Good night."

Then he faced about in order to locate the *Annie Mine.* She was fully a mile away, and in the darkness it was no easy task to get her bearings. First, he settled upon a blaze of lights which he knew nothing but a man-of-war could make. That must be the United States war-ship *Lancaster.* Somewhere to the left and beyond should be the *Annie Mine.* But to the left he made out three lights close together. That could not be the schooner. For the moment he was confused. He rolled over on his back and shut his eyes, striving to construct a mental picture of the harbor as he had seen it in daytime. With a snort of satisfaction he rolled back again. The three lights evidently belonged to the big English tramp steamer. Therefore the schooner must lie somewhere between the three lights and the *Lancaster.* He gazed long and steadily, and there, very dim and low, but at the point he expected, burned a single light—the anchor light of the *Annie Mine.*

And it was a fine swim under the starshine. The air was warm as the water, and the water as warm as tepid milk. The good salt taste of it was in his mouth, the tingling of it along his limbs; and the steady beat of his heart, heavy and strong, made him glad for living.

But beyond being glorious the swim was uneventful. On the right hand he passed the many-lighted *Lancaster,* on the left hand the English tramp, and ere long the *Annie Mine* loomed large above him. He grasped the hanging rope ladder and drew himself noiselessly on deck.

There was no one in sight. He saw a light in the galley, and knew that the captain's son, who kept the lonely anchor watch, was making coffee. Alf went forward to the forecastle. The men were snoring in their bunks, and in that confined space the heat seemed to him insufferable. So he put on a thin cotton shirt and a pair of dungaree trousers, tucked blanket and pillow under his arm, and went up on deck and out on the forecastle-head.

Hardly had he begun to doze when he was roused by a boat coming alongside and hailing the anchor watch. It was the police boat, and to Alf it was given to enjoy the excited conversation that ensued. Yes, the captain's son recognized the clothes. They belonged to Alf Davis, one of the seamen. What had happened? No; Alf Davis had not come aboard. He was ashore. He was not ashore? Then he must be drowned. Here both the lieutenant and the captain's son talked at the same time, and Alf could make out nothing. Then he heard them come forward and rouse out the crew. The crew grumbled sleepily and said that Alf Davis was not in the forecastle; whereupon the captain's son waxed indignant at the Yokohama police and their ways, and the lieutenant quoted rules and regulations in despairing accents.

Alf rose up from the forecastlehead and extended his hand, saying:

"I guess I'll take those clothes. Thank you for bringing them aboard so promptly."

"I don't see why he couldn't have brought you aboard inside of them," said the captain's son.

And the police lieutenant said nothing, though he turned the clothes over somewhat sheepishly to their rightful owner.

 The next day, when Alf started to go ashore, he found himself surrounded by shouting and gesticulating, though very respectful, sampan men, all extraordinarily anxious to have him for a passenger. Nor did the one he selected say, "You pay now," when he entered his boat. When Alf prepared to step out on to the pier, he offered the man the customary ten sen. But the man drew himself up and shook his head.

"You all right," he said. "You no pay. You never no pay. You bully boy and all right."

And for the rest of the *Annie Mine's* stay in port, the sampan men refused money at Alf Davis's hand. Out of admiration for his pluck and independence, they had given him the freedom of the harbor.

AN ADVENTURE IN THE UPPER SEA

I am a retired captain of the upper sea. That is to say, when I was a younger man (which is not so long ago) I was an aeronaut and navigated that aerial ocean which is all around about us and above us. Naturally it is a hazardous profession, and naturally I have had many thrilling experiences, the most thrilling, or at least the most nerve-racking, being the one I am about to relate.

It happened before I went in for hydrogen gas balloons, all of varnished silk, doubled and lined, and all that, and fit for voyages of days instead of mere hours. The *Little Nassau* (named after the *Great Nassau* of many years back) was the balloon I was making ascents in at the time. It was a fair-sized, hot-air affair, of single thickness, good for an hour's flight or so and capable of attaining an altitude of a mile or more. It answered my purpose, for my act at the time was making half-mile parachute jumps at recreation parks and country fairs. I was in Oakland, a California town, filling a summer's engagement with a street railway company. The company owned a large park outside the city, and of course it was

to its interest to provide attractions which would send
the townspeople over its line when they went out to get a whiff of country air. My contract called for two ascensions weekly, and my act was an especially taking feature, for it was on my days that the largest crowds were drawn.

Before you can understand what happened, I must first explain a bit about the nature of the hot-air balloon which is used for parachute jumping. If you have ever witnessed such a jump, you will remember that directly the parachute was cut loose the balloon turned upside down, emptied itself of its smoke and heated air, flattened out and fell straight down, beating the parachute to the ground. Thus there is no chasing a big deserted bag for miles and miles across the country, and much time, as well as trouble, is thereby saved. This maneuver is accomplished by attaching a weight, at the end of a long rope, to the top of the balloon. The aeronaut, with his parachute and trapeze, hangs to the bottom of the balloon, and, weighing more, keeps it right side down. But when he lets go, the weight attached to the top immediately drags the top down, and the bottom, which is the open mouth, goes up, the heated air pouring out. The weight used for this purpose on the *Little Nassau* was a bag of sand.

But to return. On the particular day I have in mind there was an unusually large crowd in attendance, and the police had their hands full keeping the people back. There was much pushing and shoving, and the ropes were bulging with the pressure of men, women and children. As I came down from the dressing room I noticed two girls outside the ropes, of about fourteen and sixteen, and inside the rope a youngster of eight or nine. They were holding him by the hands, and he was struggling, excitedly and half in laughter, to get away from them. I thought nothing of it at the time—just a bit of childish play, no more; and it was only in the light of after events that the scene was impressed vividly upon me.

"Keep them cleared out, George!" I called to my assistant. "We don't want any accidents."

"Ay," he answered, "that I will, Charley."

George Guppy had helped me in no end of ascents, and because of his coolness, judgment and absolute reliability I had come to trust my life in his hands with the utmost confidence. His business it was to overlook the inflating of the balloon, and to see that everything about the parachute was in perfect working order.

The *Little Nassau* was already filled and straining at the guys. The parachute lay flat along the ground and beyond it the trapeze. I tossed aside my overcoat, took my position, and gave the signal to let go. As you know, the first rush upward from the earth is very sudden, and this time the balloon, when it first caught the wind, heeled violently over and was longer than usual in righting. I looked down at the old familiar sight of the world rushing away from me. And there were the thousands of people, every face silently upturned. And the silence startled me, for, as crowds went, this was the time for them to catch their first breath and send up a roar of applause. But there was no hand-clapping, whistling, cheering—only silence. And instead, clear as a bell and distinct, without the slightest shake or quaver, came George's voice through the megaphone:

"Ride her down, Charley! Ride the balloon down!"

What had happened? I waved my hand to show that I had heard, and began to think. Had something gone wrong with the parachute? Why should I ride the balloon down instead of making the jump which thousands were waiting to see? What was the matter? And as I puzzled, I received another start. The earth was a thousand feet beneath, and yet I heard a child crying softly, and seemingly very close to hand. And though the *Little Nassau* was shooting skyward like a rocket, the crying did not grow fainter and fainter and die away. I confess I was almost on the edge of a funk, when, unconsciously following up the noise with my eyes, I looked above me and saw a boy astride the sandbag which was to bring the *Little Nassau* to earth. And it was the same little boy I had seen struggling with the two girls—his sisters, as I afterward learned.

There he was, astride the sandbag and holding on to the rope for dear life. A puff of wind heeled the balloon slightly, and he swung out into space for ten or a dozen feet, and back again, fetching up against the tight canvas with a thud which even shook me, thirty feet or more beneath. I thought to see him dashed loose, but he clung on and whimpered. They told me afterward, how, at the moment they were casting off the balloon, the little fellow had torn away from his sisters, ducked under the rope, and deliberately jumped astride the sandbag. It has always been a wonder to me that he was not jerked off in the first rush.

Well, I felt sick all over as I looked at him there, and I understood why the balloon had taken longer to right itself, and why George had called after me to ride her down. Should I cut loose with the parachute, the bag would at once turn upside down, empty itself, and begin its swift descent. The only hope lay in my riding her down and in the boy holding on. There was no possible way for me to reach him. No man could climb the slim, closed parachute; and even if a man could, and made the mouth of the balloon, what could he do? Straight out, and fifteen feet away, trailed the boy on his ticklish perch, and those fifteen feet were empty space.

I thought far more quickly than it takes to tell all this, and realized on the instant that the boy's attention must be called away from his terrible danger. Exercising all the self-control I possessed, and striving to make myself very calm, I said cheerily:

"Hello, up there, who are you?"

He looked down at me, choking back his tears and brightening up, but just then the balloon ran into a cross-current, turned half around and lay over. This set him swinging back and forth, and he fetched the canvas another bump. Then he began to cry again.

"Isn't it great?" I asked heartily, as though it was the most enjoyable thing in the world; and, without waiting for him to answer: "What's your name?"

"Tommy Dermott," he answered.

"Glad to make your acquaintance, Tommy Dermott," I went on. "But I'd like to know who said you could ride up with me?"

He laughed and said he just thought he'd ride up for the fun of it. And so we went on, I sick with fear for him, and cudgeling my brains to keep up the conversation. I knew that it was all I could do, and that his life depended upon my ability to keep his mind off his danger. I pointed out to him the great panorama spreading away to the ho-

rizon and four thousand feet beneath us. There lay San
Francisco Bay like a great placid lake, the haze of smoke over the city, the Golden Gate, the ocean fog rim beyond, the Mount Tamalpais over all, clear-cut and sharp against the sky. Directly below us I could see a buggy, apparently crawling, but I knew from experience that the men in it were lashing the horses on our trail.

But he grew tired of looking around, and I could see he was beginning to get frightened.

"How would you like to go in for the business?" I asked.

He cheered up at once and asked, "Do you get good pay?"

But the *Little Nassau,* beginning to cool, had started on its long descent, and ran into counter currents which bobbed it roughly about. This swung the boy around pretty lively, smashing him into the bag once quite severely. His lip began to tremble at this, and he was crying again. I tried to joke and laugh, but it was no use. His pluck was oozing out, and at any moment I was prepared to see him go shooting past me.

I was in despair. Then, suddenly, I remembered how one fright could destroy another fright, and I frowned up at him and shouted sternly:

"You just hold on to that rope! If you don't I'll thrash you within an inch of your life when I get you down on the ground! Understand?"

"Ye-ye-yes, sir," he whimpered, and I saw that the thing had worked. I was nearer to him than the earth, and he was more afraid of me than of falling.

"Why, you've got a snap up there on that soft bag," I rattled on.

 "Yes," I assured him, "this bar down here is hard and narrow, and it hurts to sit on it."

Then a thought struck him, and he forgot all about his aching fingers.

"When are you going to jump?" he asked. "That's what I came up to see."

I was sorry to disappoint him, but I wasn't going to make any jump.

But he objected to that. "It said so in the papers," he said.

"I don't care," I answered. "I'm feeling sort of lazy to-day, and I'm just going to ride down the balloon. It's my balloon and I guess I can do as I please about it. And, anyway, we're almost down now."

And we were, too, and sinking fast. And right there and then that youngster began to argue with me as to whether it was right for me to disappoint the people, and to urge their claims upon me. And it was with a happy heart that I held up my end of it, justifying myself in a thousand different ways, till we shot over a grove of eucalyptus trees and dipped to meet the earth.

"Hold on tight!" I shouted, swinging down from the trapeze by my hands in order to make a landing on my feet.

We skimmed past a barn, missed a mesh of clothesline, frightened the barnyard chickens into a panic, and rose up again clear over a haystack—all this almost quicker than it takes to tell. Then we came down in an orchard, and when my feet had touched the ground I fetched up the balloon by a couple of turns of the trapeze around an apple tree.

I have had my balloon catch fire in mid air, I have

hung on the cornice of a ten-story house, I have dropped like a bullet for six hundred feet when a parachute was slow in opening; but never have I felt so weak and faint and sick as when I staggered toward the unscratched boy and gripped him by the arm.

"Tommy Dermott," I said, when I had got my nerves back somewhat. "Tommy Dermott, I'm going to lay you across my knee and give you the greatest thrashing a boy ever got in the world's history."

"No, you don't," he answered, squirming around. "You said you wouldn't if I held on tight."

"That's all right," I said, "but I'm going to, just the same. The fellows who go up in balloons are bad, unprincipled men, and I'm going to give you a lesson right now to make you stay away from them, and from balloons, too."

And then I gave it to him, and if it wasn't the greatest thrashing in the world, it was the greatest he ever got.

But it took all the grit out of me, left me nerve-broken, that experience. I canceled the engagement with the street railway company, and later on went in for gas. Gas is much the safer, anyway.

CHARLIE'S COUP

Perhaps our most laughable exploit on the fish patrol, and at the same time our most dangerous one, was when we rounded in, at a single haul, an even score of wrathful fishermen. Charley called it a "coop," having heard Neil Partington use the term; but I think he misunderstood the word, and thought it meant "coop," to catch, to trap. The fishermen, however, coup or coop, must have called it a Waterloo, for it was the severest stroke ever dealt them by the fish patrol, while they had invited it by open and impudent defiance of the law.

During what is called the "open season" the fishermen might catch as many salmon as their luck allowed and their boats could hold. But there was one important restriction. From sundown Saturday night to sunup Monday morning, they were not permitted to set a net. This was a wise provision on the part of the Fish Commission, for it was necessary to give the spawning salmon some opportunity to ascend the river and lay their eggs. And this law, with only an occasional violation, had been obediently observed by the Greek fishermen who caught salmon for the canneries and the market.

148 One Sunday morning, Charley received a telephone call from a friend in Collinsville, who told him that the full force of fishermen was out with its nets. Charley and I jumped into our salmon boat and started for the scene of the trouble. With a light favoring wind at our back we went through the Carquinez Straits, crossed Suisun Bay, passed the Ship Island Light, and came upon the whole fleet at work.

But first let me describe the method by which they worked. The net used is what is known as a gill net. It has a simple diamond-shaped mesh which measures at least seven and one-half inches between the knots. From five to seven and even eight hundred feet in length, these nets are only a few feet wide. They are not stationary, but float with the current, the upper edge supported on the surface by floats, the lower edge sunk by means of leaden weights.

This arrangement keeps the net upright in the current and effectually prevents all but the smaller fish from ascending the river. The salmon, swimming near the surface, as is their custom, run their heads through these meshes, and are prevented from going on through by their larger girth of body, and from going back because of their gills, which catch in the mesh. It requires two fishermen to set such a net,—one to row the boat, while the other, standing in the stern, carefully pays out the net. When it is all out, stretching directly across the stream, the men make their boat fast to one end of the net and drift along with it.

As we came upon the fleet of law-breaking fishermen, each boat two or three hundred yards from its neighbors, and boats and nets dotting the river as far as we could

see, Charley said, "I've only one regret, lad, and that is
that I haven't a thousand arms so as to be able to catch them all. As it is, we'll only be able to catch one boat, for while we are tackling that one it will be up nets and away with the rest."

As we drew closer, we observed none of the usual flurry and excitement which our appearance invariably produced. Instead, each boat lay quietly by its net, while the fishermen favored us with not the slightest attention.

"It's curious," Charley muttered. "Can it be they don't recognize us?"

I said that it was impossible, and Charley agreed; yet there was a whole fleet, manned by men who knew us only too well, and who took no more notice of us than if we were a hay scow or a pleasure yacht.

This did not continue to be the case, however, for as we bore down upon the nearest net, the men to whom it belonged detached their boat and rowed slowly toward the shore. The rest of the boats showed no sign of uneasiness.

"That's funny," was Charley's remark. "But we can confiscate the net, at any rate."

We lowered sail, picked up one end of the net, and began to heave it into the boat. But at the first heave we heard a bullet zip-zipping past us on the water, followed by the faint report of a rifle. The men who had rowed ashore were shooting at us. At the next heave a second bullet went zipping past, perilously near. Charley took a turn around a pin and sat down. There were no more shots. But as soon as he began to heave in, the shooting recommenced.

"That settles it," he said, flinging the end of the net

overboard. "You fellows want it worse than we do, and you can have it."

We rowed over toward the next net, for Charley was intent on finding out whether or not we were face to face with an organized defiance. As we approached, the two fishermen proceeded to cast off from their net and row ashore, while the first two rowed back and made fast to the net we had abandoned. And at the second net we were greeted by rifle shots till we desisted and went on to the third, where the maneuver was again repeated.

Then we gave it up, completely routed, and hoisted sail and started on the long windward beat back to Benicia. A number of Sundays went by, on each of which the law was persistently violated. Yet, short of an armed force of soldiers, we could do nothing. The fishermen had hit upon a new idea and were using it for all it was worth, while there seemed no way by which we could get the better of them.

About this time Neil Partington happened along from the Lower Bay, where he had been for a number of weeks. With him was Nicholas, the Greek boy who had helped us in our raid on the oyster pirates, and the pair of them took a hand. We made our arrangements carefully. It was planned that while Charley and I tackled the nets, they were to be hidden ashore so as to ambush the fishermen who landed to shoot at us.

It was a pretty plan. Even Charley said it was. But we reckoned not half so well as the Greeks. They forestalled us by ambushing Neil and Nicholas and taking them prisoners, while, as of old, bullets whistled about our ears when Charley and I attempted to take possession of the nets. When we were again beaten off, Neil Partington and Nicholas were released. They were rather shame-faced when they put in an appearance, and Charley chaffed them unmercifully. But Neil chaffed back, demanding to know why Charley's imagination had not long since overcome the difficulty.

"Just you wait; the idea'll come all right," Charley promised.

"Most probably," Neil agreed. "But I'm afraid the salmon will be exterminated first, and then there will be no need for it when it does come."

Neil Partington, highly disgusted with his adventure, departed for the Lower Bay, taking Nicholas with him, and Charley and I were left to our own resources. This meant that the Sunday fishing would be left to itself, too, until such time as Charley's idea happened along. I puzzled my head a good deal to find out some way of checkmating the Greeks, as also did Charley, and we broached a thousand expedients which on discussion proved worthless.

The fishermen, on the other hand, were in high feather, and their boasts went up and down the river to add to our discomfiture. Among all classes of them we became aware of a growing insubordination. We were beaten, and they were losing respect for us. With the loss of respect, contempt began to arise. Charley began to be spoken of as the "olda woman," and I received my rating as the "pee-wee kid." The situation was fast becoming unbearable, and we knew that we should have to deliver a stunning stroke at the Greeks in order to regain the old-time respect in which we had stood.

Then one morning the idea came. We were down on Steamboat Wharf, where the river steamers made their landings, and where we found a group of amused longshoremen and loafers listening to the hard-luck tale of a sleepy-eyed young fellow in long sea boots. He was a sort of amateur fisherman, he said, fishing for the local market of Berkeley. Now Berkeley was on the Lower Bay, thirty miles away. On the previous night, he said, he had set his net and dozed off to sleep in the bottom of the boat.

The next he knew it was morning, and he opened his eyes to find his boat rubbing softly against the piles of Steamboat Wharf at Benicia. Also he saw the river steamer *Apache* lying ahead of him, and a couple of deck-hands disentangling the shreds of his net from the paddle-wheel. In short, after he had gone to sleep, his fisherman's riding light had gone out, and the *Apache* had run over his net. Though torn pretty well to pieces, the net in some way still remained foul, and he had had a thirty-mile tow out of his course.

Charley nudged me with his elbow. I grasped his thought on the instant, but objected:

"We can't charter a steamboat."

"Don't intend to," he rejoined. "But let's run over to Turner's Shipyard. I've something in my mind there that may be of use to us."

And over we went to the shipyard, where Charley led the way to the *Mary Rebecca,* lying hauled out on the ways, where she was being cleaned and overhauled. She was a scow schooner we both knew well, carrying a cargo of one hundred and forty tons and a spread of canvas greater than any other schooner on the bay.

"How d'ye do, Ole," Charley greeted a big blue-shirted Swede who was greasing the jaws of the main gaff with a piece of pork rind.

Ole grunted, puffed away at his pipe, and went on greasing. The captain of a bay schooner is supposed to work with his hands just as well as the men.

Ole Ericsen verified Charley's conjecture that the *Mary Rebecca*, as soon as launched, would run up the San Joaquin River nearly to Stockton for a load of wheat. Then Charley made his proposition, and Ole Ericsen shook his head.

"Just a hook, one good-sized hook," Charley pleaded.

"No, Ay tank not," said Ole Ericsen. "Der *Mary Rebecca* yust hang up on efery mud bank with that hook. Ay don't want to lose der *Mary Rebecca*. She's all Ay got."

"No, no," Charley hurried to explain. "We can put the end of the hook through the bottom from the outside, and fasten it on the inside with a nut. After it's done its work, why, all we have to do is to go down into the hold, unscrew the nut, and out drops the hook. Then drive a wooden peg into the hole, and the *Mary Rebecca* will be all right again."

Ole Ericsen was obstinate for a long time; but in the end, after we had had dinner with him, he was brought round to consent.

"Ay do it, by Yupiter!" he said, striking one huge fist into the palm of the other hand. "But yust hurry you up with der hook. Der *Mary Rebecca* slides into der water tonight."

It was Saturday, and Charley had need to hurry. We headed for the shipyard blacksmith shop, where, under Charley's directions, a most generously curved hook of heavy steel was made. Back we hastened to the *Mary Rebecca*. Aft of the great centerboard case, through what was properly her keel, a hole was bored. The end of the hook was inserted from the outside, and Charley, on the inside, screwed the nut on tightly. As it stood complete, the hook projected over a foot beneath the bottom of the schooner. Its curve was something like the curve of a sickle, but deeper.

In the late afternoon the *Mary Rebecca* was launched, and preparations were finished for the start upriver next morning. Charley and Ole intently studied the evening sky for signs of wind, for without a good breeze our project was doomed to failure. They agreed that there were all the signs of a stiff westerly wind—not the ordinary afternoon sea breeze, but a half gale, which even then was springing up.

Next morning found their predictions verified. The sun was shining brightly, but something more than a half gale was shrieking up the Carquinez Straits, and the *Mary Rebecca* got under way with two reefs in her mainsail and one in her foresail. We found it quite rough in the Straits and in Suisun Bay; but as the water grew more landlocked it became calm, though without letup in the wind.

Off Ship Island Light the reefs were shaken out, and at Charley's suggestion a big fisherman's staysail was made all ready for hoisting, and the maintopsail, bunched into a cap at the masthead, was overhauled so that it could be set on an instant's notice.

We were tearing along, wing and wing, before the wind, foresail to starboard and mainsail to port, as we came upon the salmon fleet. There they were, boats and nets, as on that first Sunday when they had bested us, strung out evenly over the river as far as we could see. A narrow space on the right-hand side of the channel was left clear for steamboats, but the rest of the river was covered with the wide-stretching nets. The narrow space was our logical course, but Charley, at the wheel, steered the *Mary Rebecca* straight for the nets.

This did not cause any alarm among the fishermen, because upriver sailing craft are always provided with "shoes" on the ends of their keels, which permit them to slip over the nets without fouling them.

"Now she takes it!" Charley cried, as we dashed across the middle of a line of floats which marked a net. At one end of this line was a small barrel buoy, at the other the two fishermen in their boat. Buoy and boat at once began to draw together, and the fishermen to cry out, as they were jerked after us. A couple of minutes later we hooked a second net, and then a third, and in this fashion we tore straight up through the centre of the fleet.

The consternation we spread among the fishermen was tremendous. As fast as we hooked a net the two ends of it, buoy and boat, came together as they dragged out astern; and so many buoys and boats, coming together at such breakneck speed, kept the fishermen on the jump to avoid smashing into one another. Also, they shouted at us like mad to heave to into the wind, for they took it as some drunken prank on the part of scow sailors, little dreaming that we were the fish patrol.

The drag of a single net is very heavy, and Charley and Ole Ericsen decided that even in such a wind ten nets were all the *Mary Rebecca* could take along with her. So when we had hooked ten nets, with ten boats containing twenty men streaming along behind us, we veered to the left out of the fleet and headed toward Collinsville.

We were all jubilant. Charley was handling the wheel as though he were steering the winning yacht home in a race. The two sailors who made up the crew of the *Mary Rebecca*, were grinning and joking. Ole Ericsen was rubbing his huge hands in childlike glee.

"Ay tank you fish patrol fallers never ban so lucky as when you sail with Ole Ericsen," he was saying, when a rifle cracked sharply astern, and a bullet gouged along the newly painted cabin, glanced on a nail, and sang shrilly onward into space.

This was too much for Ole Ericsen. At sight of his beloved paintwork thus defaced, he jumped up and shook his fist at the fishermen; but a second bullet smashed into the cabin not six inches from his head, and he dropped down to the deck under cover of the rail.

All the fishermen had rifles, and they now opened a general fusillade. We were all driven to cover—even Charley, who was compelled to desert the wheel. Had it not been for the heavy drag of the nets, we would inevitably have broached to at the mercy of the enraged fishermen. But the nets, fastened to the bottom of the *Mary Rebecca* well aft, held her stern into the wind, and she continued to plough on, though somewhat erratically.

Charley, lying on the deck, could just manage to reach the lower spokes of the wheel; but while he could steer after a fashion, it was very awkward. Ole Ericsen bethought himself of a large piece of sheet steel in the empty hold. It was in fact a plate from the side of the *New Jersey*, a steamer which had recently been wrecked outside the Golden Gate, and in the salving of which the *Mary Rebecca* had taken part.

Crawling carefully along the deck, the two sailors, Ole, and myself got the heavy plate on deck and aft, where we reared it as a shield between the wheel and the fishermen. The bullets whanged and banged against it till it rang like a bull's-eye, but Charley grinned in its shelter, and coolly went on steering.

So we raced along, behind us a howling, screaming bedlam of wrathful Greeks, Collinsville ahead, and bullets spat-spatting all around us.

"Ole," Charley said in a faint voice, "I don't know what we're going to do."

Ole Ericsen, lying on his back close to the rail and grinning upward at the sky, turned over on his side and looked at him. "Ay tank we go into Collinsville yust der same," he said.

"But we can't stop," Charley groaned. "I never thought of it, but we can't stop."

A look of consternation slowly overspread Ole Ericsen's broad face. It was only too true. We had a hornet's nest on our hands, and to stop at Collinsville would be to have it about our ears.

"Every man Jack of them has a gun," one of the sailors remarked cheerfully.

"Yes, and a knife, too," the other sailor added.

It was Ole Ericsen's turn to groan. "What for a Svaidish faller like me monkey with none of my biziness, I don't know," he soliloquized.

A bullet glanced on the stern and sang off to starboard like a spiteful bee. "There's nothing to do but plump the *Mary Rebecca* ashore and run for it," was the verdict of the first cheerful sailor.

"And leaf der *Mary Rebecca*?" Ole demanded, with unspeakable horror in his voice.

"Not unless you want to," was the response. "But I don't want to be within a thousand miles of her when those fellers come aboard"—indicating the bedlam of excited Greeks towing behind.

We were right in at Collinsville then, and went foaming by within biscuit-toss of the wharf.

"I only hope the wind holds out," Charley said, stealing a glance at our prisoners.

"What of der wind?" Ole demanded disconsolately. "Der river will not hold out, and then . . . and then . . ."

"It's head for tall timber, and the Greeks take the hindermost," adjudged the cheerful sailor, while Ole was stuttering over what would happen when we came to the end of the river.

We had now reached a dividing of the ways. To the left was the mouth of the Sacramento River, to the right the mouth of the San Joaquin. The cheerful sailor crept forward and jibed over the foresail as Charley put the helm to starboard and we swerved to the right into the San Joaquin. The wind, from which we had been running away on an even keel, now caught us on our beam, and the *Mary Rebecca* was pressed down on her port side as if she were about to capsize.

Still we dashed on, and still the fishermen dashed on behind. The value of their nets was greater than the fines they would have to pay for violating the fish laws; so to cast off from their nets and escape, which they could easily do, would profit them nothing. Further, they remained by their nets instinctively, as a sailor remains by his ship. And still further, the desire for vengeance was roused, and we could depend upon it that they would follow us to the ends of the earth, if we undertook to tow them that far.

The rifle firing had ceased, and we looked astern to see

what our prisoners were doing. The boats were strung along at unequal distances apart, and we saw the four nearest ones bunching together. This was done by the boat ahead trailing a small rope astern to the one behind. When this was caught, they would cast off from their net and heave in on the line till they were brought up to the boat in front. So great was the speed at which we were travelling, however, that this was very slow work. Sometimes the men would strain to their utmost and fail to get in an inch of the rope; at other times they came ahead more rapidly.

When the four boats were near enough together for a man to pass from one to another, one Greek from each of three got into the nearest boat to us, taking his rifle with him. This made five in the foremost boat, and it was plain that their intention was to board us. This they undertook to do, by main strength and sweat, running hand over hand the float line of a net. And though it was slow, and they stopped frequently to rest they gradually drew nearer.

Charley smiled at their efforts, and said, "Give her the topsail, Ole."

The cap at the mainmast head was broken out, and sheet and downhaul pulled flat, amid a scattering rifle fire from the boats; and the *Mary Rebecca* lay over and sprang ahead faster than ever.

But the Greeks were undaunted. Unable, at the increased speed, to draw themselves nearer by means of their hands, they rigged from the blocks of their boat sail what sailors call a "watch tackle." One of them, held by the legs by his mates, would lean far over the bow and make the tackle fast to the float line. Then they would heave in on the tackle till the blocks were together, when the maneuver would be repeated.

"Have to give her the staysail," Charley said.

Ole Ericsen looked at the straining *Mary Rebecca* and shook his head. "It will take der masts out of her," he said.

"And we'll be taken out of her if you don't," Charley replied.

Ole shot an anxious glance at his masts, another at the boat load of armed Greeks, and consented.

The five men were in the bow of the boat—a bad place when a craft is towing. I was watching the behavior of their boat as the great fisherman's staysail, far, far larger than the topsail and used only in light breezes, was broken out. As the *Mary Rebecca* lurched forward with a tremendous jerk, the nose of the boat ducked down into the water, and the men tumbled over one another in a wild rush into the stern to save the boat from being dragged sheer under water.

"That settles them!" Charley remarked, though he was anxiously studying the behavior of the *Mary Rebecca*, which was being driven under far more canvas than she was rightly able to carry.

"Next stop is Antioch!" announced the cheerful sailor, after the manner of a railway conductor. "And next comes Merryweather!"

"Come here, quick," Charley said to me.

I crawled across the deck and stood upright beside him in the shelter of the sheet steel.

"Feel in my inside pocket," he commanded, "and get my notebook. That's right. Tear out a blank page and write what I tell you."

And this is what I wrote:

> Telephone to Merryweather, to the sheriff, the constable, or the judge. Tell them we are coming and to turn out the town. Arm everybody. Have them down on the wharf to meet us or we are gone gooses.

"Now make it good and fast to that marlinspike, and stand by to toss it ashore."

I did as he directed. By then we were close to Antioch. The wind was shouting through our rigging, the *Mary Rebecca* was half over on her side and rushing ahead like an ocean greyhound. The seafaring folk of Antioch had seen us breaking out topsail and staysail, a most reckless performance in such weather, and had hurried to the wharf-ends in little groups to find out what was the matter.

Straight down the water front we boomed, Charley edging in till a man could almost leap ashore. When he gave the signal I tossed the marlinspike. It struck the planking of the wharf a resounding smash, bounced along fifteen or twenty feet, and was pounced upon by the amazed onlookers.

It all happened in a flash, for the next minute Antioch was behind and we were heeling it up the San Joaquin toward Merryweather, six miles away. The river straightened out here into its general easterly course, and we squared away before the wind, wing and wing once more, the foresail bellying out to starboard.

Ole Ericsen seemed sunk into a state of stolid despair. Charley and the two sailors were looking hopeful, as they had good reason to be. Merryweather was a coal-mining town, and, it being Sunday, it was reasonable to expect the men to be in town. Further, the coal miners had never lost any love for the Greek fishermen, and were pretty certain to render us hearty assistance.

We strained our eyes for a glimpse of the town, and the first sight we caught of it gave us immense relief. The wharves were black with men. As we came closer, we could see them still arriving, stringing down the main street, guns in their hands and on the run. Charley glanced astern at the fisherman with a look of ownership in his eye which till then had been missing. The Greeks were plainly overawed by the display of armed strength and were putting their own rifles away.

We took in topsail and staysail, dropped the main peak, and as we got abreast of the principal wharf jibed the mainsail. The *Mary Rebecca* shot around into the wind, the captive fishermen describing a great arc behind her, and forged ahead till she lost way, when lines were flung ashore and she was made fast. This was accomplished under a hurricane of cheers from the delighted miners.

Ole Ericsen heaved a great sigh. "Ay never tank Ay see my wife never again," he confessed.

"Why, we were never in any danger," said Charley.

Ole looked at him incredulously.

"Sure, I mean it," Charley went on. "All we had to do, any time, was to let go our end–as I am going to do now, so that those Greeks can untangle their nets."

He went below with a monkey wrench, unscrewed the nut, and let the hook drop off. When the Greeks had hauled their nets into their boats and made everything shipshape, a posse of citizens took them off our hands and led them away to jail.

"Ay tank Ay ban a great big fool," said Ole Ericsen. But he changed his mind when the admiring townspeople crowded aboard to shake hands with him, and a couple of enterprising newspaper men took photographs of the *Mary Rebecca* and her captain.

ALL GOLD CANYON

It was the green heart of the canyon, where the walls swerved back from the rigid plan and relieved their harshness of line by making a little sheltered nook and filling it to the brim with sweetness and roundness and softness. Here all things rested. Even the narrow stream ceased its turbulent downrush long enough to form a quiet pool. Knee-deep in the water, with drooping head and half-shut eyes, drowsed a red-coated, many-antlered buck.

On one side, beginning at the very lip of the pool, was a tiny meadow, a cool, resilient surface of green that extended to the base of the frowning wall. Beyond the pool a gentle slope of earth ran up and up to meet the opposing wall. Fine grass covered the slope—grass that was spangled with flowers, with here and there patches of color, orange and purple and golden. Below, the canyon was shut in. There was no view. The walls leaned together abruptly and the canyon ended in a chaos of rocks, moss-covered and hidden by a green screen of vines and creepers and boughs of trees. Up the canyon rose far hills and peaks, the big foothills, pine-covered and remote. And far beyond, like clouds upon the border of the sky,

166 towered minarets of white, where the Sierra's eternal snows flashed austerely the blazes of the sun.

There was no dust in the canyon. The leaves and flowers were clean and virginal. The grass was young velvet. Over the pool three cottonwoods sent their snowy fluffs fluttering down the quiet air. On the slope the blossoms of the wine-wooded manzanita filled the air with springtime odors, while the leaves, wise with experience, were already beginning their vertical twist against the coming aridity of summer. In the open spaces on the slope, beyond the farthest shadow reach of the manzanita, poised the mariposa lilies, like so many flights of jeweled moths suddenly arrested and on the verge of trembling into flight again. Here and there that woods harlequin, the madroña, permitting itself to be caught in the act of changing its pea-green truck to madder red, breathed its fragrance into the air from great clusters of waxen bells. Creamy white were these bells, shaped like lilies of the valley, with the sweetness of perfume that is of the springtime.

There was not a sigh of wind. The air was drowsy with its weight of perfume. It was a sweetness that would have been cloying had the air been heavy and humid. But the air was sharp and thin. It was as starlight transmuted into atmosphere, shot through and warmed by sunshine, and flower-drenched with sweetness.

An occasional butterfly drifted in and out through the patches of light and shade. And from all about rose the low and sleepy hum of mountain bees—feasting sybarites that jostled one another good-naturedly at the board, nor found time for rough discourtesy. So quietly did the little steam drip and ripple its way through the canyon that it spoke only in faint and occasional gurgles. The voice of the stream was as a drowsy whisper, ever interrupted by dozings and silences, ever lifted again in the awakenings.

The motion of all things was a drifting in the heart of the canyon. Sunshine and butterflies drifted in and out among the trees. The hum of the bees and the whisper of the stream were a drifting of sound. And the drifting sound and drifting color seemed to weave together in the making of a delicate and intangible fabric which was the spirit of the place. It was a spirit of peace that was not of death, but of smooth-pulsing life, of quietude that was not silence, of movement that was not action, of repose that was quick with existence without being violent with struggle and travail. The spirit of the place was the spirit of the peace of the living, somnolent with the easement and content of prosperity, and undisturbed by rumors of far wars.

The red-coated, many-antlered buck acknowledged the lordship of the spirit of the place and dozed knee-deep in the cool, shaded pool. There seemed no flies to vex him and he was languid with rest. Sometimes his ears moved when the stream awoke and whispered; but they moved lazily, with foreknowledge that it was merely the stream grown garrulous at discovery that it had slept.

But there came a time when the buck's ears lifted and tensed with swift eagerness for sound. His head was turned down the canyon. His sensitive, quivering nostrils scented the air. His eyes could not pierce the green screen through which the stream rippled away, but to his ears came the voice of a man. It was a steady, monotonous, singsong voice. Once the buck heard the harsh clash of metal upon rock. At the sound he snorted with a sudden start that jerked him through the air from water to meadow, and his feet sank into the young velvet, while he pricked his ears and again scented the air. Then he stole across the tiny meadow, pausing once and again to listen, and faded away out of the canyon like a wraith, soft-footed and without sound.

The clash of steel-shod soles against the rocks began to be heard, and the man's voice grew louder. It was raised in a sort of chant and became distinct with nearness, so that the words could be heard:

'Tu'n around an' tu'n yo' face
Untoe them sweet hills of grace.
(D' pow'rs of sin yo' am scornin'!)
Look about an' look aroun',
Fling yo' sin pack on d' groun'.
(Yo' will meet wid d' Lord in d' mornin'!)'

A sound of scrambling accompanied the song, and the spirit of the place fled away on the heels of the red-coated buck. The green screen was burst asunder, and a man peered out at the meadow and the pool and the sloping sidehill. He was a deliberate sort of man. He took in the scene with one embracing glance, then ran his eyes over the details to verify the general impression. Then, and not until then, did he open his mouth in vivid and solemn approval:

"Smoke of life an' snakes of purgatory! Will you just look at that! Wood an' water an' grass an' a sidehill! A pocket hunter's delight an' a cayuse's paradise! Cool green for tired eyes! Pink pills for pale people ain't in it. A secret pasture for prospectors and a resting place for tired burros, by damn!"

He was a sandy-complexioned man in whose face geniality and humor seemed the salient characteristices. It was a mobile face, quick-changing to inward mood and thought. Thinking was in him a visible process. Ideas chased across his face like windflaws across the surface of a lake. His hair, sparse and unkempt of growth, was an indeterminate and colorless as his complexion. It would seem that all the color of his frame had gone into his eyes, for they were startlingly blue. Also they were laughing and merry eyes, within them much of the naiveté and wonder of the child; and yet, in an unassertive way, they contained much of calm self-reliance and strength of purpose founded upon self-experience and experience of the world.

From out the screen of vines and creepers he flung ahead of him a miner's pick and shovel and gold pan. Then he crawled out himself into the open. He was clad in faded overalls and black cotton shirt, with hobnailed brogans on his feet, and on his head a hat whose shapelessness and stains advertised the rough usage of wind and rain and sun and camp smoke. He stood erect, seeing wide-eyed the secrecy of the scene and sensuously inhaling the warm, sweet breath of the canyon garden through nostrils that dilated and quivered with delight. His eyes narrowed to laughing slits of blue, his face wreathed itself in joy, and his mouth curled in a smile as he cried aloud:

"Jumping dandelions and happy hollyhocks, but that smells good to me! Talk about your attar o' roses an' cologne factories! They ain't in it!"

He had the habit of soliloquy. His quick-changing facial expressions might tell every thought and mood, but the tongue, perforce, ran hard after, repeating, like a second Boswell.

The man lay down on the lip of the pool and drank long and deep of its water. "Tastes good to me," he murmured, lifting his head and gazing across the pool at the sidehill, while he wiped his mouth with the back of his hand. The sidehill attracted his attention. Still lying on his stomach, he studied the hill formation long and carefully. It was a practiced eye that travelled up the slope to the crumbling canyon wall and back and down again to the edge of the pool. He scrambled to his feet and favored the sidehill with a second survey.

"Looks good to me," he concluded, picking up his pick and shovel and gold pan.

He crossed the stream below the pool, stepping agilely from stone to stone. Where the sidehill touched the water he dug up a shovelful of dirt and put it into the gold pan. He squatted down, holding the pan in his two hands, and partly immersing it in the stream. Then he imparted to the pan a deft circular motion that sent the water sluicing in and out through the dirt and gravel. The larger and the lighter particles worked to the surface, and these, by a skillful dipping movement of the pan, he spilled out and over the edge. Occasionally, to expedite matters, he rested the pan and with his fingers raked out the large pebbles and pieces of rock.

The contents of the pan diminished rapidly until only fine dirt and the smallest bits of gravel remained. At this stage he began to work very deliberately and carefully. It was fine washing, and he washed fine and finer, with a keen scrutiny and delicate and fastidious touch. At last the pan seemed empty of everything but water; but with a quick semicircular flirt that sent the water flying over the shallow rim into the stream he disclosed a layer of black sand on the bottom of the pan. So thin was this layer that it was like a streak of paint. He examined it closely. In the midst of it was a tiny golden speck. He dribbled a little water in over the depressed edge of the pan. With a quick flirt he sent the water sluicing across the bottom, turning the grains of black sand over and over. A second tiny golden speck rewarded his effort.

The washing had now become very fine—fine beyond all need of ordinary placer mining. He worked the black sand, a small portion at a time, up the shallow rim of the pan. Each small portion he examined sharply, so that his eyes saw every grain of it before he allowed it to slide over the edge and away. Jealously, bit by bit, he let the black sand slip away. A golden speck, no larger than a pin point, appeared on the rim, and by his manipulation of the water it returned to the bottom of the pan. And in such fashion another speck was disclosed, and another. Great was his care of them. Like a shepherd he herded his flock of golden specks so that not one should be lost. At last, of the pan of dirt nothing remained but his golden herd. He counted it, and then, after all his labor, sent it flying out of the pan with one final swirl of water.

But his blue eyes were shining with desire as he rose to his feet. "Seven," he muttered aloud, asserting the sum of the specks for which he had toiled so hard and which he had so wantonly thrown away. "Seven," he repeated, with the emphasis of one trying to impress a number on his memory.

He stood still a long while, surveying the hillside. In his eyes was a curiosity, new-aroused and burning. There

172 was an exultance about his bearing and a keenness like that of a hunting animal catching the fresh scent of game.

He moved down the stream a few steps and took a second panful of dirt.

Again came the careful washing, the jealous herding of the golden specks, and the wantonness with which he sent them flying into the stream when he had counted their number.

"Five," he muttered, and repeated, "five."

He could not forbear another survey of the hill before filling the pan farther down the stream. His golden herds diminished. "Four, three, two, two, one," were his memory tabulations as he moved down the stream. When but one speck of gold rewarded his washing he stopped and built a fire of dry twigs. Into this he thrust the gold pan and burned it till it was blue-black. He held up the pan and examined it critically. Then he nodded approbation. Against such a color background he could defy the tiniest yellow speck to elude him.

Still moving down the stream, he panned again. A single speck was his reward. A third pan contained no gold at all. Not satisfied with this, he panned three times again, taking his shovels of dirt within a foot of one another. Each pan proved empty of gold, and the fact, instead of discouraging him, seemed to give him satisfaction. His elation increased with each barren washing, until he arose, exclaiming jubilantly, "If it ain't the real thing, may God knock off my head with sour apples!"

Returning to where he had started operations, he began to pan up the stream. At first his golden herds increased—increased prodigiously. "Fourteen, eighteen, twenty-one, twenty-six," ran his memory tabulations. Just above the pool he struck his richest pan—thirty-five colors.

"Almost enough to save," he remarked regretfully as he allowed the water to sweep them away.

The sun climbed to the top of the sky. The man worked on. Pan by pan he went up the stream, the tally of results steadily decreasing.

"It's just booful, the way it peters out," he exulted when a shovelful of dirt contained no more than a single speck of gold.

And when no specks at all were found in several pans he straightened up and favored the hillside with a confident glance.

"Aha! Mr. Pocket!" he cried out as though to an auditor hidden somewhere above him beneath the surface of the slope. "Aha! Mr. Pocket! I'm a-comin', I'm a-comin', an' I'm shorely gwine to get yer! You heah me, Mr. Pocket! I'm gwine to get yer as shore as punkins ain't cauliflowers!"

He turned and flung a measuring glance at the sun poised above him in the azure of the cloudless sky. Then he went down the canyon, following the line of shovel holes he had made in filling the pans. He crossed the stream below the pool and disappeared through the green screen. There was little opportunity for the spirit of the place to return with its quietude and repose, for the man's voice, raised in ragtime song, still dominated the canyon with possession.

After a time, with a greater clashing of steel-shod feet on rock, he returned. The green screen was tremendously agitated. It surged back and forth in the throes of a struggle. There was a loud grating and clanging of metal.

The man's voice leaped to a higher pitch and was sharp with imperativeness. A large body plunged and panted. There was a snapping and ripping and rending, and amid a shower of falling leaves a horse burst through the screen. On its back was a pack, and from this trailed broken vines and torn creepers. The animal gazed with astonished eyes at the scene into which it has been precipitated, then dropped its head to the grass and began contentedly to graze. A second horse scrambled into view, slipping once on the mossy rocks and regaining equilibrium when its hoofs sank into the yielding surface of the meadow. It was riderless, though on its back was a high-horned Mexican saddle, scarred and discolored by long usage.

The man brought up the rear. He threw off pack and saddle, with an eye to camp location, and gave the animals their freedom to graze. He unpacked his food and got out frying pan and coffeepot. He gathered an armful of dry wood, and with a few stones made a place for his fire.

"My," he said, "but I've got an appetite! I could scoff iron filings an' horseshoe nails an' thank you kindly, ma'am, for a second helpin'."

He straightened up, and while he reached for matches in the pocket of his overalls his eyes travelled, across the pool to the sidehill. His fingers had clutched the matchbox, but they relaxed their hold and the hand came out empty. The man wavered perceptibly. He looked at his preparations for cooking and he looked at the hill.

"Guess I'll take another whack at her," he concluded, starting to cross the stream.

"They ain't no sense in it, I know," he mumbled apologetically. "But keepin' grub back an hour ain't goin' to hurt none, I reckon."

A few feet back from his first line of test pans he started a second line. The sun dropped down the western sky, the shadows lengthened, but the man worked on. He began a third line of test pans. He was crosscutting the hillside, line by line, as he ascended. The center of each line produced the richest pans, while the ends came where no colors showed in the pan. And as he ascended the hillside the lines grew perceptibly shorter. The regularity with which their length diminished served to indicate that somewhere up the slope the last line would be so short as to have scarcely length at all, and that beyond could come only a point. The design was growing into an inverted V. The converging sides of this V marked the boundaries of the gold-bearing dirt.

The apex of the V was evidently the man's goal. Often he ran his eye along the converging sides and on up the hill, trying to divine the apex, the point where the gold-bearing dirt must cease. Here resided "Mr. Pocket"—for so the man familiarly addressed the imaginary point above him on the slope, crying out:

"Come down out o' that, Mr. Pocket! Be right smart an' agreeable, an' come down!"

"All right," he would add later, in a voice resigned to determination. "All right, Mr. Pocket. It's plain to me I got to come right up an' snatch you out bald-headed. An' I'll do it! I'll do it!" he would threaten still later.

Each pan he carried down to the water to wash, and as he went higher up the hill the pans grew richer, until he began to save the gold in an empty baking powder can which he carried carelessly in his lap pocket. So en-

176 grossed was he in his toil that he did not notice the long twilight of oncoming night. It was not until he tried vainly to see the gold colors in the bottom of the pan that he realized the passage of time. He straightened up abruptly. An expression of whimsical wonderment and awe overspread his face as he drawled:

"Gosh darn my buttons, if I didn't plumb forget dinner!"

He stumbled across the stream in the darkness and lighted his long-delayed fire. Flapjacks and bacon and warmed-over beans constituted his supper. Then he smoked a pipe by the smoldering coals, listening to the night noises and watching the moonlight stream through the canyon. After that he unrolled his bed, took off his heavy shoes, and pulled the blankets up to his chin. His face showed white in the moonlight, like the face of a corpse. But it was a corpse that knew its resurrection, for the man rose suddenly on one elbow and gazed across at his hillside.

"Good night, Mr. Pocket," he called sleepily. "Good night."

He slept through the early gray of morning until the direct rays of the sun smote his closed eyelids, when he awoke with a start and looked about him until he had established the continuity of his existence and identified his present self with the days previously lived.

To dress, he had merely to buckle on his shoes. He glanced at his fireplace and at his hillside, wavered, but fought down the temptation and started the fire.

"Keep yer shirt on, Bill; keep yer shirt on," he admonished himself. "What's the good of rushin'? No use in get-tin' all het up an' sweaty. Mr. Pocket'll wait for you. He ain't a-runnin' away before you can get yer breakfast. Now what you want, Bill, is something fresh in yer bill o' fare. So it's up to you to go an' get it."

He cut a short pole at the water's edge and drew from one of his pockets a bit of line and a draggled fly that had once been a royal coachman.

"Mebbe they'll bite in the early morning," he muttered as he made his first cast into the pool. And a moment later he was gleefully crying: "What'd I tell you, eh? What'd I tell you?"

He had no reel nor any inclination to waste time, and by main strength, and swiftly, he drew out of the water a flashing ten-inch trout. Three more, caught in rapid succession, furnished his breakfast. When he came to the steppingstones on his way to his hillside, he was struck by a sudden thought, and paused.

"I'd just better take a hike downstream a ways," he said, "There's no tellin' what cuss may be snoopin' around."

But he crossed over on the stones, and with a "I really oughter take that hike" the need of the precaution passed out of his mind and he fell to work.

At nightfall he straightened up. The small of his back was stiff from stooping toil, and as he put his hand behind him to soothe the protesting muscles he said, "Now what d'ye think of that, by damn? I clean forgot my dinner again! If I don't watch out I'll sure be degeneratin' into a two-meal-a-day crank."

"Pockets is the damnedest things I ever see for makin' a man absent-minded," he communed that night as he crawled into his blankets. Nor did he forget to call up the hillside, "Good night, Mr. Pocket! Good night!"

Rising with the sun, and snatching a hasty breakfast, he was early at work. A fever seemed to be growing in him, nor did the increasing richness of the test pans allay this fever. There was a flush in his cheek other than that made by the heat of the sun, and he was oblivious to fatigue and the passage of time. When he filled a pan with dirt he ran down the hill to wash it; nor could he forbear running up the hill again, panting and stumbling profanely, to refill the pan.

He was now a hundred yards from the water, and the inverted V was assuming definite proportions. The width of the pay dirt steadily decreased, and the man extended in his mind's eye the sides of the V to their meeting place far up the hill. This was his goal, the apex of the V, and he panned many times to locate it.

"Just about two yards above that manzanita bush an' a yard to the right," he finally concluded.

Then the temptation seized him. "As plain as the nose on your face," he said as he abandoned his laborious crosscutting and climbed to the indicated apex. He filled a pan and carried it down the hill to wash. It contained no trace of gold. He dug deep, and he dug shallow, filling and washing a dozen pans, and was unrewarded even by the tiniest golden speck. He was enraged at having yielded to the temptation, and cursed himself blasphemously and pridelessly. Then he went down the hill and took up the crosscutting.

"Slow an' certain, Bill; slow an' certain," he crooned. "Short cuts to fortune ain't in your line, an' it's about time you know it. Get wise, Bill; get wise. Slow an' certain's the only hand you can play; so go to it, an' keep to it, too."

As the crosscuts decreased, showing that the sides of the V were converging, the depth of the V increased. The gold trace was dipping into the hill. It was only at thirty inches beneath the surface that he could get colors in his pan. The dirt he found at twenty-five inches from the surface, and at thirty-five inches, yielded barren pans. At the base of the V, by the water's edge, he had found the gold colors at the grass roots. The higher he went up the hill, the deeper the gold dipped. To dig a hole three feet deep in order to get one test pan was a task of no mean magnitude; while between the man and the apex intervened an untold number of such holes to be dug. "An' there's no tellin' how much deeper it'll pitch," he sighed in a moment's pause, while his fingers soothed his aching back.

Feverish with desire, with aching back and stiffening muscles, with pick and shovel gouging and mauling the soft brown earth, the man toiled up the hill. Before him was the smooth slope, spangled with flowers and made sweet with their breath. Behind him was devastation. It looked like some terrible eruption breaking out on the smooth skin of the hill. His slow progress was like that of a slug, befouling beauty with a monstrous trail.

Though the dipping gold trace increased the man's work, he found consolation in the increasing richness of the pans. Twenty cents, thirty cents, fifty cents, sixty cents, were the values of the gold found in the pans, and at nightfall he washed his banner pan, which gave him a dollar's worth of gold dust from a shovelful of dirt.

"I'll just bet it's my luck to have some inquisitive cuss come buttin' in here on my pasture," he mumbled sleepily that night as he pulled the blankets up to his chin.

Suddenly he sat upright. "Bill!" he called sharply. "Now listen to me, Bill; d'ye hear! It's up to you, tomorrow morning', to mosey round an' see what you can see. Understand? Tomorrow morning, an' don't you forget it!"

He yawned and glanced across his sidehill. "Good night, Mr. Pocket," he called.

In the morning he stole a march on the sun, for he had finished breakfast when its first rays caught him, and he was climbing the wall of the canyon where it crumbled away and gave footing. From the outlook at the top he found himself in the midst of loneliness. As far as he could see, chain after chain of mountains heaved themselves into his vision. To the east his eyes, leaping the miles between range and range and between many ranges, brought up at last against the white-peaked Sierras—the main crest, where the backbone of the Western world reared itself against the sky. To the north and south he could see more distinctly the cross systems that broke through the main trend of the sea of mountains. To the west the ranges fell away, one behind the other, diminishing and fading into the gentle foothills that, in turn, descended into the great valley which he could not see.

And in all that mighty sweep of earth he saw no sign of man nor of the handiwork of man—save only the torn bosom of the hillside at his feet. The man looked long and carefully. Once, far down his own canyon, he thought he saw in the air a faint hint of smoke. He looked again and decided that it was the purple haze of the hills made dark by a convolution of the canyon wall at its back.

"Hey, you, Mr. Pocket!" he called down into the canyon. "Stand out from under! I'm a-comin', Mr. Pocket! I'm a-comin'!"

The heavy brogans on the man's feet made him appear clumsy-footed, but he swung down from the giddy height as lightly and airily as a mountain goat. A rock, turning under his foot on the edge of the precipice, did not disconcert him. He seemed to know the precise time required for the turn to culminate in disaster, and in the meantime he utilized the false footing itself for the momentary earth contact necessary to carry him on into safety. Where the earth sloped so steeply that it was impossible to stand for a second upright, the man did not hesitate. His foot pressed the impossible surface for but a fraction of the fatal second and gave him the bound that carried him onward. Again, where even the fraction of a second's footing was out of the question, he would swing his body past by a moment's handgrip on a jutting knob of rock, a crevice, or a precariously rooted shrub. At last, with a wild leap and yell, he exchanged the face of the wall for an earth slide and finished the descent in the midst of several tons of sliding earth and gravel.

His first pan of the morning washed out over two dollars in coarse gold. It was from the center of the V. To either side the diminution in the values of the pans was swift. His lines of crosscutting holes were growing very short. The converging sides of the inverted V were only a few yards apart. Their meeting point was only a few yards above him. But the pay streak was dipping deeper and deeper into the earth. By early afternoon he was sinking the test holes five feet before the pans could show the gold trace.

For that matter the gold trace had become something

 more than a trace; it was a placer mine in itself, and the man resolved to come back after he had found the pocket and work over the ground. But the increasing richness of the pans began to worry him. By late afternoon the worth of the pans had grown to three and four dollars. The man scratched his head perplexedly and looked a few feet up the hill at the manzanita bush that marked approximately the apex of the V. He nodded his head and said oracularly:

"It's one o' two things, Bill; one o' two things. Either Mr. Pocket's spilled himself all out an' down the hill, or else Mr. Pocket's that damned rich you maybe won't be able to carry him all away with you. And that'd be hell, wouldn't it, now?" He chuckled at contemplation of so pleasant a dilemma.

Nightfall found him by the edge of the stream, his eyes wrestling with the gathering darkness over the washing of a five-dollar pan.

"Wisht I had an electric light to go on working," he said.

He found sleep difficult that night. Many times he composed himself and closed his eyes for slumber to overtake him; but his blood pounded with too strong desire, and as many times his eyes opened and he murmured wearily, "Wisht it was sunup."

Sleep came to him in the end, but his eyes were open with the first paling of the stars, and the gray of dawn caught him with breakfast finished and climbing the hillside in the direction of the secret abiding place of Mr. Pocket.

The first crosscut the man made, there was space for only three holes, so narrow had become the pay streak and so close was he to the fountainhead of the golden stream he had been following for four days.

"Be ca'm, Bill; be ca'm," he admonished himself as he broke ground for the final hole where the sides of the V had at last come together in a point.

"I've got the almighty cinch on you, Mr. Pocket, an' you can't lose me," he said many times as he sank the hole deeper and deeper.

Four feet, five feet, six feet, he dug his way down into the earth. The digging grew harder. His pick grated on broken rock. He examined the rock. "Rotten quartz," was his conclusion as, with the shovel, he cleared the bottom of the hole of loose dirt. He attacked the crumbling quartz with the pick, bursting the disintegrating rock asunder with every stroke.

He thrust his shovel into the loose mass. His eye caught a gleam of yellow. He dropped the shovel and squatted suddenly on his heels. As a farmer rubs the clinging earth from fresh-dug potatoes, so the man, a piece of rotten quartz held in both hands, rubbed the dirt away.

"Sufferin' Sardanopolis!" he cried. "Lumps an' chunks of it! Lumps an' chunks of it!"

It was only half rock he held in his hand. The other half was virgin gold. He dropped it into his pan and examined another piece. Little yellow was to be seen, but with his strong fingers he crumbled the rotten quartz away till both hands were filled with glowing yellow. He rubbed the dirt away from fragment after fragment, tossing them into the gold pan. It was a treasure hole. So much had the quartz rotted away that there was less of it than there was of gold. Now and again he found a piece to which no rock clung—a piece that was all gold. A

184 chunk, where the pick had laid open the heart of the gold, glittered like a handful of yellow jewels, and he cocked his head at it and slowly turned it around and over to observe the rich play of the light upon it.

"Talk about yer Too Much Gold diggin's!" the man snorted contemptuously. "Why, this diggin'd make it look like thirty cents. This diggin' is all gold. An' right here an' now I name this yere canyon 'All Gold Canyon,' b' gosh!"

Still squatting on his heels, he continued examining the fragments and tossing them into the pan. Suddenly there came to him a premonition of danger. It seemed a shadow had fallen upon him. But there was no shadow. His heart had given a great jump up into his throat and was choking him. Then his blood slowly chilled and he felt the sweat of his shirt cold against his flesh.

He did not spring up nor look around. He did not move. He was considering the nature of the premonition he had received, trying to locate the source of the mysterious force that had warned him, striving to sense the imperative presence of the unseen thing that threatened him. There is an aura of things hostile, made manifest by messengers too refined for the senses to know; and this aura he felt, but knew not how he felt it. His was the feeling as when a cloud passes over the sun. It seemed that between him and life had passed something dark and smothering and menacing; a gloom, as it were, that swallowed up life and made for death—his death.

Every force of his being impelled him to spring up and confront the unseen danger, but his soul dominated the panic, and he remained squatting on his heels, in his hands a chunk of gold. He did not dare to look around, but he knew by now that there was something behind him and above him. He made believe to be interested in the gold in his hand. He examined it critically, turned it over and over, and rubbed the dirt from it. And all the time he knew that something behind him was looking at the gold over his shoulder.

Still feigning interest in the chunk of gold in his hand, he listened intently and he heard the breathing of the thing behind him. His eyes searched the ground in front of him for a weapon, but they saw only the uprooted gold, worthless to him now in his extremity. There was his pick, a handy weapon on occasion; but this was not such an occasion. The man realized his predicament. He was in a narrow hole that was seven feet deep. His head did not come to the surface of the ground. He was in a trap.

He remained squatting on his heels. He was quite cool and collected; but his mind, considering every factor, showed him only his helplessness. He continued rubbing the dirt from the quartz fragments and throwing the gold into the pan. There was nothing else for him to do. Yet he knew that he would have to rise up, sooner or later, and face the danger that breathed at his back. The minutes passed, and with the passage of each minute he knew that by so much he was nearer the time when he must stand up or else—and his wet shirt went cold against his flesh again at the thought—or else he might receive death as he stooped there over his treasure.

Still he squatted on his heels, rubbing dirt from gold and debating in just what manner he should rise up. He might rise up with a rush and claw his way out of the hole to meet whatever threatened on the even footing aboveground. Or he might rise up slowly and carelessly, and feign casually to discover the thing that breathed at his back. His instinct and every fighting fibre of his body favored the mad, clawing rush to the surface. His intellect, and the craft thereof, favored the slow and cautious meeting with the thing that menaced and which he could not see. And while he debated, a loud, crashing noise burst on his ear. At the same instant he received a stunning blow on the left side of the back, and from the point of impact felt a rush of flame through his flesh. He sprang up in the air, but halfway to his feet collapsed. His body crumpled in like a leaf withered in sudden heat, and he came down, his chest across his pan of gold, his face in the dirt and rock, his legs tangled and twisted because of the restricted space at the bottom of the hole. His legs twitched convulsively several times. His body was shaken as with a mighty ague. There was a slow expansion of the lungs, accompanied by a deep sigh. Then the air was slowly, very slowly, exhaled, and his body as slowly flattened itself down into inertness.

Above, revolver in hand, a man was peering down over the edge of the hole. He peered for a long time at the prone and motionless body beneath him. After a while the stranger sat down on the edge of the hole so that he could see into it, and rested the revolver on his knee. Reaching his hand into a pocket, he drew out a wisp of brown paper. Into this he dropped a few crumbs of tobacco. The combination became a cigarette, brown and squat, with the ends turned in. Not once did he take his eyes from the body at the bottom of the hole. He lighted the cigarette and drew its smoke into his lungs with a caressing intake of the breath. He smoked slowly. Once the cigarette went out and he relighted it. And all the while he studied the body beneath him.

In the end he tossed the cigarette stub away and rose to his feet. He moved to the edge of the hole. Spanning it, a hand resting on each edge, and with the revolver still in the right hand, he muscled his body down into the hole. While his feet were yet a yard from the bottom he released his hands and dropped down.

At the instant his feet struck bottom he saw the pocket miner's arm leap out, and his own legs knew a swift, jerking grip that overthrew him. In the nature of the jump his revolver hand was above his head. Swiftly as the grip had flashed about his legs, just as swiftly he brought the revolver down. He was still in the air, his fall in process of completion, when he pulled the trigger. The explosion was deafening in the confined space. The smoke filled the hole so that he could see nothing. He struck the bottom on his back, and like a cat's the pocket miner's body was on top of him. Even as the miner's body passed on top, the stranger crooked in his right arm to fire; and even in that instant the miner, with a quick thrust of elbow, struck his wrist. The muzzle was thrown up and the bullet thudded into the dirt of the side of the hole.

The next instant the stranger felt the miner's hand grip his wrist. The struggle was now for the revolver. Each man strove to turn it against the other's body. The smoke in the hole was clearing. The stranger, lying on his back, was beginning to see dimly. But suddenly he was blinded by a handful of dirt deliberately flung into his eyes by his antagonist. In that moment of shock his grip on the revolver was broken. In the next moment he felt a smashing darkness descend upon his brain, and in the midst of the darkness even the darkness ceased.

But the pocket miner fired again and again, until the revolver was empty. Then he tossed it from him and, breathing heavily, sat down on the dead man's legs.

The miner was sobbing and struggling for breath. "Measly skunk!" he panted; "a-campin' on my trail an' lettin' me do the work, an' then shootin' me in the back!"

He was half crying from anger and exhaustion. He peered at the face of the dead man. It was sprinkled with loose dirt and gravel, and it was difficult to distinguish the features.

"Never laid eyes on him before," the miner concluded his scrutiny. "Just a common an' ordinary thief, damn him! An' he shot me in the back! He shot me in the back!"

He opened his shirt and felt himself, front and back, on his left side.

"Went clean through, and no harm done!" he cried jubilantly. "I'll bet he aimed all right, all right; but he drew the gun over when he pulled the trigger—the cuss! But I fixed 'm! Oh, I fixed 'm!"

His fingers were investigating the bullet hole in his side, and a shade of regret passed over his face. "It's goin' to be stiffer'n hell," he said. "An' it's up to me to get mended an' get out o' here."

He crawled out of the hole and went down the hill to his camp. Half an hour later he returned, leading his pack horse. His open shirt disclosed the rude bandages with which he had dressed his wound. He was slow and awkward with his left-hand movements, but that did not prevent his using the arm.

The bight of the pack rope under the dead man's shoulders enabled him to heave the body out of the hole. Then he set to work gathering up his gold. He worked steadily for several hours, pausing often to rest his stiffening shoulder and to exclaim:

"He shot me in the back, the measly skunk! He shot me in the back!"

When his treasure was quite cleaned up and wrapped securely into a number of blanket-covered parcels, he made an estimate of its value.

"Four hundred pounds, or I'm a Hottentot," he concluded. "Say two hundred in quartz an' dirt—that leaves two hundred pounds of gold. Bill! Wake up! Two hundred pounds of gold! Forty thousand dollars! An' it's yourn—all yourn!"

He scratched his head delightedly and his fingers blundered into an unfamiliar groove. They quested along it for several inches. It was a crease through his scalp where the second bullet had plowed.

He walked angrily over to the dead man.

"You would, would you?" he bullied. "You would, eh? Well, I fixed you good an' plenty, an' I'll give you decent burial, too. That's more'n you'd have done for me."

He dragged the body to the edge of the hole and toppled it in. It struck the bottom with a dull crash, on its side, the face twisted up to the light. The miner peered down at it.

"An' you shot me in the back!" he said accusingly.

With pick and shovel he filled the hole. Then he loaded

 the gold on his horse. It was too great a load for the animal, and when he had gained his camp he transferred part of it to his saddle horse. Even so, he was compelled to abandon a portion of his outfit—pick and shovel and gold pan, extra food and cooking utensils, and divers odds and ends.

The sun was at the zenith when the man forced the horses at the screen of vines and creepers. To climb the huge boulders the animals were compelled to uprear and struggle blindly through the tangled mass of vegetation. Once the saddle horse fell heavily and the man removed the pack to get the animal on its feet. After it started on its way again the man thrust his head out from among the leaves and peered up at the hillside.

"The measly skunk!" he said, and disappeared.

There was a ripping and tearing of vines and boughs. The trees surged back and forth, marking the passage of the animals through the midst of them. There was a clashing of steel-shod hoofs on stone, and now and again an oath or a sharp cry of command. Then the voice of the man was raised in song:

'Tu'n around an' tu'n yo' face
Untoe them sweet hills of grace.
(D' pow'rs of sin yo' am scornin'!)
Look about an' look aroun',
Fling yo' sin pack on d' groun'.
(Yo' will meet wid d' Lord in d' mornin'!)

The song grew faint and fainter, and through the silence crept back the spirit of the place. The stream once more drowsed and whispered; the hum of the mountain bees rose sleepily. Down through the perfume-weighted air fluttered the snowy fluffs of the cottonwoods. The butterflies drifted in and out among the trees, and over all blazed the quiet sunshine. Only remained the hoofmarks in the meadow and the torn hillside to mark the boisterous trail of the life that had broken the peace of the place and passed on.

TO BUILD A FIRE

Day had broken cold and gray, exceedingly cold and gray, when the man turned aside from the main Yukon trail and climbed the high earth-bank, where a dim and little-travelled trail led eastward through the fat spruce timberland. It was a steep bank, and he paused for breath at the top, excusing the act to himself by looking at his watch. It was nine o'clock. There was no sun nor hint of sun, though there was not a cloud in the sky. It was a clear day, and yet there seemed an intangible pall over the face of things, a subtle gloom that made the day dark, and that was due to the absence of sun. This fact did not worry the man. He was used to the lack of sun. It had been days since he had seen the sun, and he knew that a few more days must pass before that cheerful orb, due south, would just peep above the sky line and dip immediately from view.

The man flung a look back along the way he had come. The Yukon lay a mile wide and hidden under three feet of ice. On top of this ice were as many feet of snow. It was all pure white, rolling in gentle undulations where

194 the ice jams of the freeze-up had formed. North and south, as far as his eye could see, it was unbrokenewhite, save for a dark hairline that curved and twisted from around the spruce-covered island to the south, and that curved and twisted away into the north, where it disappeared behind another spruce-covered island. This dark hairline was the trail—the main trail—that led south five hundred miles to the Chilkoot Pass, Dyea, and Salt Water; and that led north seventy miles to Dawson, and still on to the north a thousand miles to Nulato, and finally to St. Michael, on Bering Sea, a thousand miles and half a thousand more.

But all this—the mysterious, far-reaching hairline trail, the absence of sun from the sky, the tremendous cold, and the strangeness and weirdness of it all—made no impression on the man. It was not because he was long used to it. He was a newcomer in the land, a cheechako and this was his first winter. The trouble with him was that he was without imagination. He was quick and alert in the things of life, but only in the things, and not in the significances. Fifty degrees below zero meant eighty-odd degrees of frost. Such fact impressed him as being cold and uncomfortable, and that was all. It did not lead him to meditate upon his frailty as a creature of temperature, and upon man's frailty in general, able only to live within certain narrow limits of heat and cold; and from there on it did not lead him to the conjectural field of immortality and man's place in the universe. Fifty degrees below zero stood for a bite of frost that hurt and that must be guarded against by the use of mittens, ear flaps, warm moccasins, and thick socks. Fifty degrees below zero was to him just precisely fifty degrees below zero. That there should be anything more to it than that was a thought that never entered his head.

As he turned to go on, he spat speculatively. There was a sharp, explosive crackle that startled him. He spat again. And again, in the air, before it could fall to the snow, the spittle crackled. He knew that at fifty below spittle crackled on the snow, but his spittle had crackled in the air. Undoubtedly it was colder than fifty below—how much colder he did not know. But the temperature did not matter. He was bound for the old claim on the left fork of Henderson Creek, where the boys were already. They had come over across the divide from the Indian Creek country, while he had come the roundabout way to take a look at the possibilities of getting out logs in the spring from the islands in the Yukon. He would be in to camp by six o'clock; a bit after dark, it was true, but the boys would be there, a fire would be going, and a hot supper would be ready. As for lunch, he pressed his hand against the protruding bundle under his jacket. It was also under his shirt, wrapped up in a handkerchief and lying against the naked skin. It was the only way to keep the biscuits from freezing. He smiled agreeably to himself as he thought of those biscuits, each cut open and sopped in bacon grease, and each enclosing a generous slice of fried bacon.

He plunged in among the big spruce trees. The trail was faint. A foot of snow had fallen since the last sled had passed over, and he was glad he was without a sled, travelling light. In fact, he carried nothing but the lunch wrapped in the handkerchief. He was surprised, however, at the cold. It certainly was cold, he concluded, as he rubbed his numb nose and cheekbones with his mittened

196 hand. He was a warm-whiskered man, but the hair on his face did not protect the high cheekbones and the eager nose that thrust itself aggressively into the frosty air.

At the man's heels trotted a dog, a big native husky, the proper wolf dog, gray-coated and without any visible or temperamental difference from its brother, the wild wolf. The animal was depressed by the tremendous cold. It knew that it was no time for travelling. Its instinct told it a truer tale than was told to the man by the man's judgment. In reality, it was not merely colder than fifty below zero; it was colder than sixty below, than seventy below. It was seventy-five below zero. Since the freezing point is thirty-two above zero, it meant that one hundred and seven degrees of frost obtained. The dog did not know anything about thermometers. Possibly in its brain there was no sharp consciousness of a condition of very cold such as was in the man's brain. But the brute had its instinct. It experienced a vague but menacing apprehension that subdued it and made it slink along at the man's heels, and that made it question eagerly every unwonted movement of the man as if expecting him to go into camp or to seek shelter somewhere and build a fire. The dog had learned fire, and it wanted fire, or else to burrow under the snow and cuddle its warmth away from the air.

The frozen moisture of its breathing had settled on its fur in a fine powder of frost, and especially were its jowls, muzzle, and eyelashes whitened by its crystalled breath. The man's red beard and mustache were likewise frosted, but more solidly, the deposit taking the form of ice and increasing with every warm, moist breath he exhaled. Also, the man was chewing tobacco, and the muzzle of ice held his lips so rigidly that he was unable to clear his chin when he expelled the juice. The result was that a crystal beard of the color and solidity of amber was increasing its length on his chin. If he fell down it would shatter itself, like glass, into brittle fragments. But he did not mind the appendage. It was the penalty all tobacco chewers paid in that country, and he had been out before in two cold snaps. They had not been so cold as this, he knew, but by the spirit thermometer at Sixty Mile he knew they had been registered at fifty below and at fifty-five.

He held on through the level stretch of woods for several miles, crossed a wide flat, and dropped down a bank to the frozen bed of a small stream. This was Henderson Creek, and he knew he was ten miles from the forks. He looked at his watch. It was ten o'clock. He was making four miles an hour, and he calculated that he would arrive at the forks at half-past twelve. He decided to celebrate that event by eating his lunch there.

The dog dropped in again at his heels, with a tail drooping discouragement, as the man swung along the creek bed. The furrow of the old sled trail was plainly visible, but a dozen inches of snow covered the marks of the last runners. In a month no man had come up or down that silent creek. The man held steadily on. He was not much given to thinking, and just then particularly he had nothing to think about save that he would eat lunch at the forks and that at six o'clock he would be in camp with the boys. There was nobody to talk to; and, had there been, speech would have been impossible because of the ice muzzle on his mouth. So he continued monotonously to chew tobacco and to increase the length of his amber beard.

198 Once in a while the thought reiterated itself that it was very cold and that he had never experienced such cold. As he walked along he rubbed his cheekbones and nose with the back of his mittened hand. He did this automatically, now and again changing hands. But, rub as he would, the instant he stopped his cheekbones went numb, and the following instant the end of his nose went numb. He was sure to frost his cheeks; he knew that, and experienced a pang of regret that he had not devised a nose strap of the sort Bud wore in cold snaps. Such a strap passed across the cheeks, as well, and saved them. But it didn't matter much, after all. What were frosted cheeks? A bit painful, that was all; they were never serious.

Empty as the man's mind was of thoughts, he was keenly observant, and he noticed the changes in the creek, the curves and bends and timber jams, and always he sharply noted where he placed his feet. Once, coming around a bend, he shied abruptly, like a startled horse, curved away from the place where he had been walking, and retreated several paces back along the trail. The creek he knew was frozen clear to the bottom—no creek could contain water in that arctic winter—but he knew also that there were springs that bubbled out from the hillsides and ran along under the snow and on top the ice of the creek. He knew that the coldest snaps never froze these springs, and he knew likewise their danger. They were traps. They hid pools of water under the snow that might be three inches deep, or three feet. Sometimes a skin of ice half an inch thick covered them, and in turn was covered by the snow. Sometimes there were alternate layers of water and ice skin, so that when one broke through he kept on breaking through for a while, sometimes wetting himself to the waist.

That was why he had shied in such panic. He had felt the give under his feet and heard the crackle of a snow-hidden ice skin. And to get his feet wet in such a temperature meant trouble and danger. At the very least it meant delay, for he would be forced to stop and build a fire, and under its protection to bare his feet while he dried his socks and moccasins. He stood and studied the creek bed and its banks, and decided that the flow of water came from the right. He reflected awhile, rubbing his nose and cheeks, then skirted to the left, stepping gingerly and testing the footing for each step. Once clear of the danger, he took a fresh chew of tobacco and swung along at his four-mile gait.

In the course of the next two hours he came upon several similar traps. Usually the snow above the hidden pools had a sunken, candied appearance that advertised the danger. Once again, however, he had a close call; and once, suspecting danger, he compelled the dog to go on in front. The dog did not want to go. It hung back until the man shoved it forward, and then it went quickly across the white, unbroken surface. Suddenly it broke through, floundered to one side, and got away to firmer footing. It had wet its forefeet and legs, and almost immediately the water that clung to it turned to ice. It made quick efforts to lick the ice off its legs, then dropped down in the snow and began to bite out the ice that had formed between the toes. This was a matter of instinct. To permit the ice to remain would mean sore feet. It did not know this. It merely obeyed the mysterious prompting that arose from the deep crypts of its being. But the man knew, having achieved a judgment on the subject, and he removed the mitten from his right hand and helped tear out the ice particles. He did not expose his fingers more than a minute, and was astonished at the swift numbness that smote them. It certainly was cold. He pulled on the mitten hastily, and beat the hand savagely across his chest.

At twelve o'clock the day was at its brightest. Yet the sun was too far south on its winter journey to clear the horizon. The bulge of the earth intervened between it and Henderson Creek, where the man walked under a clear sky at noon and cast no shadow. At half-past twelve, to the minute, he arrived at the forks of the creek. He was pleased at the speed he had made. If he kept it up, he would certainly be with the boys by six. He unbuttoned his jacket and shirt and drew forth his lunch. The action consumed no more than a quarter of a minute, yet in that brief moment the numbness laid hold of the exposed fingers. He did not put the mitten on, but, instead, struck the fingers a dozen sharp smashes against his leg. Then he sat down on a snow-covered log to eat. The sting that followed upon the striking of his fingers against his leg ceased so quickly that he was startled. He had had no chance to take a bite of biscuit. He struck the fingers repeatedly and returned them to the mitten, baring the other hand for the purpose of eating. He tried to take a mouthful, but the ice muzzle prevented. He had forgotten to build a fire and thaw out. He chuckled at his foolishness, and as he chuckled he noted the numbness creeping into the exposed fingers. Also, he noted that the stinging which had first come to his toes when he sat down was already passing away. He wondered whether the toes were warm or numb. He moved them inside the moccasins and decided that they were numb.

He pulled the mitten on hurriedly and stood up. He was a bit frightened. He stamped up and down until the stinging returned into the feet. It certainly was cold, was his thought. That man from Sulphur Creek had spoken the truth when telling how cold it sometimes got in the country. And he had laughed at him at the time! That showed one must not be too sure of things. There was no mistake about it, it *was* cold. He strode up and down, stamping his feet and threshing his arms, until reassured by the returning warmth. Then he got out matches and proceeded to make a fire. From the undergrowth, where high water of the previous spring had lodged a supply of seasoned twigs, he got his firewood. Working carefully from a small beginning, he soon had a roaring fire, over which he thawed the ice from his face and in the protection of which he ate his biscuits. For the moment the cold of space was outwitted. The dog took satisfaction in the fire, stretching out close enough for warmth and far enough away to escape being singed.

When the man had finished, he filled his pipe and took his comfortable time over a smoke. Then he pulled on his mittens, settled the ear flaps of his cap firmly about his ears, and took the creek trail up the left fork. The dog was disappointed and yearned back toward the fire. This man did not know cold. Possibly all the generations of his ancestry had been ignorant of cold, of real cold, of cold one hundred and seven degrees below freezing point. But the dog knew; all its ancestry knew, and it had inherited the knowledge. And it knew that it was not good to walk abroad in such fearful cold. It was the time to lie snug in a hole in the snow and wait for a curtain of cloud to be drawn across the face of outer space whence this cold came. On the other hand, there was no keen intimacy between the dog and the man. The one was the toil-slave of the other, and the only caresses it had ever received were the caresses of the whip lash and of harsh and menacing throat sounds that threatened the whip lash. So the dog made no effort to communicate its apprehension to the man. It was not concerned in the welfare of the man; it was for its own sake that it yearned back toward the fire. But the man whistled, and spoke to it with the sound of whip lashes, and the dog swung in at the man's heels and followed after.

The man took a chew of tobacco and proceeded to start a new amber beard. Also, his moist breath quickly powdered with white his mustache, eyebrows, and lashes. There did not seem to be so many springs on the left fork of the Henderson, and for half an hour the man saw no signs of any. And then it happened. At a place where there were no signs, where the soft, unbroken snow seemed to advertise solidity beneath, the man broke through. It was not deep. He wet himself half-way to the knees before he floundered out to the firm crust.

He was angry, and cursed his luck aloud. He had hoped to get into camp with the boys at six o'clock, and this would delay him an hour, for he would have to build a fire and dry out his footgear. This was imperative at that low temperature–he knew that much; and he turned aside to the bank, which he climbed. On top, tangled in the underbrush about the trunks of several small spruce trees, was a high-water deposit of dry firewood–sticks and twigs, principally, but also larger portions of seasoned branches and fine, dry, last year's grasses. He threw down several large pieces on top of the snow. This served for a foundation and prevented the young flame from drowning itself in the snow it otherwise would melt. The flame he got by touching a match to a small shred of birch bark that he took from his pocket. This burned even more readily than paper. Placing it on the foundation, he fed the young flame with wisps of dry grass and with the tiniest dry twigs.

He worked slowly and carefully, keenly aware of his danger. Gradually, as the flame grew stronger, he increased the size of the twigs with which he fed it. He squatted in the snow, pulling the twigs out from their entanglement in the brush and feeding directly to the flame. He knew there must be no failure. When it is seventy-five below zero, a man must not fail in his first attempt to build a fire—that is, if his feet are wet. If his feet are dry, and he fails, he can run along the trail for half a mile and restore his circulation. But the circulation of wet and freezing feet cannot be restored by running when it is seventy-five below. No matter how fast he runs, the wet feet will freeze the harder.

All this the man knew. The old-timer on Sulphur Creek had told him about it the previous fall, and now he was appreciating the advice. Already all sensation had gone out of his feet. To build the fire he had been forced to remove his mittens, and the fingers had quickly gone numb. His pace of four miles an hour had kept his heart pumping blood to the surface of his body and to all the extremities. But the instant he stopped, the action of the pump eased down. The cold of space smote the unprotected tip of the planet, and he, being on that unprotected tip, received the full force of the blow. The blood of his body recoiled before it. The blood was alive, like the dog, and like the dog it wanted to hide away and cover itself up from the fearful cold. So long as he walked four miles an hour, he pumped that blood, willy-nilly, to the surface; but now it ebbed away and sank down into the recesses of his body. The extremities were the first to feel its absence. His wet feet froze the faster, and his exposed fingers numbed the faster, though they had not yet begun to freeze. Nose and cheeks were already freezing, while the skin of all his body chilled as it lost its blood.

But he was safe. Toes and nose and cheeks would be only touched by the frost, for the fire was beginning to burn with strength. He was feeding it with twigs the size of his finger. In another minute he would be able to feed it with branches the size of his wrist, and then he could remove his wet footgear, and, while it dried, he could keep his naked feet warm by the fire, rubbing them at first, of course, with snow. The fire was a success. He was safe. He remembered the advice of the old-timer on Sulphur Creek, and smiled. The old-timer had been very serious in laying down the law that no man must travel alone in the Klondike after fifty below. Well, here he was, he had had the accident; he was alone; and he had saved himself. Those old-timers were rather womanish, some of them, he thought. All a man had to do was to keep his head, and he was all right. Any man who was a man could travel alone. But it was surprising, the rapidity with which his cheeks and nose were freezing. And he had not thought his fingers could go lifeless in so short a time. Lifeless they were, for he could scarcely make them move together to grip a twig, and they seemed remote from his body and from him. When he touched a twig, he had to look and see whether or not he had hold of it. The wires were pretty well down between him and his finger ends.

All of which counted for little. There was the fire, snapping and crackling and promising life with every dancing flame. He started to untie his moccasins. They were coated with ice; the thick German socks were like sheaths of iron halfway to the knees; and the moccasin strings were like rods of steel all twisted and knotted as by some conflagration. For a moment he tugged with his numb fingers, then, realizing the folly of it, he drew his sheath knife.

But before he could cut the strings, it happened. It was his own fault or, rather, his mistake. He should not have built the fire under the spruce tree. He should have built it in the open. But it had been easier to pull the twigs from the brush and drop them directly on the fire. Now the tree under which he had done this carried a weight of snow on its boughs. No wind had blown for weeks, and each bough was fully freighted. Each time he had pulled a twig he had communicated a slight agitation to the tree–an imperceptible agitation, so far as he was concerned, but an agitation sufficient to bring about the disaster. High up in the tree one bough capsized its load of snow. This fell on the boughs beneath, capsizing them. This process continued, spreading out and involving the whole tree. It grew like an avalanche, and it descended without warning upon the man and the fire, and the fire was blotted out! Where it had burned was a mantle of fresh and disordered snow.

The man was shocked. It was as though he had just heard his own sentence of death. For a moment he sat and stared at the spot where the fire had been. Then he grew very calm. Perhaps the old-timer on Sulphur Creek was right. If he had only had a trail mate he would have been in no danger now. The trail mate could have built the fire. Well, it was up to him to build the fire over again, and this second time there must be no failure. Even if he succeeded, he would most likely lose some toes. His feet must be badly frozen by now, and there would be some time before the second fire was ready.

Such were his thoughts, but he did not sit and think them. He was busy all the time they were passing through his mind. He made a new foundation for a fire, this time in the open, where no treacherous tree could blot it out. Next he gathered dry grasses and tiny twigs from the high-water flotsam. He could not bring his fingers together to pull them out, but he was able to gather them by the handful. In this way he got many rotten twigs and bits of green moss that were undesirable, but it was the best he could do. He worked methodically, even collecting an armful of the larger branches to be used later when the fire gathered strength. And all the while the dog sat and watched him, a certain yearning wistfulness in its eyes, for it looked upon him as the fire provider, and the fire was slow in coming.

When all was ready, the man reached in his pocket for a second piece of birch bark. He knew the bark was there, and, though he could not feel it with his fingers, he could hear its crisp rustling as he fumbled for it. Try as he would, he could not clutch hold of it. And all the time, in his consciousness, was the knowledge that each instant his feet were freezing. This thought tended to put him in a panic, but he fought against it and kept calm. He pulled on his mittens with his teeth, and threshed his arms back and forth, beating his hands with all his might against his sides. He did this sitting down, and he stood up to do it; and all the while the dog sat in the snow, its wolf brush of a tail curled around warmly over its forefeet, its sharp wolf ears pricked forward intently as it watched the man. And the man, as he beat and threshed with his arms and hands, felt a great surge of envy as he regarded the creature that was warm and secure in its natural covering.

After a time he was aware of the first faraway signals of sensation in his beaten fingers. The faint tingling grew stronger till it evolved into a stinging ache that was excruciating, but which the man hailed with satisfaction. He stripped the mitten from his right hand and fetched forth the birch bark. The exposed fingers were quickly going numb again. Next he brought out his bunch of sulphur matches. But the tremendous cold had already driven the life out of his fingers. In his effort to separate one match from the others, the whole bunch fell in the snow. He tried to pick it out of the snow, but failed. The dead fingers could neither touch nor clutch. He was very careful. He drove the thought of his freezing feet, and nose, and cheeks, out of his mind, devoting his whole soul to the matches. He watched, using the sense of vision in place of that of touch, and when he saw his fingers on each side the bunch, he closed them—that is, he willed to close them, for the wires were down, and the fingers did not obey. He pulled the mitten on the right hand, and beat it fiercely against his knee. Then, with both mittened hands, he scooped the bunch of matches, along with much snow, into his lap. Yet he was no better off.

After some manipulation he managed to get the bunch

 between the heels of his mittened hands. In this fashion he carried it to his mouth. The ice crackled and snapped when by a violent effort he opened his mouth. He drew the lower jaw in, curled the upper lip out of the way, and scraped the bunch with his upper teeth in order to separate a match. He succeeded in getting one, which he dropped on his lap. He was no better off. He could not pick it up. Then he devised a way. He picked it up in his teeth and scratched it on his leg. Twenty times he scratched before he succeeded in lighting it. As it flamed he held it with his teeth to the birch bark. But the burning brimstone went up his nostrils and into his lungs, causing him to cough spasmodically. The match fell into the snow and went out.

The old-timer of Sulphur Creek was right, he thought in the moment of controlled despair that ensued: after fifty below, a man should travel with a partner. He beat his hands, but failed in exciting any sensation. Suddenly he bared both hands, removing the mittens with his teeth. He caught the whole bunch between the heels of his hands. His arm muscles not being frozen enable him to press the hand heels tightly against the matches. Then he scratched the bunch along his leg. It flared into flame, seventy sulphur matches at once! There was no wind to blow them out. He kept his head to one side to escape the strangling fumes, and held the blazing bunch to the birch bark. As he so held it, he became aware of sensation in his hand. His flesh was burning. He could smell it. Deep down below the surface he could feel it. The sensation developed into pain that grew acute. And still he endured it, holding the flame of the matches clumsily to the bark that would not light readily because his own burning hands were in the way, absorbing most of the flame.

At last, when he could endure no more, he jerked his hands apart. The blazing matches fell sizzling into the snow, but the birch bark was alight. He began laying dry grasses and the tiniest twigs on the flame. He could not pick and choose, for he had to lift the fuel between the heels of his hands. Small pieces of rotten wood and green moss clung to the twigs, and he bit them off as well as he could with his teeth. He cherished the flame carefully and awkwardly. It meant life, and it must not perish. The withdrawl of blood from the surface of his body now made him begin to shiver, and he grew more awkward. A large piece of green moss fell squarely on the little fire. He tried to poke it out with his fingers, but his shivering frame made him poke too far, and he disrupted the nucleus of the fire, the burning grasses and tiny twigs separating and scattering. He tried to poke them together again, but in spite of the tenseness of the effort, his shivering got away with him, and the twigs were hopelessly scattered. Each twig gushed a puff of smoke and went out. The fire provider had failed. As he looked apathetically about him, his eyes chanced on the dog, sitting across the ruins of the fire from him, in the snow, making restless, hunching movements, slightly lifting one forefoot and then the other, shifting its weight back and forth on them with wistful eagerness.

The sight of the dog put a wild idea into his head. He remembered the tale of the man, caught in a blizzard, who killed a steer and crawled inside the carcass, and so was saved. He would kill the dog and bury his hands in the warm body until the numbness went out of them. Then he could build another fire. He spoke to the dog, calling it to him; but in his voice was a strange note of fear that frightened the animal, who had never known the man to speak in such way before. Something was the matter, and its suspicious nature sensed danger—it knew not what danger, but somewhere, somehow, in its brain arose an apprehension of the man. It flattened its ears down at the sound of the man's voice, and its restless, hunching movements and the liftings and shiftings of his forefeet became more pronounced; but it would not come to the man. He got on his hands and knees and crawled toward the dog. This unusual posture again excited suspicion, and the animal sidled mincingly away.

The man sat up in the snow for a moment and struggled for calmness. Then he pulled on his mittens, by means of his teeth, and got upon his feet. He glanced down at first in order to assure himself that he was really standing up, for the absence of sensation in his feet left him unrelated to the earth. His erect position in itself started to drive the webs of suspicion from the dog's mind; and when he spoke peremptorily, with the sound of whip lashes in his voice, the dog rendered its customary allegiance and came to him. As it came within reaching distance, the man lost his control. His arms flashed out to the dog, and he experienced genuine surprise when he discovered that his hands could not clutch, that there was neither bend nor feeling in the fingers. He had forgotten for the moment that they were frozen and that they were freezing more and more. All this happened quickly, and before the animal could get away, he encircled its body with his arms. He sat down in the snow, and in this fashion held the dog, while it snarled and whined and struggled.

But it was all he could do, hold its body encircled in his arms and sit there. He realized that he could not kill the dog. There was no way to do it. With his helpless hands he could neither draw nor hold his sheath knife nor throttle the animal. He released it, and it plunged wildly away, with tail between its legs, and still snarling. It halted forty feet away and surveyed him curiously, with ears sharply pricked forward.

The man looked down at his hands in order to locate them, and found them hanging on the ends of his arms. It struck him as curious that one should have to use his eyes in order to find out where his hands were. He began threshing his arms back and forth, beating the mittened hands against his sides. He did this for five minutes, violently, and his heart pumped enough blood up to the surface to put a stop to his shivering. But no sensation was aroused in the hands. He had an impression that they hung like weights on the ends of his arms, but when he tried to run the impression down, he could not find it.

A certain fear of death, dull and oppressive, came to him. This fear quickly became poignant as he realized that it was no longer a mere matter of freezing his fingers or toes, or of losing his hands and feet, but that it was matter of life and death with the chances against him. This threw him into a panic, and he turned and ran up the creek bed along the old, dim trail. The dog joined in behind and kept up with him. He ran blindly, without intention, in fear such as he had never known in his life. Slowly, as he plowed and floundered through the snow, he began to see things again—the banks of the creek, the old timber jams, the leafless aspens, and the sky. The running made him feel better. He did not shiver. Maybe, if he ran on, his feet would thaw out; and, anyway, if he ran far enough, he would reach camp and the boys. Without doubt he would lose some fingers and toes and some of his face; but the boys would take care of him, and save the rest of him when he got there. And at the same time there was another thought in his mind that said he would never get to the camp and the boys; that it was too many miles away, that the freezing had too great a start on him, and that he would soon be stiff and dead. This thought he kept in the background and refused to consider. Sometimes it pushed itself forward and demanded to be heard, but he thrust it back and strove to think of other things.

It struck him as curious that he could run at all on feet so frozen that he could not feel them when they struck the earth and took the weight of his body. He seemed to himself to skim along above the surface, and to have no connection with the earth. Somewhere he had once seen a winged Mercury, and he wondered if Mercury felt as he felt when skimming over the earth.

His theory of running until he reached camp and the boys had one flaw in it: he lacked the endurance. Several times he stumbled, and finally he tottered, crumpled up, and fell. When he tried to rise, he failed. He must sit and rest, he decided, and next time he would merely walk and keep on going. As he sat and regained his breath, he noted that he was feeling quite warm and comfortable. He was not shivering, and it even seemed that a warm glow had come to his chest and trunk. And yet, when he touched his nose or cheeks, there was no sensation. Running would not thaw them out. Nor would it thaw out his hands and feet. Then the thought came to him that the frozen portions of his body must be extending. He tried to keep this thought down, to forget it, to think of something else; he was aware of the panicky feeling that it caused, and he was afraid of the panic. But the thought asserted itself, and persisted, until it produced a vision of his body totally frozen. This was too much, and he made another wild run along the trail. Once he slowed down to a walk, but the thought of the freezing extending itself made him run again.

And all the time the dog ran with him, at his heels. When he fell down a second time, it curled its tail over its forefeet and sat in front of him, facing him curiously eager and intent. The warmth and security of the animal angered him, and he cursed it till it flattened down its ears appeasingly. This time the shivering came more quickly upon the man. He was losing in his battle with the frost. It was creeping into his body from all sides. The thought of it drove him on, but he ran no more than a hundred feet, when he staggered and pitched headlong. It was his last panic. When he had recovered his breath and control, he sat up and entertained in his mind the conception of meeting death with dignity. However, the conception did not come to him in such terms. His idea of it was that he had been making a fool of himself, running around like a chicken with its head cut off—such was the simile that occurred to him. Well, he was bound to freeze anyway, and he might as well take it decently. With this new-found peace of mind came the first glimmerings of drowsiness. A good idea, he thought, to sleep off to death. It was like taking an anesthetic. Freezing was not so bad as people thought. There were lots worse ways to die.

 He pictured the boys finding his body next day. Suddenly he found himself with them, coming along the trail and looking for himself. And, still with them, he came around a turn in the trail and found himself lying in the snow. He did not belong with himself any more, for even then he was out of himself, standing with the boys and looking at himself in the snow. It certainly was cold, was his thought. When he got back to the States he could tell the folks what real cold was. He drifted on from this to a vision of the old-timer on Sulphur Creek. He could see him quite clearly, warm and comfortable, and smoking a pipe.

"You were right, old hoss; you were right," the man mumbled to the old-timer of Sulphur Creek.

Then the man drowsed off into what seemed to him the most comfortable and satisfying sleep he had ever known. The dog sat facing him and waiting. The brief day drew to a close in a long, slow twilight. There were no signs of a fire to be made, and, besides, never in the dog's experience had it known a man to sit like that in the snow and make no fire. As the twilight drew on, its eager yearning for the fire mastered it, and with a great lifting and shifting of forefeet, it whined softly, then flattened its ears down in anticipation of being chidden by the man. But the man remained silent. Later the dog whined loudly. And still later it crept close to the man and caught the scent of death. This made the animal bristle and back away. A little longer it delayed, howling under the stars that leaped and danced and shone brightly in the cold sky. Then it turned and trotted up the trail in the direction of the camp it knew, where were the other food providers and fire providers.

LOVE OF LIFE

> This out of all will remain—
> They have lived and have tossed:
> So much of the game will be gain,
> Though the gold of the dice has been lost.

They limped painfully down the bank, and once the foremost of the two men staggered among the rough-strewn rocks. They were tired and weak, and their faces had the drawn expression of patience which comes of hardship long endured. They were heavily burdened with blanket packs which were strapped to their shoulders. Head straps, passing across the forehead, helped support these packs. Each man carried a rifle. They walked in a stooped posture, the shoulders well forward, the head still farther forward, the eyes bent upon the ground.

"I wish we had just about two of them cartridges that's layin' in that cache of ourn," said the second man.

His voice was utterly and drearily expressionless. He spoke without enthusiasm; and the first man, limping into the milky stream that foamed over the rocks, vouchsafed no reply.

LOVE OF LIFE

This out of all will remain—
  They have lived and have tossed:
So much of the game will be gain,
  Though the gold of the dice has been lost.

They limped painfully down the bank, and once the foremost of the two men staggered among the rough-strewn rocks. They were tired and weak, and their faces had the drawn expression of patience which comes of hardship long endured. They were heavily burdened with blanket packs which were strapped to their shoulders. Head straps, passing across the forehead, helped support these packs. Each man carried a rifle. They walked in a stooped posture, the shoulders well forward, the head still farther forward, the eyes bent upon the ground.

"I wish we had just about two of them cartridges that's layin' in that cache of ourn," said the second man.

His voice was utterly and drearily expressionless. He spoke without enthusiasm; and the first man, limping into the milky stream that foamed over the rocks, vouchsafed no reply.

The other man followed at his heels. They did not remove their footgear, though the water was icy cold—so cold that their ankles ached and their feet went numb. In places the water dashed against their knees, and both men staggered for footing.

The man who followed slipped on a smooth boulder, nearly fell, but recovered himself with a violent effort, at the same time uttering a sharp exclamation of pain. He seemed faint and dizzy and put out his free hand while he reeled, as though seeking support against the air. When he had steadied himself he stepped forward, but reeled again and nearly fell. Then he stood still and looked at the other man, who had never turned his head.

The man stood still for fully a minute, as though debating with himself. Then he called out, "I say, Bill, I've sprained my ankle."

Bill staggered on through the milky water. He did not look around. The man watched him go, and though his face was expressionless as ever, his eyes were like the eyes of a wounded deer.

The other man limped up the farther bank and continued straight on without looking back. The man in the stream watched him. His lips trembled a little, so that the rough thatch of brown hair which covered them was visibly agitated. His tongue even strayed out to moisten them.

"Bill!" he cried out.

It was the pleading cry of a strong man in distress, but Bill's head did not turn. The man watched him go, limping grotesquely and lurching forward with stammering gait up the slow slope toward the soft sky line of the low-lying hill. He watched him go till he passed over the crest and disappeared. Then he turned his gaze and slowly took in the circle of the world that remained to him now that Bill was gone.

Near the horizon the sun was smoldering dimly, almost obscured by formless mists and vapors, which gave an impression of mass and density without outline or tangibility. The man pulled out his watch, the while resting his weight on one leg. It was four o'clock, and as the season was near the last of July or first of August—he did not know the precise date within a week or two—he knew that the sun roughly marked the northwest. He looked to the south and knew that somewhere beyond those bleak hills lay the Great Bear Lake; also he knew that in that direction the Arctic Circle cut its forbidding way across the Canadian Barrens. This stream in which he stood was a feeder to the Coppermine River, which in turn flowed north and emptied into Coronation Gulf and the Arctic Ocean. He had never been there, but he had seen it, once, on a Hudson's Bay Company chart.

Again his gaze completed the circle of the world about him. It was not a heartening spectacle. Everywhere was soft sky line. The hills were all low-lying. There were no trees, no shrubs, no grasses—naught but a tremendous and terrible desolation that sent fear swiftly dawning into his eyes.

"Bill!" he whispered, once and twice; "Bill!"

He cowered in the midst of the milky water, as though the vastness were pressing in upon him with overwhelming force, brutally crushing him with its complacent awfulness. He began to shake as with an ague fit, till the gun fell from his hand with a splash. This served to rouse him. He fought with his fear and pulled himself together, groping in the water and recovering the weapon. He hitched his pack farther over on his left shoulder, so as to take a portion of its weight from off the injured ankle. Then he proceeded, slowly and carefully, wincing with pain, to the bank.

He did not stop. With a desperation that was madness, unmindful of the pain, he hurried up the slope to the crest of the hill over which his comrade had disappeared—more grotesque and comical by far than that limping, jerking comrade. But at the crest he saw a shallow valley, empty of life. He fought with his fear again, overcame it, hitched the pack still farther over on his left shoulder, and lurched on down the slope.

The bottom of the valley was soggy with water, which the thick moss held, spongelike, close to the surface. This water squirted out from under his feet at every step, and each time he lifted a foot the action culminated in a sucking sound as the wet moss reluctantly released its grip. He picked his way from muskeg to muskeg, and followed the other man's footsteps along and across the rocky ledges which thrust like islets through the sea of moss.

Though alone, he was not lost. Farther on, he knew, he would come to where dead spruce and fir, very small and wizened, bordered the shore of a little lake, the *titchinnichilie*, in the tongue of the country, the "land of little sticks." And into that lake flowed a small stream, the water of which was not milky. There was rush grass on that stream—this he remembered well—but no timber, and he would follow it till its first trickle ceased at a divide. He would cross this divide to the first trickle of another stream, flowing to the west, which he would follow until it emptied into the river Dease, and here he would find a cache under an upturned canoe and piled over with many rocks. And in this cache would be ammunition for his empty gun, fishhooks and lines, a small net—all the utilities for the killing and snaring of food. Also he would find flour—not much—a piece of bacon, and some beans.

Bill would be waiting for him there, and they would paddle away south down the Dease to the Great Bear Lake. And south across the lake they would go, ever south, till they gained the Mackenzie. And south, still south, they would go, while the winter raced vainly after them, and the ice formed in the eddies, and the days grew chill and crisp, south to some warm Hudson's Bay Company post, where timber grew tall and generous and there was grub without end.

These were the thoughts of the man as he strove onward. But hard as he strove with his body, he strove equally hard with his mind, trying to think that Bill had not deserted him, that Bill would surely wait for him at the cache. He was compelled to think this thought, or else there would not be any use to strive, and he would have lain down and died. And as the dim ball of the sun sank slowly into the northwest he covered every inch—and many times—of his and Bill's flight south before the downcoming winter. And he conned the grub of the cache and the grub of the Hudson's Bay Company post over and over again. He had not eaten for two days; for a far longer time he had not had all he wanted to eat. Often he stooped and picked pale muskeg berries, put them into his mouth, and chewed and swallowed them. A muskeg berry is a bit of seed enclosed in a bit of water. In the mouth the water melts away and the seed chews sharp and bitter. The man knew there was no nourishment in the berries, but he chewed them patiently with a hope greater than knowledge and defying experience.

At nine o'clock he stubbed his toe on a rocky ledge, and from sheer weariness and weakness staggered and fell. He lay for some time, without movement, on his side. Then he slipped out of the pack straps and clumsily dragged himself into a sitting posture. It was not yet dark, and in the lingering twilight he groped about among the rocks for shreds of dry moss. When he had gathered a heap he built a fire—a smoldering, smudgy fire—and put a tin pot of water on to boil.

He unwrapped his pack and the first thing he did was to count his matches. There were sixty-seven. He counted them three times to make sure. He divided them into several portions, wrapping them in oil paper, disposing of one bunch in his empty tobacco pouch, of another bunch in the inside band of his battered hat, of a third bunch under his shirt on the chest. This accomplished, a panic came upon him, and he unwrapped them all and counted them again. There were still sixty-seven.

He dried his wet footgear by the fire. The moccasins were in soggy shreds. The blanket socks were worn through in places, and his feet were raw and bleeding. His ankle was throbbing, and he gave it an examination. It had swollen to the size of his knee. He tore a long strip from one of his two blankets and bound the ankle tightly. He tore other strips and bound them about his feet to serve for both moccasins and socks. Then he drank the pot of water, steaming hot, wound his watch, and crawled between his blankets.

He slept like a dead man. The brief darkness around midnight came and went. The sun arose in the north-east—at least the day dawned in that quarter, for the sun was hidden by gray clouds.

At six o'clock he awoke, quietly lying on his back. He gazed straight up into the gray sky and knew that he was hungry. As he rolled over on his elbow he was startled by a loud snort, and saw a bull caribou regarding him with alert curiosity. The animal was not more than fifty feet away, and instantly into the man's mind leaped the vision and the savor of a caribou steak sizzling and frying over a fire. Mechanically he reached for the empty gun, drew a bead, and pulled the trigger. The bull snorted and leaped away, his hoofs rattling and clattering as he fled across the ledges.

The man cursed and flung the empty gun from him. He groaned aloud as he started to drag himself to his feet. It was a slow and arduous task. His joints were like rusty hinges. They worked harshly in their sockets, with much friction, and each bending or unbending was accomplished only through a sheer exertion of will. When he finally gained his feet, another minute or so was consumed in straightening up, so that he could stand erect as a man should stand.

He crawled up a small knoll and surveyed the prospect. There were no trees, no bushes, nothing but a gray sea of moss scarcely diversified by gray rocks, gray lakelets, and gray streamlets. The sky was gray. There was no sun nor hint of sun. He had no idea of north, and he had forgotten the way he had come to this spot the night before. But he was not lost. He knew that. Soon he would come to the land of the little sticks. He felt that it lay off to the left somewhere, not far—possibly just over the next low hill.

He went back to put his pack into shape for traveling. He assured himself of the existence of his three separate parcels of matches, though he did not stop to count them. But he did linger, debating, over a squat moose-hide sack. It was not large. He could hide it under his two hands. He knew that it weighed fifteen pounds—as much as all the rest of the pack—and it worried him. He finally set it to one side and proceeded to roll the pack. He paused to gaze at the squat moose-hide sack. He picked it up hastily with a defiant glance about him, as though the desolation were trying to rob him of it; and when he rose to his feet to stagger on into the day, it was included in the pack on his back.

He bore away to the left, stopping now and again to eat muskeg berries. His ankle had stiffened, his limp was more pronounced, but the pain of it was as nothing compared with the pain of his stomach. The hunger pains were sharp. They gnawed and gnawed until he could not keep his mind steady on the course he must pursue to gain the land of little sticks. The muskeg berries did not allay this gnawing, while they made his tongue and the roof of his mouth sore with their irritating bite.

He came upon a valley where rock ptarmigan rose on whirring wings from the ledges and muskegs. "Ker—ker—ker" was the cry they made. He threw stones at them but could not hit them. He placed his pack on the ground and stalked them as a cat stalks a sparrow. The sharp rocks cut through his pants legs till his knees left a trail of blood; but the hurt was lost in the hurt of his hunger. He squirmed over the wet moss, saturating his clothes and chilling his body; but he was not aware of it, so great was his fever for food. And always the ptarmigan rose, whirring, before him, till their "Ker–ker–ker" became a mock to him, and he cursed them and cried aloud at them with their own cry.

Once he crawled upon one that must have been asleep. He did not see it till it shot up in his face from its rocky nook. He made a clutch as startled as was the rise of the ptarmigan, and there remained in his hand three tail feathers. As he watched its flight he hated it, as though it had done him some terrible wrong. Then he returned and shouldered his pack.

As the day wore along he came into valleys or swales where game was more plentiful. A band of caribou passed by, twenty and odd animals, tantalizingly within rifle range. He felt a wild desire to run after them, a certitude that he could run them down. A black fox came toward him, carrying a ptarmigan in his mouth. The man shouted. It was a fearful cry, but the fox, leaping away in fright, did not drop the ptarmigan.

Late in the afternoon he followed a stream, milky with lime, which ran through sparse patches of rush grass. Grasping these rushes firmly near the root, he pulled up what resembled a young onion sprout no larger than a shingle nail. It was tender, and his teeth sank into it with a crunch that promised deliciously of food. But its fibres were tough. It was composed of stringy filaments saturated with water, like the berries, and devoid of nourishment. He threw off his pack and went into the rush grass on hands and knees, crunching and munching, like some bovine creature.

He was very weary and often wished to rest–to lie down and sleep; but he was continually driven on, not so much by his desire to gain the land of little sticks as by his hunger. He searched little ponds for frogs and dug up the earth with his nails for worms, though he knew in spite that neither frogs nor worms existed so far north.

He looked into every pool of water vainly, until, as the long twilight came on, he discovered a solitary fish, the size of a minnow, in such a pool. He plunged his arm in up to the shoulder, but it eluded him. He reached for it with both hands and stirred up the milky mud at the bottom. In his excitement he fell in, wetting himself to the waist. Then the water was too muddy to admit of his seeing the fish, and he was compelled to wait until the sediment had settled.

The pursuit was renewed, till the water was again muddied. But he could not wait. He unstrapped the tin bucket and began to bail the pool. He bailed wildly at first, splashing himself and flinging the water so short a distance that it ran back into the pool. He worked more carefully, striving to be cool, though his heart was pounding against his chest and his hands were trembling. At the end of half an hour the pool was nearly dry. Not a cupful of water remained. And there was no fish. He found a hidden crevice among the stones through which it had escaped to the adjoining and larger pool—a pool which he could not empty in a night and a day. Had he known of the crevice, he could have closed it with a rock at the beginning and the fish would have been his.

Thus he thought, and crumpled up and sank down upon the wet earth. At first he cried softly to himself, then he cried loudly to the pitiless desolation that ringed him around; and for a long time after he was shaken by great dry sobs.

He built a fire and warmed himself by drinking quarts

226 of hot water, and made camp on a rocky ledge in the same fashion he had the night before. The last thing he did was to see that his matches were dry and to wind his watch. The blankets were wet and clammy. His ankle pulsed with pain. But he knew only that he was hungry, and through his restless sleep he dreamed of feasts and banquets and of food served and spread in all imaginable ways.

He awoke chilled and sick. There was no sun. The gray of earth and sky had become deeper, more profound. A raw wind was blowing, and the first flurries of snow were whitening the hilltops. The air about him thickened and grew white while he made a fire and boiled more water. It was wet snow, half rain, and the flakes were large and soggy. At first they melted as soon as they came in contact with the earth, but ever more fell, covering the ground, putting out the fire, spoiling his supply of moss fuel.

This was a signal for him to strap on his pack and stumble onward, he knew not where. He was not concerned with the land of little sticks, nor with Bill and the cache under the upturned canoe by the river Dease. He was mastered by the verb "to eat." He was hunger-mad. He took no heed of the course he pursued, so long as that course led him through the swale bottoms. He felt his way through the wet snow to the watery muskeg berries, and went by feel as he pulled up the rush grass by the roots. But it was tasteless stuff and did not satisfy. He found a weed that tasted sour and he ate all he could find of it, which was not much, for it was a creeping growth, easily hidden under the several inches of snow.

He had no fire that night, nor hot water, and crawled

under his blanket to sleep the broken hunger sleep. The snow turned into a cold rain. He awakened many times to feel it falling on his upturned face. Day came—a gray day and no sun. It had ceased raining. The keenness of his hunger had departed. Sensibility, as far as concerned the yearning for food, had been exhausted. There was a dull, heavy ache in his stomach, but it did not bother him so much. He was more rational, and once more he was chiefly interested in the land of little sticks and the cache by the river Dease.

He ripped the remnant or one of his blankets into strips and bound his bleeding feet. Also he recinched the injured ankle and prepared himself for a day of travel. When he came to his pack he paused long over the squat moose-hide sack, but in the end it went with him.

The snow had melted under the rain, and only the hilltops showed white. The sun came out, and he succeeded in locating the points of the compass, though he knew now that he was lost. Perhaps, in his previous days' wanderings, he had edged away too far to the left. He now bore off to the right to counteract the possible deviation from his true course.

Though the hunger pangs were no longer so exquisite, he realized that he was weak. He was compelled to pause for frequent rests, when he attacked the muskeg berries and rush-grass patches. His tongue felt dry and large, as though covered with a fine hairy growth, and it tasted bitter in his mouth. His heart gave him a great deal of trouble. When he had travelled a few minutes it would begin a remorseless thump, thump, thump, and then leap up and away in a painful flutter of beats that choked him and made him go faint and dizzy.

 In the middle of the day he found two minnows in a large pool. It was impossible to bail it, but he was calmer now and managed to catch them in his tin bucket. They were no longer than his little finger, but he was not particularly hungry. The dull ache in his stomach had been growing duller and fainter. It seemed almost that his stomach was dozing. He ate the fish raw, masticating with painstaking care, for the eating was an act of pure reason. While he had no desire to eat, he knew that he must eat to live.

In the evening he caught three more minnows, eating two and saving the third for breakfast. The sun had dried stray shreds of moss, and he was able to warm himself with hot water. He had not covered more than ten miles that day; and the next day, travelling whenever his heart permitted him, he covered no more than five miles. But his stomach did not give him the slightest uneasiness. It had gone to sleep. He was in a strange country, too, and the caribou were growing more plentiful, also the wolves. Often their yelps drifted across the desolation, and once he saw three of them slinking away before his path.

Another night; and in the morning, being more rational, he untied the leather string that fastened the squat moose-hide sack. From its open mouth poured a yellow stream of coarse gold dust and nuggets. He roughly divided the gold in halves, caching one half on a prominent ledge, wrapped in a piece of blanket, and returning the other half to the sack. He also began to use strips of the one remaining blanket for his feet. He still clung to his gun, for there were cartridges in that cache by the river Dease.

This was a day of fog, and this day hunger awoke in

him again. He was very weak and was afflicted with a giddiness which at times blinded him. It was no uncommon thing now for him to stumble and fall; and stumbling once, he fell squarely into a ptarmigan nest. There were four newly hatched chicks, a day old—little specks of pulsating life no more than a mouthful; and he ate them ravenously, thrusting them alive into his mouth and crunching them like eggshells between his teeth. The mother ptarmigan beat about him with great outcry. He used his gun as a club with which to knock her over, but she dodged out of reach. He threw stones at her and with one chance shot broke a wing. Then she fluttered away, running, trailing the broken wing, with him in pursuit.

The little chicks had no more than whetted his appetite. He hopped and bobbed clumsily along on his injured ankle, throwing stones and screaming hoarsely at times; at other times hopping and bobbing silently along, picking himself up grimly and patiently when he fell, or rubbing his eyes with his hand when the giddiness threatened to overpower him.

The chase led him across swampy ground in the bottom of the valley, and he came upon footprints in the soggy moss. They were not his own—he could see that. They must be Bill's. But he could not stop, for the mother ptarmigan was running on. He would catch her first, then he would return and investigate.

He exhausted the mother ptarmigan; but he exhausted himself. She lay panting on her side. He lay panting on his side, a dozen feet away, unable to crawl to her. And as he recovered she recovered, fluttering out of reach as his hungry hand went out to her. The chase was resumed. Night settled down and she escaped. He stumbled from

230 weakness and pitched head foremost on his face, cutting his cheek, his pack upon his back. He did not move for a long while; then he rolled over on his side, wound his watch, and lay there until morning.

Another day of fog. Half of his last blanket had gone into foot wrappings. He failed to pick up Bill's trail. It did not matter. His hunger was driving him too compellingly—only—only he wondered if Bill, too, were lost. By midday the irk of his pack became too oppressive. Again he divided the gold, this time merely spilling half of it on the ground. In the afternoon he threw the rest of it away, there remaining to him only the half blanket, the tin bucket, and the rifle.

A hallucination began to trouble him. He felt confident that one cartridge remained to him. It was in the chamber of the rifle and he had overlooked it. On the other hand, he knew all the time that the chamber was empty. But the hallucination persisted. He fought it off for hours, then threw his rifle open and was confronted with emptiness. The disappointment was as bitter as though he had really expected to find the cartridge.

He plodded on for half an hour, when the hallucination arose again. Again he fought it, and still it persisted, till for very relief he opened his rifle to unconvince himself. At times his mind wandered farther afield, and he plodded on, a mere automaton, strange conceits and whimsicalities gnawing at his brain like worms. But these excursions out of the real were of brief duration, for ever the pangs of the hunger bite called him back. He was jerked back abruptly once from such an excursion by a sight that caused him nearly to faint. He reeled and swayed, doddering like a drunken man to keep from falling. Before him stood a horse. A horse! He could not believe his eyes. A thick mist was in them, intershot with sparkling points of light. He rubbed his eyes savagely to clear his vision, and beheld not a horse but a great brown bear. The animal was studying him with bellicose curiosity.

The man had brought his gun halfway to his shoulder before he realized. He lowered it and drew his hunting knife from its beaded sheath at his hip. Before him was meat and life. He ran his thumb along the edge of his knife. It was sharp. The point was sharp. He would fling himself upon the bear and kill it. But his heart began its warning thump, thump, thump. Then followed the wild upward leap and tattoo of flutters, the pressing as of an iron band about his forehead, the creeping of the dizziness into his brain.

His desperate courage was evicted by a great surge of fear. In his weakness, what if the animal attacked him? He drew himself up to his most imposing stature, gripping the knife and staring hard at the bear. The bear advanced clumsily a couple of steps, reared up, and gave vent to a tentative growl. If the man ran, he would run after him; but the man did not run. He was animated now with the courage of fear. He, too, growled, savagely, terribly, voicing the fear that is to life germane and that lies twisted about life's deepest roots.

The bear edged away to one side, growling menacingly, himself appalled by this mysterious creature that appeared upright and unafraid. But the man did not move. He stood like a statue till the danger was past, when he yielded to a fit of trembling and sank down into the wet moss.

 He pulled himself together and went on, afraid now in a new way. It was not the fear that he should die passively from lack of food, but that he should be destroyed violently before starvation had exhausted the last particle of the endeavor in him that made toward surviving. There were the wolves. Back and forth across the desolation drifted their howls, weaving the very air into a fabric of menace that was so tangible that he found himself, arms in the air, pressing it back from him as it might be the walls of a wind-blown tent.

Now and again the wolves, in packs of two and three, crossed his path. But they sheered clear of him. They were not in sufficient numbers, and besides, they were hunting the caribou, which did not battle, while this strange creature that walked erect might scratch and bite.

In the late afternoon he came upon scattered bones where the wolves had made a kill. The debris had been a caribou calf an hour before, squawking and running and very much alive. He contemplated the bones, clean-picked and polished, pink with the cell life in them which had not yet died. Could it possibly be that he might be that ere the day was done! Such was life, eh? A vain and fleeting thing. It was only life that pained. There was no hurt in death. To die was to sleep. It meant cessation, rest. Then why was he not content to die?

But he did not moralize long. He was squatting in the moss, a bone in his mouth, sucking at the shreds of life that still dyed it faintly pink. The sweet meaty taste, thin and elusive almost as a memory, maddened him. He closed his jaws on the bones and crunched. Sometimes it was the bone that broke, sometimes his teeth. Then he crushed the bones between rocks, pounded them to a pulp, and swallowed them. He pounded his fingers, too, in his haste, and yet found a moment in which to feel surprise at the fact that his fingers did not hurt much when caught under the descending rock.

Came frightful days of snow and rain. He did not know when he made camp, when he broke camp. He travelled in the night as much as in the day. He rested wherever he fell, crawled on whenever the dying life in him flickered up and burned less dimly. He, as a man, no longer strove. It was the life in him, unwilling to die, that drove him on. He did not suffer. His nerves had become blunted, numb, while his mind was filled with weird visions and delicious dreams.

But ever he sucked and chewed on the crushed bones of the caribou calf, the least remnants of which he had gathered up and carried with him. He crossed no more hills or divides, but automatically followed a large stream which flowed through a wide and shallow valley. He did not see this stream nor this valley. He saw nothing save visions. Soul and body walked or crawled side by side, yet apart, so slender was the thread that bound them.

He awoke in his right mind, lying on his back on a rocky ledge. The sun was shining bright and warm. Afar off he heard the squawking of caribou calves. He was aware of vague memories of rain and wind and snow, but whether he had been beaten by the storm for two days or two weeks he did not know.

For some time he lay without movement, the genial sunshine pouring upon him and saturating his miserable body with its warmth. A fine day, he thought. Perhaps he could manage to locate himself. By a painful effort he rolled over on his side. Below him flowed a wide and sluggish river. Its unfamiliarity puzzled him. Slowly he followed it with his eyes, winding in wide sweeps among the bleak, bare hills, bleaker and barer and lower-lying than any hills he had yet encountered. Slowly, deliberately, without excitement or more than the most casual interest, he followed the course of the strange stream toward the sky line and saw it emptying into a bright and shining sea. He was still unexcited. Most unusual, he thought, a vision or a mirage—more likely a vision, a trick of his disordered mind. He was confirmed in this by sight of a ship lying at anchor in the midst of the shining sea. He closed his eyes for a while, then opened them. Strange how the vision persisted! Yet not strange. He knew there were no seas or ships in the heart of the barren lands, just as he had known there was no cartridge in the empty rifle.

He heard a snuffle behind him—a half-choking gasp or cough. Very slowly, because of his exceeding weakness and stiffness, he rolled over on his other side. He could see nothing near at hand, but he waited patiently. Again came the snuffle and cough, and outlined between two jagged rocks not a score of feet away he made out the gray head of a wolf. The sharp ears were not pricked so sharply as he had seen them on other wolves; the eyes were bleared and bloodshot, the head seemed to droop limply and forlornly. The animal blinked continually in the sunshine. It seemed sick. As he looked it snuffled and coughed again.

This, at least, was real, he thought, and turned on the other side so that he might see the reality of the world which had been veiled from him before by the vision. But the sea still shone in the distance and the ship was plainly discernible. Was it reality after all? He closed his eyes for a long while and thought, and then it came to him. He had been making north by east, away from the Dease Divide and into the Coppermine Valley. This wide and sluggish river was the Coppermine. That shining sea was the Arctic Ocean. That ship was a whaler, strayed east, far east, from the mouth of the Mackenzie, and it was lying at anchor in Coronation Gulf. He remembered the Hudson's Bay Company chart he had seen long ago, and it was all clear and reasonable to him.

He sat up and turned his attention to immediate affairs. He had worn through the blanket wrappings, and his feet were shapeless lumps of raw meat. His last blanket was gone. Rifle and knife were both missing. He had lost his hat somewhere, with the bunch of matches in the band, but the matches against his chest were safe and dry inside the tobacco pouch and oil paper. He looked at his watch. It marked eleven o'clock and was still running. Evidently he had kept it wound.

He was calm and collected. Though extremely weak, he had no sensation of pain. He was not hungry. The thought of food was not even pleasant to him, and whatever he did was done by his reason alone. He ripped off his pants legs to the knees and bound them about his feet. Somehow he had succeeded in retaining the tin bucket. He would have some hot water before he began what he foresaw was to be a terrible journey to the ship.

His movements were slow. He shook as with a palsy. When he started to collect dry moss he found he could not rise to his feet. He tried again and again, then contented himself with crawling about on hands and knees. Once he crawled near to the sick wolf. The animal dragged itself reluctantly out of his way, licking its chops with a tongue which seemed hardly to have the strength to curl. The man noticed that the tongue was not the customary healthy red. It was a yellowish brown and seemed coated with a rough and half-dry mucus.

After he had drunk a quart of hot water the man found he was able to stand, and even to walk as well as a dying man might be supposed to walk. Every minute or so he was compelled to rest. His steps were feeble and uncertain, just as the wolf's that trailed him were feeble and uncertain; and that night, when the shining sea was blotted out by blackness, he knew he was nearer to it by no more than four miles.

Throughout the night he heard the cough of the sick wolf, and now and then the squawking of the caribou calves. There was life all around him, but it was strong life, very much alive and well, and he knew the sick wolf clung to the sick man's trail in the hope that the man would die first. In the morning, on opening his eyes, he beheld it regarding him with a wistful and hungry stare. It stood crouched, with tail between its legs, like a miserable and woebegone dog. It shivered in the chill morning wind and grinned dispiritedly when the man spoke to it in a voice that achieved no more than a hoarse whisper.

The sun rose brightly, and all morning the man tottered and fell toward the ship on the shining sea. The weather was perfect. It was the brief Indian summer of the high latitudes. It might last a week. Tomorrow or next day it might be gone.

In the afternoon the man came upon a trail. It was of another man, who did not walk, but who dragged himself on all fours. The man thought it might be Bill, but he thought in a dull, uninterested way. He had no curiosity. In fact sensation and emotion had left him. He was no longer susceptible to pain. Stomach and nerves had gone to sleep. Yet the life that was in him drove him on. He was very weary, but it refused to die. It was because it refused to die that he still ate muskeg berries and minnows, drank his hot water, and kept a wary eye on the sick wolf.

He followed the trail of the other man who dragged himself along, and soon came to the end of it—a few fresh-picked bones where the soggy moss was marked by the foot pads of many wolves. He saw a squat moose-hide sack, mate to his own, which had been torn by sharp teeth. He picked it up, though its weight was almost too much for his feeble fingers. Bill had carried it to the last. Ha-ha! He would have the laugh on Bill. He would survive and carry it to the ship in the shining sea. His mirth was hoarse and ghastly, like a raven's croak, and the sick wolf joined him, howling lugubriously. The man ceased suddenly. How could he have the laugh on Bill if that were Bill; if those bones, so pinky-white and clean, were Bill?

He turned away. Well, Bill had deserted him; but he would not take the gold, nor would he suck Bill's bones. Bill would have, though, had it been the other way around, he mused as he staggered on.

He came to a pool of water. Stooping over in quest of minnows, he jerked his head back as though he had been stung. He had caught sight of his reflected face. So horrible was it that sensibility awoke long enough to be shocked. There were three minnows in the pool, which was too large to drain; and after several ineffectual attempts to catch them in the tin bucket he forbore. He was afraid, because of his great weakness, that he might fall in and drown. It was for this reason that he did not trust himself to the river astride one of the many drift logs which lined its sandspits.

That day he decreased the distance between him and the ship by three miles; the next day by two—for he was crawling now as Bill had crawled; and the end of the fifth day found the ship still seven miles away and him unable to make even a mile a day. Still the Indian summer held on, and he continued to crawl and faint, turn and turn about; and ever the sick wolf coughed and wheezed at his heels. His knees had become raw meat like his feet, and though he padded them with the shirt from his back it was a red track he left behind him on the moss and stones. Once, glancing back, he saw the wolf licking hungrily his bleeding trail, and he saw sharply what his own end might be—unless—unless he could get the wolf. Then he began as grim a tragedy of existence as was ever played—a sick man that crawled, a sick wolf that limped, two creatures dragging their dying carcasses across the desolation and hunting each other's lives.

Had it been a well wolf, it would not have mattered so much to the man; but the thought of going to feed the maw of that loathsome and all but dead thing was repugnant to him. He was finicky. His mind had begun to wander again and to be perplexed by hallucinations, while his lucid intervals grew rarer and shorter.

He was awakened once from a faint by a wheeze close in his ear. The wolf leaped lamely back, losing its footing and falling in its weakness. It was ludicrous, but he was not amused. Nor was he even afraid. He was too far gone for that. But his mind was for the moment clear, and he lay and considered. The ship was no more than four miles away. He could see it quite distinctly when he rubbed the mists out of his eyes, and he could see the white sail of a small boat cutting the water of the shining sea. But he could never crawl those four miles. He knew that, and was very calm in the knowledge. He knew that he could not crawl half a mile. And yet he wanted to live. It was unreasonable that he should die after all he had undergone. Fate asked too much of him. And, dying, he declined to die. It was stark madness, perhaps, but in the very grip of death he defied death and refused to die.

He closed his eyes and composed himself with infinite precaution. He steeled himself to keep above the suffocating languor that lapped like a rising tide through all the wells of his being. It was very like a sea, this deadly languor that rose and rose and drowned his consciousness bit by bit. Sometimes he was all but submerged, swimming through oblivion with a faltering stroke; and again, by some strange alchemy of soul, he would find another shred of will and strike out more strongly.

Without movement he lay on his back, and he could hear, slowly drawing near and nearer, the wheezing intake and output of the sick wolf's breath. It drew closer, ever closer, through an infinitude of time, and he did not move. It was at his ear. The harsh dry tongue grated like sandpaper against his cheek. His hands shot out—or at least he willed them to shoot out. The fingers were curved like talons, but they closed on empty air. Swiftness and certitude require strength, and the man had not this strength.

The patience of the wolf was terrible. The man's patience was no less terrible. For half a day he lay motionless, fighting off unconsciousness and waiting for the thing that was to feed upon him and upon which he wished to feed. Sometimes the languid sea rose over him and he dreamed long dreams; but ever through it all, waking and dreaming, he waited for the wheezing breath and the harsh caress of the tongue.

He did not hear the breath, and he slipped slowly from some dream to the feel of the tongue along his hand. He waited. The fangs pressed softly; the pressure increased; the wolf was exerting its last strength in an effort to sink teeth in the food for which it had waited so long. But the man had waited long, and the lacerated hand closed on the jaw. Slowly, while the wolf struggled feebly and the hand clutched feebly, the other hand crept across to a grip. Five minutes later the whole weight of the man's body was on top of the wolf. The hands had not sufficient strength to choke the wolf, but the face of the man was pressed close to the throat of the wolf and the mouth of the man was full of hair. At the end of half an hour the man was aware of a warm trickle in his throat. It was not pleasant. It was like molten lead being forced into his stomach, and it was forced by his will alone. Later the man rolled over on his back and slept.

There were some members of a scientific expedition on the whaleship *Bedford.* From the deck they remarked a strange object on the shore. It was moving down the beach toward the water. They were unable to classify it, and, being scientific men, they climbed into the whaleboat alongside and went ashore to see. And they saw something that was alive but which could hardly be called a man. It was blind, unconscious. It squirmed along the ground like some monstrous worm. Most of its efforts were ineffectual, but it was persistent, and it writhed and twisted and went ahead perhaps a score of feet an hour.

Three weeks afterward the man lay in a bunk on the whaleship *Bedford*, and with tears streaming down his wasted cheeks told who he was and what he had undergone. He also babbled incoherently of his mother, of sunny southern California, and a home among the orange groves and flowers.

The days were not many after that when he sat at table with the scientific men and ship's officers. He gloated over the spectacle of so much food, watching it anxiously as it went into the mouths of others. With the disappearance of each mouthful an expression of deep regret came into his eyes. He was quite sane, yet he hated those men at mealtime. He was haunted by a fear that the food would not last. He inquired of the cook, the cabin boy, the captain, concerning the food stores. They reassured him countless times; but he could not believe them, and pried cunningly about the lazaret to see with his own eyes.

It was noticed that the man was getting fat. He grew stouter with each day. The scientific men shook their heads and theorized. They limited the man at his meals, but still his girth increased and he swelled prodigiously under his shirt.

The sailors grinned. They knew. And when the scientific men set a watch on the man they knew. They saw him slouch for'ard after breakfast, and, like a mendicant,

242 with outstretched palm, accost a sailor. The sailor grinned and passed him a fragment of sea biscuit. He clutched it avariciously, looked at it as a miser looks at gold, and thrust it into his shirt bosom. Similar were the donations from other grinning sailors.

The scientific men were discreet. They let him alone. But they privily examined his bunk. It was lined with hardtack; the mattress was stuffed with hardtack; every nook and cranny was filled with hardtack. Yet he was sane. He was taking precautions against another possible famine—that was all. He would recover from it, the scientific men said; and he did, ere the *Bedford's* anchor rumbled down in San Francisco Bay.

STUDY GUIDE

by
John Creasy
for

THE CALL OF THE WILD
AND OTHER STORIES

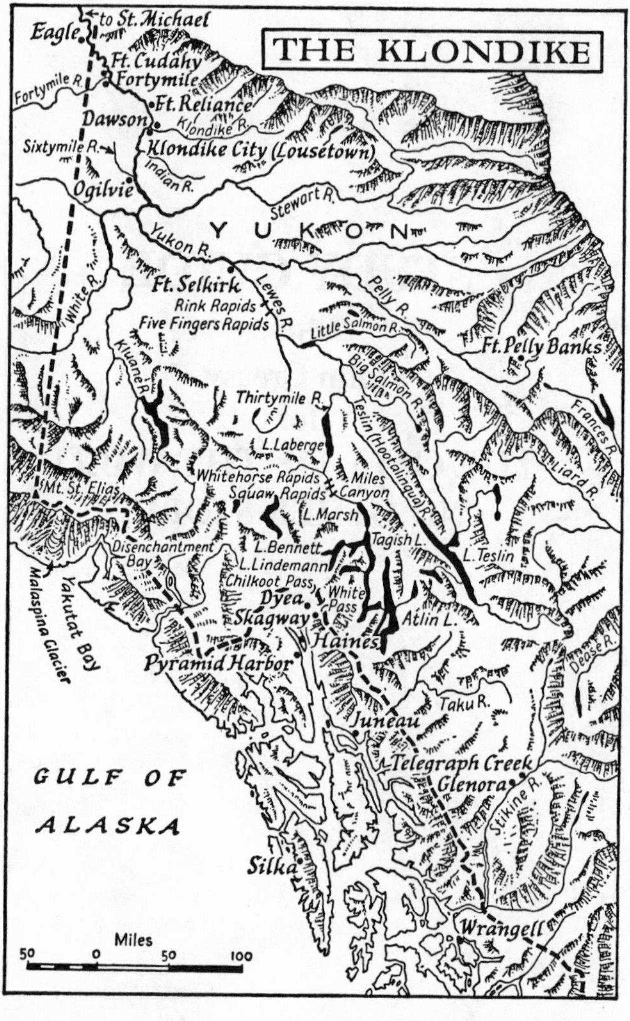
THE KLONDIKE
to St. Michael
Eagle
Ft. Cudahy
Fortymile
Fortymile R.
Ft. Reliance
Dawson
Klondike R.
Sixtymile R.
Klondike City (Lousetown)
Indian R.
Ogilvie
Stewart R.
YUKON
Yukon R.
White R.
Ft. Selkirk
Lewes R.
Rink Rapids
Five Fingers Rapids
Pelly R.
Little Salmon R.
Ft. Pelly Banks
Kluane R.
Big Salmon R.
Thirtymile R.
Teslin (Hootalinqua) R.
Frances R.
L. Laberge
Liard R.
Whitehorse Rapids
Miles Canyon
Squaw Rapids
Mt. St. Elias
L. Marsh
Tagish L.
Disenchantment Bay
L. Bennett
L. Lindemann
Chilkoot Pass
L. Teslin
Malaspina Glacier
Yakutat Bay
Dyea
White Pass
Skagway
Atlin L.
Haines
Dease R.
Pyramid Harbor
Taku R.
Juneau
Telegraph Creek
Glenora
Stikine R.
GULF OF ALASKA
Silka
Wrangell
Miles
50 0 50 100

About the Author

Born in San Francisco, California, on January 12, 1876, *G3* Jack London was the son of Professor William Chaney, an astrologist lecturer-writer, and Flora Wellman, a music tutor and spiritualist (one who tries to make contact with the spirits of people who have died). Later his mother married John London. The young boy took his stepfather's name but insisted on the romantic nickname "Jack" despite the objections of teachers and editors.

While growing up Jack London lived on many farms and ranches in California because his family moved from place to place, unable to pay the rent. He was ten when money problems forced the London family to move to Oakland, and Jack helped support the family. Weekdays before and after school he delivered newspapers, Saturdays he delivered ice, and Sundays he set up pins at the bowling alley. At this time Jack discovered the Oakland Public Library. Books of romantic adventures, deep-sea voyages, and rags-to-riches stories incited his imagination and became more real to him than his own exhausting and uneventful existence.

By the age of thirteen Jack had managed to save six dollars in pennies and nickels and bought a small, leaky skiff. Bailing as he sailed and steered, Jack took his skiff out in the worst storms, even when veteran sailors warned him it was suicidal. He learned to sail skillfully in the tricky currents and sudden squalls of San Francisco Bay. Ships from all over the world sailed by him, feeding his imagination with their magic names. Someday, he thought, he would slip through the pinching fingers of land that encircled the bay and sail out into the world beyond.

Jack quit school at fourteen when his injured father was unable to work. For the next five years, he endured G4 various low-paying, back-breaking jobs, laboring at least ten hours a day as a canner, as a jute mill worker, and later as a coal shoveler.

But some of his work was daring and even thrilling. At fifteen Jack London borrowed $300, purchased his own sloop, the *Razzle Dazzle,* and became an oyster pirate, robbing oyster beds in the San Francisco Bay. Later he switched to the other side of the law and worked for the state fish patrol. Some of the thieves he caught were the same oyster pirates he had gone on raids with.

In Jack's character, rebellion and discipline were continually at war with each other. At seventeen he became an able-bodied seaman for a seven-month seal-hunting expedition to Japan, Korea, and Siberia. After returning home he wrote, "Story of a Typhoon off the Coast of Japan," an article that won the $25 first prize for a newspaper writing-contest in the San Francisco *Morning Call.* For adventure, a year later he traveled cross-country as a hobo riding the rails and briefly joined some of the thousands who had lost their jobs after the Depression of 1893. In Niagara Falls, New York, he was arrested for vagrancy and sentenced to a thirty-day jail term.

This experience convinced Jack London of the need to escape a life in which he seemed to be continually overworked and underpaid. He wanted to be a writer—famous, rich, and respected. To do that he knew he would need an education. At nineteen he entered the freshman class at Oakland High School. After high school graduation he crammed for three months and passed the college entrance exam. Yet he left the University of California after one semester, once again heeding the call for money and adventure.

In 1897 Jack London decided to join the gold rush to the Klondike, an area in northwest Canada near the Alaskan border (see map). In less than two weeks he had bor- G5
rowed $1,500, had equipped himself with a ton of supplies, and had boarded a boat to Skagway, Alaska. Although he spent a year in the frozen North, he discovered no gold. But his experiences provided him the raw material for a lifetime of stories—stories that would later establish his name and fortune. After the winter he returned home with only five dollars in his pocket and avidly began writing as a profession.

This period of concentrated activity was later detailed in his autobiographical novel *Martin Eden* (1909). It describes the struggles of a rough-hewn, impoverished sailor who drives himself to study, write, and work eighteen hours a day and finally transforms himself into a knowledgeable, successful author. London's stories began appearing in newspapers and magazines. In 1900 he published his first collection of short stories, *Son of Wolf*, recounting some of his northland adventures.

Throughout his life he continued writing prolifically, 1,000 to 4,000 words daily. In 1902 he wrote *The People of the Abyss*, his account of the wretched living conditions in the East End of London. The publication of *The Call of the Wild* (1903) brought Jack London worldwide acclaim. It was an immediate success—the first printing of 10,000 copies sold out the first day the book was published. Severely debt-ridden, London had sold all rights for *The Call of the Wild* to his publisher for $2,000. If he had instead chosen to collect royalties, he would have made over $100,000.

London had a huge ranch near Glen Ellen, California, on which he supported his family and friends. His home became a haven for reporters, hobos, artists, sailors, busi-

ness tycoons, convicts, admirers, and hard-luck ne'er-do-wells. This manner of grand living and even grander
G6 spending kept him constantly in debt.

In 1904 he traveled to Japan as a war correspondent to cover the Russo-Japanese War. With mounting financial problems he was also forced to continue writing fiction, and he produced *The Sea-Wolf* (1904), *White Fang* (1906), and *Burning Daylight* (1910).

Even toward the end of his career, Jack London still retained his restless need for adventure and his compulsive drive for success. He spent over $25,000 on a custom-built sailboat, which critics called "London's Folly", and sailed it to Hawaii and Tahiti. In the Marquesas Islands in the South Pacific he encountered lepers, headhunters, and cannibals. Still he maintained his rigorous schedule of daily writing. At last, he was forced to return home to California to recuperate from a tropical disease. Soon after, he published *John Barleycorn* (1913), his best-selling autobiographical treatise on alcoholism.

Throughout his life Jack London remained a man of opposites. He was a realist and a dreamer; a disciplined writer and a reckless adventurer; a crude barroom rowdy and a sensitive, bookish intellectual. He would grab money fiercely with one hand, then throw it away with the other. He was a rugged individualist who had to compete and win over everyone else, but he was also a fighter for social justice who defended the weak and the unsuccessful. He was a lover of life who played with death.

He died at age forty on November 22, 1916. Even his death caused controversy. Although some claim he had committed suicide with a lethal dose of sedatives, four attending physicians attributed the cause of death to uremia, a severe kidney disorder. Nonetheless, in seven-

teen years he had completed over fifty books—several published after his death—on such diverse subjects as economics, philosophy, farming, prize fighting, and prison G7
reform, as well as books of fiction. He was a great artist not only in spite of but because of his excesses. Perhaps the most fitting epitaph for his brief yet troubled career would be Franklin Walker's observation: "Jack London's best adventure story was his own life."

Historical Background

In 1876, the year Jack London was born, America celebrated her one-hundredth birthday. At that time the number of people living on farms and in small towns far outnumbered those living in cities. But that way of life would soon change. During the next fifty years America would emerge as the world's leading industrial power.

By the late nineteenth century the United States had embarked upon the Industrial Revolution. The decade from 1880 to 1890 saw the most rapid railroad expansion in American history. More than 70,000 miles of tracks were laid—enough to circle the earth nine times. Railroads both created and depended upon many other industries. They provided jobs, opened up towns, and transported people, freight, and mail.

The railroads opened up the frontier, but in doing so, they also brought an end to the Old West. By 1893 the historian Frederick Jackson Turner wrote that America had reached the end of the frontier. The land from sea to sea had been explored, and now the new territory was being settled and developed. Settlers had been lured westward in search of gold, fur, cattle, land, and adventure. The wild, unspoiled land where a family might go to escape the crowded city was rapidly vanishing.

G8 Many small farmers, in fact, were returning to the cities. Fewer and fewer farmers were growing more and more food. In 1840 it took over three hours of human work to produce a bushel of wheat; in the 1890s that time had been reduced to ten minutes. There was simply a surplus of farmers. They couldn't compete with the large farm owners who used newly invented plowing and reaping machines, often selling their harvests to city markets as Jack London's father had once done.

Big cities were where the jobs were. Thousands of farmers, educators, immigrants, artists all looking for work and a place to live crowded the cities to the bursting point. During the 1800s, 5,250,000 newcomers landed on America's shores. With so many competing for the same jobs, employers could get away with paying starvation wages. Two dollars was considered a good wage for a twelve-hour day. Many poorly lit, overcrowded, unsafe factories were referred to as "sweat shops." By 1900 almost two million children were working sixty-to-seventy-hour weeks—as Jack London himself had once done. Children, often exhausted and undernourished, received from $1.50 to $2.50 weekly. And many competed with adults for the same jobs.

Meanwhile marvelous advances were occurring in science and technology. The telegraph, the typewriter, and the telephone speeded communication and thereby helped the growth of industry. The age of industry, steel, and electricity was also an era of great inventions. In 1879 Thomas A. Edison perfected the incandescent light bulb and later helped develop the movie projector, the phonograph, and the dictating machine. In 1892 Charles and Franklin Duryea produced the first motor car. Soon

the automobile industry would be revolutionalized by Henry Ford. And in December 1903 Orville and Wilbur Wright collaborated in their historic flight at Kitty G9
Hawk.

Nineteenth-century America was a period of tremendous economic and territorial expansion. Multimillionaires like John D. Rockefeller, Andrew Carnegie, and J. P. Morgan dominated American finance by building monopolies—exclusive ownership choking out competing industries—in oil, railroads, and steel. The Industrial Revolution also contributed to *imperialism*, a movement toward acquiring new colonies. After the Spanish-American War (1898), the United States annexed Hawaii and acquired the Spanish colonies of Cuba, Puerto Rico, Guam, and the Philippines. In 1900 America declared an Open Door policy in China that gave American ships equal trading rights with any other country in the Far East. Acquiring new territories extended the economic frontier (the limits of the economy) by providing sources for new markets, investments, and raw materials.

This period of rapid growth produced alarming extremes—enormous wealth and bitter proverty, great progress and intense misery. In 1892 the country had 4,000 millionaires and countless paupers. In that same year began a severe economic depression that would continue for the next four years. Cries for social reform were everywhere. Strikes, riots, and protest marches were common. In 1893 six hundred banks closed; fifteen thousand business firms failed. During 1893 about 1,500 people from Kelly's Industrial Army, a group of unemployed workers from California, arrived in Washington, D.C., to demand relief for the poor and the jobless. During 1894, 750,000 United States workers went on strike for higher wages and shorter hours.

By the summer of 1897 thousands of Americans had
G10 caught a fever that was spreading across the country. Gold had been discovered at the Klondike River in northwestern Canada, near the Alaskan border. By the following year 18,000 gold seekers were camped in the Klondike area. Many had used up their entire savings, sold all their possessions, and plunged into debt to finance the adventure. In all around 100,000 men and women made the trip. By the end of 1897 the Klondike field had yielded more than $22 million worth of gold. But most of the prospectors, like Jack London, returned home penniless, if they were lucky enough to come home alive.

What drove these men and women on this mad scramble for the pot of gold at the end of the rainbow, hundreds of miles to the frozen North? Pulling at them was the American dream itself, the unshakable belief that everyone had a right to a better way of life. With hard work, a little daring, and just a bit of luck, you could get rich—in fact, you *should* get rich!

This dream had lured adventurous people to America from the beginning. It was still doing so, for newcomers were arriving by the hundreds of thousands every year. And if the streets were not paved with gold, as many of the immigrants had been led to believe, then many would seek their elusive riches northward in the Canadian Klondike. The desperate attempt to escape poverty drove many families in search of gold. But also it was the dissatisfaction of people on the move, people prompted by a sense of optimism, restlessness, and adventure. This spirited determination to take risks, make sacrifices, and venture forth also caused many to immigrate to a strange new land, expand westward, build giant industries, and seek gold in the far North.

About this Book

Jack London remains one of the world's most popular writers. And *The Call of the Wild*, first published in 1903, made London a famous author almost overnight. Throughout his life he wrote over fifty books, yet *The Call of the Wild* has always been the best loved and most widely read. What is it that makes this book a favorite with readers of all ages? G11

First of all, there is Buck, the main character. He is a big lovable dog, half St. Bernard, half Scotch Shepherd. Most of the story is told from his point of view. That is, you see everything through Buck's eyes. You feel his sadness, his pain, and his rage as he is kidnapped from the sheltered warmth of fireside comforts and human companions only to be forced into a strange, frigid, and frightening world. You share his fear, and then his triumph, as he faces and overcomes the dangers of this new life. You share, too, the strange, haunting "memories" that this new life seems to bring to him of a world that existed long before he was born.

Therefore, the novel succeeds only to the degree you believe in its hero Buck, a dog who describes his *own* "thoughts" and "feelings" as if he were human. You may not know for certain how or even if a dog thinks and feels. But the author gets you to emphathize with a dog, sharing in his thoughts and feelings as if you were inside his character. Thus through the skill and imagination of Jack London's writing, you may experience Buck's responses to an alien and often cruel environment.

Buck's story takes place in a spellbinding setting—the stark, terrifying beauty of the land bordering the Arctic wilderness. The graphic description of time and place, the 1897 Klondike gold strikes, is written from the au-

thor's own experience. And Jack London never tires of portraying the flaming northern lights, the crystal land-
G12 scapes, the dancing stars, and the ghostly moonlit glaciers. He creates a setting that not only convinces you he has lived the life he is describing but also recreates the excitement so that you experience it along with him.

Intriguing, too, is the central idea, or theme of the book. It explores the fascinating question: How much have animals (and people) really changed from their "primordial state"—that is, from the way their ancestors looked and acted thousands of years ago? Could they ever return to that state? Chapter by chapter you can see Buck changing. His once ordinary teeth seem to lengthen into slashing fangs; his once fleshy soft body becomes tautly muscular. But more than that, it is Buck's personality—the way he thinks and acts—that changes.

Buck changes in order to survive. In his southland home he had been given food, shelter, and loving care in return for being obedient, gentle, honest, and fair. But to survive in the wild North, he must learn to be fierce instead of gentle, crafty instead of honest, and strong rather than fair. Once again, you see the story from Buck's point of view, and you see that at first he does not plan, or even want, these changes in himself. In order to survive against nature, Buck must drastically adapt himself to an indifferent and often cruel environment that gives him little food and no shelter; with brutal people who have no love; against other dogs who think gentleness is a sign of weakness.

The struggles for survival in *The Call of the Wild* are accentuated by the mad rush for gold. Without the prospect of discovered gold, Buck would never have been kidnapped and later sold to pull a dogsled in the Klondike.

The book's descriptions of life and death in the rugged

wilderness have captivated some and angered others. If this novel is, as some critics say, brutally bloodthirsty, it is also sometimes idealistic and sentimental. Nevertheless *G13*
most readers have been enticed by its portrayal of life at a time and place in which mostly the strong and the fit survived, when just staying alive was a daily battle, and life itself was a triumph.

Through these pages you yourself can explore the frozen frontier—where nature wears down an individual's endurance and threatens even the will to survive. This challenge of the wilderness has already called out irresistibly to Buck. Since then, the wilderness call has been heard millions of times by people around the world who have read Buck's story. You too may wish to yield to your own sleepy longings and heed the power of the primitive. Listen . . . now it is calling you.

CHAPTER NOTES AND QUESTIONS

Chapter 1

burmal Occurring in the winter.

ferine Savage; beastlike; having escaped domestication and become wild.

hydrophoby Mispronunciation for hydrophobia (rabies).

waxed Grew; increased.

weazened Wizened; withered; shriveled.

Barrens Barren Grounds: the tundra area of northwestern Canada.

Buck, half Scotch shepherd, half St. Bernard, is a proud, protective, and pampered pet on a California estate. But Buck's days of leisure in the sun are numbered. Danger lurks outside the garden gate.

1. The book opens with a four-line poem. It refers to the awakening of the sleeping animal instinct. How does the poem relate to what happens to Buck in Chapter 1? How does the chapter title, "Into the Primitive," refer to Buck?
2. Who is Manuel and what kind of person is he? Why do you think he kidnaps Buck?
3. In the story Buck has an unforgettable confrontation with the man in the red sweater. Buck "learned the lesson, and in all his life he never forgot it." What happens to Buck? What is it that Buck learns?
4. Briefly describe the *setting*, or physical surroundings, at the start and at the end of Chapter 1. List at least three ways in which the two differ.
5. One of the more striking elements of the book is the *point of view;* that is, the reader sees everything through Buck's eyes. At the end of the chapter, Buck experiences snow for the first time. Describe his reactions.

Chapter 2

primordial Primitive; existing at the very beginning.

retrogression A going back; returning to a lower or less developed state.

unmolested Untouched; undistrubed.

Already "flung into the heart of things primordial," Buck has painfully learned the law of the club—a dog must submit to a man with a club. Now from the other dogs, Buck will soon discover the law of the fang. He must fight back. There is no place to hide.

1. In Chapter 2 Buck furthers his instruction in primitive survival. Five important incidents occur. Choose any three events and explain what he learns from each one: (a) from Curly's death, (b) from pulling the sled, (c) from approaching Sol-leks, (d) from Billee's insulation against the nighttime cold, (e) from Pike's remedy for hunger.
2. In this chapter what does Spitz do that makes Buck hate him?
3. How do the personalities of Billee and Joe differ?

Chapter 3

rove To join with a slight twist, forming a loose rope.

paradox Contradiction.

aurora borealis The northern lights; patches and streamers of colored lights appearing most clearly from the Arctic skies.

quarter Mercy shown a defeated opponent.

inexorable Relentless; unstoppable.

When it is kill or be killed, there is only one choice. The clash between Buck and Spitz was just a matter of time.

1. Why is the title, "The Dominant Primordial Beast," a good one for this chapter? To whom or to what does it refer?
2. Twice Spitz attacks when Buck is exhausted. Describe these two incidents. What do these actions reveal

about the character of Spitz?

3. What does Buck do that enables him to kill Spitz?
G16 What does Buck's victory over Spitz show about the transformation in Buck's character?

Chapter 4

trace Harness strap.

lugubriously Mournfully.

fly A piece of canvas extending over the ridge pole of a tent, forming an outer roof.

Buck has proved himself as a masterful sled dog—or has he? Dave gives him an example of what might happen to a dog who stays in the traces too long.

1. When Perrault starts to harness up the dogs in the morning, what does Buck do? How do Buck's actions here show that he has become more sophisticated in the face of the law of the club?
2. In Skagway, Alaska, François and Perrault have "passed out of Buck's life for good." Why? Who takes their place?
3. What does the new Scottish master finally do with Dave? Do you think what he does is right? Why or why not?

Chapter 5

salient Noticeable; outstanding; prominent.

callowness Inexperience; lack of adult sophistication.

Pullman Luxurious railway sleeping coaches created by

George Pullman. Hardy Alaskans thought traveling in Pullman cars was strictly for posh "tenderfeet."

impeachment Serious accusations discrediting someone's motives or conduct.

Q. E. D. Latin abbreviation for *quod erat demonstrandum* (which was to be proved).

Footsore and bone-tired, the dogs think they can endure no more. But they have yet to meet their new masters. To a team of dogs in the icy wilderness, inexperienced masters are more dangerous than cruel ones.

1. Charles and Hal already have eight dogs; later they buy six Outside dogs—fourteen in all. They calculate the days and miles and then figure out the food needed for the dogs and humans. What is wrong with their calculations?
2. Why do you think these three people fail to adapt to their new environment? How are they similar to Buck? How do they differ from Buck?
3. Even though Buck is being beaten with the club, why has he "made up his mind not to get up"?
4. Why does John Thorton become so enraged at Hal? What does Thornton do?

Chapter 6

haw; gee; mush Commands for animals to go to the left, to the right, or straight ahead.

miners' meeting A quick citizens' meeting to conduct trials or settle disputes in the absence of full-time courts.

Eldorado Saloon Bar named after Eldorado, a legendary city of gold and great riches sought by early explorers in South America.

G18 **Bonanza King** One who had made a fortune at Bonanza Creek in one of the early gold mine strikes.

In the cruel Northland, Buck has learned to put his own needs first. Strange, then, that he also learns love and loyalty of a kind he has never known before. Now this love and loyalty will be put to the extreme test.

1. Although Buck has become part of Thornton's family, what specific signs show that Buck is still heeding the ways of the primitive?
2. In four incidents Buck proves his love for John Thornton. Which incident demands the greatest sacrifice from Buck? Why, do you think, is Buck so devoted to Thornton?
3. Being caring and sensitive does not prevent Thornton from functioning well in the harsh wilderness. Which of Thornton's actions show that he can adapt to life in the wilds?

Chapter 7

unwonted Rare; unusual; uncommon.

time-graven Carved or engraved by time.

placer A place where gold dust and nuggets are mixed with loose sand and gravel.

excrescence An abnormal outgrowth or enlargement.

sluice boxes Long sloping troughs with flowing water used to wash gold from sand or gravel.

Only Buck's love for John Thornton ties him to the civilized life he once knew. If that tie is broken, the Northland's claim on him will be complete.

G19

1. What are Thornton and his partners looking for on their trip? What finally happens to them?
2. How does Buck communicate to the timber wolf that Buck's intentions are friendly?
3. Why does Buck kill the Yeehat Indians? How do you feel about what Buck does?
4. After Buck leads the wolf pack, a new breed of wolf evolves. It is a larger-than-usual wolf with a brown muzzle and white patches on its chest. What does this description suggest?

AFTER YOU READ

Fact Quiz

Read each statement below. If it is true, write *true*. If the statement is false, rewrite it to make it true.

1. Buck welcomed the opportunity to leave Judge Miller's estate.
2. François and Perrault were couriers for the United States government in Canada.
3. The dogs Billee and Joe were ferocious fighters.
4. Dave was a fair and wise dog who nipped at Buck when he delayed the sled's starting.
5. Whenever the sled broke through the ice, Perrault had to stop and build a fire.
6. The dog Dolly had to be killed because she suddenly went mad.
7. At night François massaged Buck's tender feet and even made little moccasins for them.

8. Spitz was an even greater dog team leader than Buck.
9. François wept when he left Buck for the last time.

G20 10. When Buck dreamed by the campfire, he never once thought of Judge Miller's estate.

11. The dog Dave died of exhaustion while in the harness.
12. Buck was willing to jump off the edge of a cliff at Thornton's command.
13. Buck stalked and killed a thousand-pound bull moose.
14. Buck killed four wolves from the pack before they accepted him as a member of their pack.
15. Whenever the Yeehat Indians referred to Buck, they told of a legendary Ghost Dog who robbed traps, slayed dogs, and even defied their bravest hunters.

Answer each question below.

16. What did Buck learn from Judge Miller?
17. Besides a person carrying a club, what else did Buck learn to fear?
18. Why was it inevitable that Buck and Spitz would have a fight to the death?
19. In what ways did Judge Miller and John Thornton differ as masters to Buck?
20. What did Buck learn from François and Perrault?

Interpreting the Book

1. In Chapter 1 the man in the red sweater taught Buck the savage lesson of the wilderness. The color red is a *symbol.* A symbol is something that stands for or represents another idea. For example, the color blue might represent or symbolize innocence. A lion might symbolize pride and power. In Chapter 1 what do

you think the color red symbolized? Explain.

2. Why do you think the dog Curly was destroyed?
3. In Chapter 2 the hungry Buck stole food from the pro- *G21* visions of François and Perrault. In what way did this act represent a dramatic change in Buck's personality?
4. Buck dreamed of beastlike men covered with hair. What did these visions mean? Why did Buck have these dreams?
5. What do you consider the two most important lessons that Buck learned about getting along in the Northland? Did these lessons involve getting along with nature? With people? With other dogs? Or did these lessons deal with Buck's discoveries about his own character?
6. At the end of the fight scene between Buck and Spitz, Jack London wrote, "The dark circle became a dot . . . as Buck disappeared from view." What did the author mean? Describe what happened.
7. Why do you suppose Jack London had neither Buck nor Thornton utter any feelings of sympathy after Charles, Hal, and Mercedes plunged through the ice to their death?
8. Do you think the author approved or disapproved of the complete change Buck has undergone? Give reasons for your answer.
9. Why do you think Dave so desperately wanted to remain in harness, even though it would have meant dying in the traces of the sled?
10. The title of the last chapter, "The Sounding of the Call," carries the theme, the message or main idea, of the novel. What do you think the Call means to Buck? What in your opinion does the Call mean to those pursuing gold far in the frozen North?

Personal Reactions

G22 **1.** Of all the animal and human characters—excluding Buck and Thornton—whom do you like the most? Whom do you like the least? Why?

2. Thornton and Buck shared a mutual kindness, affection, and respect. But some people believe it is impossible for a dog to feel a "human" emotion like love. Do you think it is possible for a dog and its owner to love each other? Explain.

3. By the end of the story, Buck was completely transformed. What has he lost? What has he gained? Which way do you think Buck was better off, before or after?

4. Do you believe as Jack London did that there is a "call of the wild," a primitive instinct, in animals? In human beings?

Critical Interpretations

The two excerpts below both deal with Jack London's novel *The Call of the Wild.* The first quotation deals with the theme, or main idea, of the book. The second quotation deals with some of the strengths and weaknesses of the book.

> *The Call of the Wild* was written as a demonstration of the conflict between the savage cruelty of so-called civilization and the liberty of wild life in nature.
>
> —Arthur Calder-Marshall

1. Read the above quotation. Do you agree that the novel shows the savage cruelty of civilization *vs.* the liberty of the wilderness? Or does the book more accurately show the liberty of civilization vs. the savage cruelty of the wilderness? Explain your answer, using G23 examples from the book.

> The love of Buck, the dog, for John Thornton, who saves him from an ignorant master who was driving his dogs beyond endurance, is quite natural. But London endows Buck with human qualities which no dog has shown. . . . The best scenes are those in which Buck fights for the supremacy of the pack, or in which he revenges himself upon the Yeehat Indians who have killed Thornton. Here Buck follows his instincts. But in the description of the dog's motives, London is often absurd.
>
> —Arthur Hobson Quinn

2. What do you think of London's portrayal of Buck? In what ways was it realistic? In what ways was it unrealistic?
3. What do you like most about *The Call of the Wild?* What do you like least? Briefly give reasons for each.

Be a Writer

A. A good author makes his story seem real by including many convincing details. In Chapter 1, paragraphs two, three, and four include many details—stables, servants' cottages, orchards, kennels, library, fountain—that convince you of the wealth and luxury of Judge Miller's estate. These details make you believe the author has actually been there and knows what he's talking about.

Think of a place that is special to you. Then write a

paragraph describing it so that even a stranger could form a picture of it. Include some things you have observed that others may never have noticed. Use vivid, convincing details.

B. When an author reveals what a person in a particular story is like, that technique is called *characterization.* Sometimes the author will suggest to the reader what that person is like on the inside by describing how he or she looks on the outside.

In Chapter 5, paragraph five, Jack London characterizes, or shows the character of, Charles and Hal simply by focusing on details of their appearance. The author describes Charles's "watery eyes," "twisted" mustache, and "limply drooping lip." London describes Hal's revolver and knife conspicuously strapped to his belt, a belt that broadcasts Hal's obvious inexperience in the wilds. In short, they looked as out of place in the wilds as they actually were.

Using details of dress, manner, and appearance, briefly describe any two people. They can be real or imaginary. Be sure to choose details that will suggest their personalities.

Special Projects

A. Imagine you are a movie director. Then from *The Call of the Wild,* choose a scene that you would like to film. Be sure to state who is in the scene, where they are, and what happens. You might also want to include specific directions for the shooting script, such as fade out, close up, music interlude.

B. Plan an advertisement campaign to promote the book. Create a poster, a book jacket, or a magazine ad. Whatever your choice, make sure it has an eye- *G25* catching illustration. Briefly identify the main elements of the book: title, author, main character, time, setting. Also your ad should include a one- or two-sentence description that will make a reader want to rush out to buy a copy of the book.

C. Write a diary based on one important scene or on a few days' events from the novel. Describe it as if you were one of these characters:

1. Buck
2. Spitz
3. François or Perrault
4. Mercedes
5. Hal
6. John Thornton

D. The Klondike gold rush of 1897–98 drew thousands of people from the world over. Seeking adventure and riches, the men and women pitted their strength and skills against the icy wilderness. From this northward movement came human records of misery, wealth, heroism, violence, and death. This was the stuff of which legends were made.

To find out more about this fascinating subject, read some firsthand accounts of the gold rush. Check the card catalog to locate a library book on the Klondike gold rush. Here are three highly recommended books: *The Klondike Stampede of 1897–98*, by Edwin T. Adney; *The Klondike Fever: The Life and Death of the Last Great Gold Rush*, by Pierre Berton; or *Klondike Ninety Eight: E. A. Hegg's Gold Rush Album*, by Ethel A. Becker.

Choose your favorite episode from one of these books. Then briefly summarize it in your own words.

G26 About the Story

kibosh Something that checks or stops an activity.
savvy Common sense or practical know-how.
magazine Holder on a gun for cartridges to be fed into the gun chamber.

You probably would not think that lifelong friends could split up over a dog. Then again, you probably never met the likes of that darned Spot.

Getting the Facts

1. A long, drawn-out tale that relies on exaggeration for its humor is often called a "shaggy-dog story." "That Spot" is this kind of story. Find and quote three examples of humorous exaggeration.
2. (a) Describe Spot's looks. Give details. (b) Describe Spot's personality. Give examples.
3. "He [Spot] could do everything but work." Explain.

Interpreting the Story

1. The main character is narrating, or telling the story about, what has already happened to him. Why does the narrator call Stephen Mackaye "the meanest man I ever knew"?
2. Why do the narrator and his friend both fail in killing Spot?

3. Why do you think Spot keeps coming back?
4. If you were the narrator or his friend Stephen Mackaye, how would you deal with Spot? Be specific. Tell why. G27

IN YEDDO BAY

About the Story

Yeddo The original name for Tokyo. It was based on the name Edo, the name of a powerful family who lived there about 1180.

yen A unit of money in Japan; one yen equals one hundred sen.

sen A Japanese coin. Around 1900 ten sen were worth about six cents in American money.

sealing schooner A schooner for hunting seals. It has two or more masts and fore-and-aft (front-and-back) sails.

kowtowing Kneeling and bowing to show great respect and obedience.

sampan A small boat common in Japan and China. It usually has one or two oars in the back, a single sail, and a cabin covered with mats.

forecastlehead *or* **fo′c′slehead** (for′ kas əl hed *or* fok′ səl hed) Part of the forecastle closest to the bow (front) of a ship. The forecastle is the sailors' sleeping quarters at the ship's bow.

bully Excellent or first rate; a common expression in the early 1900s.

In a crowded city near Tokyo, a sixteen-year-old boy
becomes an easy target for pickpockets. Broke and stran-
G28 ded in a strange setting, he desperately wants to return to
his sealing schooner. But how can someone be marooned
with people and ships all around? Well, Alf is—and only
pride and lack of money stand in his way.

Getting the Facts

1. At the beginning of the story what might Alf have done to keep from having his hip purse stolen?
2. Describe the restaurant owner's behavior before, and then after, Ralph finds the money to pay him. What causes the change in the owner's behavior?
3. When Alf asks for help, what do the harbor police do for him? What do they tell him? How does Alf finally get his clothes returned to him?

Interpreting the Story

1. Why does Alf refuse to sell his shirt to the boatman, or to sleep out the night on the shore?
2. The author tells us that 10 sen were worth about 6 cents in American money. Figuring that a penny then is worth at least 10 cents in today's money, the boat ride cost about 60 cents. How much did Alf's meal cost, in today's money? How much did he lose at the beginning of the story? (1 yen = 100 sen.)
3. The next time Alf goes ashore, the boatman refuses to take his money. Why?
4. What does London think of Alf's behavior? What do

you think of Alf's behavior? In both cases tell why.

5. Suppose you were in a restaurant and suddenly discovered that you did not have enough money to pay for the meal you had just eaten. What would you do? G29

AN ADVENTURE IN THE UPPER SEA

About the Story

aeronaut A pilot of an airship or balloon.

guys Ropes or wires used to steady and hold down an object, in this case a balloon.

funk Fear or panic.

fetching up Stopping; halting.

During the late 1800s balloonists like Charlie often performed at country fairs and parks. But throughout his career as an aeronaut, never before had Charley experienced such a shock. One thousand feet above ground, and suddenly—a child crying out *above* him!

Getting the Facts

1. What makes the balloon go up? What makes it finally come down again?
2. What does Charley do to keep Tommy from letting go and falling? Give some specific examples.
3. At the end of the story Charley compares this experience to some other frightening events that have happened to him before. What are they?

Interpreting the Story

G30 1. Why is everyone so quiet when the balloon takes off?
2. What would have happened if Charley had used his parachute? Explain why.
3. "I remembered how one fright could destroy another fright." What does Charley mean by this comment? How does he put it to use to help Tommy?

CHARLEY'S COUP

About the Story

coup A sudden, highly successful action or move.

Waterloo A reference to Napoleon's defeat at the Battle of Waterloo, hence any decisive or disastrous defeat.

centerboard A long retractable board lowered into the water beneath the boat. It keeps the boat moving straight ahead, instead of sliding sideways in heavy winds.

scow A large flat-bottomed boat with square ends, used mainly for transporting freight.

wing and wing With sails extended on both sides, like wings, while sailing downwind.

up-river sailing craft Boats sailing upriver *against* the current.

heave to into the wind Come to a stop by circling around so that the wind acts as a break.

broached to Turned sideways to the wind.

jibed Shifted the sails to the other side of the ship.

caught us on our beam Hit us on the side of our boat.

G31

Three men from the California fish patrol are no match for twenty treacherous salmon pirates—yet Charley thinks so, since the fish patrol can cut the pirates' illegally cast nets. But what happens when the three pursuers become the pursued?

Getting the Facts

1. This story is made up of a string of problems that Charley has to solve. His first plan to outwit the salmon pirates fails. What is the plan and what goes wrong with it?
2. What do Charley and his friends on the schooner do to protect themselves when the fishermen start shooting at them?
3. The fishermen try to pull themselves close enough to the schooner to board it. How does Charley stop them?
4. How do Charley and his friends get the message for help to the sheriff at Merryweather?
5. At the end of the story Charley says, "Why, we were never in danger." Explain what he means.

Interpreting the Story

1. How old do you think the narrator of this story is? What clues do you have about his age?
2. By fishing on Sundays, the fishermen are "killing the goose that laid the golden egg." Explain.

3. "But we can't stop," Charley groaned. Explain what would have happened if they had stopped.

G32 4. Ole says, "Der river will not hold out, and then . . ." What does he mean? What is happening to the river?

ALL GOLD CANYON

About the Story

scoff Eat heartily, chiefly British slang.

royal coachman A type of artificial fly used primarily in fishing for trout and salmon.

cayuse A range horse descended from the wild horses of the American Northwest.

nor found time for rough discourtesy And did not disturb or bother each other.

the stream grown garrulous The stream having started gurgling (become talkative).

wind-flows Ripples across the lake's surface.

Boswell James Boswell, eighteenth-century Scottish lawyer and biographer whose great biography of Dr. Samuel Johnson is a detailed record of Johnson's travels, conversations, and actions. Hence, a Boswell pays tribute to someone else by narrating that person's words and actions.

placer-mine A mixture of gold, or particles of other valuable minerals, and gravel, dirt, pebbles, mud. Refining is done by washing out the debris to leave the metal.

Sardanopolis Misspelling of Sardanapalus, the Greek name for Ashurbanipal, the legendary last king of the

Assyrian empire, around 820 B.C. He was noted for his luxuriously sensual life style.

booful Distortion of the word *beautiful.* The mispronunciation shows the speaker's lack of education.

Hottentot A tribe of pastoral people from Cape of Good Hope, South Africa. Sometimes they are wrongly confused with the South African Bushmen.

The heart of the green canyon lies sheltered and undisturbed. But a fierce gold prospector shatters the silence of the pine-bordered foothills. Beware! Wherever human greed dwells, the threat of violence soon will follow.

Getting the Facts

1. How does Bill trace down the pocket of gold in the hillside? Where are the test pans richest? Where are they poorest?
2. The closer Bill gets to the pocket, the more excited and absorbed in his work he becomes. How does the story reveal this fact? Explain what he does and what he forgets to do.
3. The author provides a detailed description of Bill being shot. Describe what he hears, then what he feels, and then what he does.

Interpreting the Story

1. The first seven paragraphs describe the canyon. Then "the spirit of the place fled away on the heels of the red-coated buck." Describe "the spirit of the place." What comes along to disrupt it?

2. While panning for gold, why is Bill happy to see the number of gold specks getting smaller as he goes G34 downstream?
3. Why does Bill blacken his gold pan in the fire?
4. Reread the last paragraph of the story. What happens to the canyon? What is the author saying here about the individual's effect upon nature? Explain.

TO BUILD A FIRE

About the Story

salt water Seawater; the ocean.

intangible pall A vague gloom. A pall is a black cloth placed over a coffin. Intangible means something that cannot be touched.

creature of temperature A warm-blooded organism, such as a human being. Human beings have a relatively high and constant body temperature that is internally regulated; their body temperatures do not adapt well to the external extremes of heat and cold. Thus "creatures of temperature" are at nature's mercy.

brute An animal, especially a creature of below-human intelligence.

spirit thermometer A thermometer that contains alcohol.

high-water flotsam Driftwood or any kind of debris washed ashore at the water's highest point.

the wires were down The person's nerves were numb; they carried no messages (like telephone or telegraph lines that are knocked down).

He had been warned by the old timer of the Yukon, a weather-wizened survivor of many blistering winters: A lone human being cannot survive in seventy-five degrees G35 below zero—one hundred seven degrees below the point of freezing. But he had intelligence, he thought. He and the dog would show them.

Getting the Facts

1. What are the main mistakes the man makes?
2. It is so cold that the man's spittle freezes even before it hits the ground, and yet he steps into a pool of unfrozen water. Where does the water come from? Describe or quote three other details that make you *feel* the cold.
3. Describe what happens to the fire the man builds under the spruce tree. Give details about how and why it happens.
4. The story describes several steps in the process of freezing to death. Pain is just the first and least serious step. What happens after that?
5. "There was no sun nor hint of sun, though there was not a cloud in the sky." Why is this? Where is the sun?

Interpreting the Story

1. The man has his good points and bad points. Do you think he is brave or just reckless? Skillful or blundering? Wise or foolish? In which ways would you like to be like him? Which of his faults would you want to avoid?
2. "He stamped up and down until the stinging returned

into his feet." Why does he want the stinging to return?

G36 3. Almost no background information is given about "the man," who even remains nameless. He ignores the old-timer's advice about traveling when colder than fifty below. Why? What do you think motivates him to make this dangerously difficult trip?

4. The man drowses off into "the most comfortable and satisfying sleep he had ever known." What is really happening?

5. Based on this story what do you think is the author's view of nature? How do the man and the dog differ in the face of the dangerous cold? What enables the dog to survive?

LOVE OF LIFE

About the Story

ague A malarial fever with chills and sweating.
vouchsafed Granted; conceded; bestowed.
lazaret A space in between a ship's decks.

Alone, injured, lost in a desolate land—how long can a man survive? How long will he even want to survive?

Getting the Facts

1. Early in the story, the man is faced with a number of very serious problems. Describe at least three of them. What does he do to try to overcome them?
2. The first time the author mentions the moose-hide

sack, he does not tell you what's in it. But he gives you several clues. What are some of these clues?

3. Why does the main character's friend Bill, desert him? What eventually happens to Bill? G37

Interpreting the Story

1. The man is panic-stricken about the number of matches he has left. If you were lost in the wilderness, what might you need a fire for? List all the uses you can think of.
2. Both men in the story carry a moose-hide sack. Bill keeps his to the very end. What does this fact tell you about him? The main character leaves his moose-hide sack behind, yet he hoards something else. What is it? What does this action by the main character tell us about people's dreams of wealth and glory?
3. Toward the end of the story how does the man finally kill the sick wolf? What does he do with it then? If the wolf had killed the man, how would it have accomplished this feat? Describe some ways in which the man and the wolf are similar.
4. The story title reveals the theme, or main idea, of the story. Explain the significance of the title in terms of the main character.

☆★☆

Be a Writer

A. In the story "That Spot," when the dog returns to his owners, London compares Spot to a storm: "I was

just sitting up in the blankets and laughing when a *tornado* hit camp." This is an example of a *meta-*
G38 *phor*–comparing two things without using like or as. Make up five metaphors of your own. Here are a few to get you started: she's a firecracker; he has the intelligence of a brick; the car made a jackrabbit start.

B. In the story "In Yeddo Bay" the author suggests that Americans thought the Japanese were "puzzling." What do you think the Japanese thought of the Americans? Write a dialogue in which the restaurant owner and the waiter talk about Alf and the "trick" they thought he tried to pull on them.

C. "An Adventure in the Upper Sea" seems very real because it includes many vivid details about the swift motion of the balloon, the bumpy air currents, the way the earth looks from far above, and so on.

Using this type of realistic description, write this same story from Tommy's point of view. Have him tell why he wants to ride on the balloon, what it feels like as it takes off, what he sees, and how scared he is. Show the thoughts and feelings as if you yourself were Tommy.

D. In "Love of Life" Jack London describes the strange setting in which the main character happens to find himself. Notice how the physical description of the place also suggests the man's feelings of confusion and desolation.

> He crawled up a small knoll and surveyed the prospect. There were no trees, no bushes, nothing but a gray sea of mass scarcely diversified by gray rocks, gray lakelets, and gray streamlets. The sky was gray. There was no sun nor hint of sun. He had no idea of north, and he had forgotten the way he had come to

this spot the night before. But he was not lost. He knew that.

Notice that the author's technique of stating what was *not* in the scene emphasizes the feeling of emptiness. Note also how the repetition of the color gray adds to the mood of being uncertain and disoriented.

Now think of a place that you know well. Then, using some of these techniques, describe it accurately. Be sure to use specific details. Carefully choose the color or colors of certain objects in order to create a certain mood. Try to make your description of the place as convincing as if you were describing an actual character.

Special Projects

A. Using "That Spot," write out a possible conversation that might occur between the two former friends if they were to meet again.

B. Based on "An Adventure in the Upper Sea," do some library research on the history of ballooning, such as early hot-air balloons, hydrogen and helium dirigibles, or modern hot-air sport balloons.

C. From "Charlie's Coup," plan your own promotional campaign to recruit fish patrollers to catch illegal salmon pirates. Think of some gimmick–adventure, prestige, community responsibility–that would attract prospective fish patrollers. Choose a project from number 1 or 2 below.

1. Write a television or radio commercial. Rehearse your commercial before acting it out. Then, if possible, tape-record or videotape it for playback to your class.

G40 **2.** Create a poster, a window banner, or a magazine ad. Make an ad that will appeal to your intended audience.

D. Tape-record or write out an interview with the main character from either "All Gold Canyon" or from "Love of Life." Ask leading questions dealing with the character's thoughts, feelings, and experiences.

Further Reading

Other Works by Jack London

The Bodley Head Jack London, vol. 1–4, edited and introduced by Arthur Calder-Marshall. Four books of London's adventures: stories of the Klondike and the South Seas, as well as a few of his novels.

Burning Daylight. Heroic adventures of Elam Harnish in the Klondike and the California frontier.

The Cruise of the Dazzler. An easy-to-read novel about a stowaway boy and the Frisco Kid aboard a sloop on a Pacific cruise.

Martin Eden. Often considered London's finest novel: autobiographical fiction about the dreams and sacrifices of a young man struggling to become a great writer.

The Sea-Wolf. A novel about the brutal sea adventures of the unforgettable and domineering hero, Wolf Larsen.

The Star Rover. London's last novel, the story of an ex-convict's ability to endure the brutalities of prison life.

White Fang. The story of the wild wolf White Fang whose incredible journey begins in the heartless wilderness of the icy North.

Works About Jack London

Calder-Marshall, Arthur. *Lone Wolf: The Story of Jack London.* A short, simple, and balanced rendering of London's chaotic life.

Jack London Newsletter. A periodical of critical essays, book reviews, bibliographies, and personal reminiscences on London and his writings.

Labor, Earle. *Jack London.* An indispensable guide to the man and his writings by a noteworthy London scholar.

London, Joan. *Jack London and His Times.* Well-organized work by London's daughter, dealing with the times in which the author lived.

Stone, Irving. *Sailor on Horseback.* Exciting and popular "biographical novel" that provides much drama yet fictionalizes parts of Jack London's life.

Walker, Franklin. *Jack London and the Klondike: The Genesis of an American Writer.* Well-written treatment of London's Klondike writings and adventures.

Audiovisual Resources

Records and Cassettes

The Call of the Wild—Begley. Caedmon. Record, cassette.

To Build a Fire—Toppo. C M S. Record, cassette.

*Films (16mm)**

All Gold Canyon. Weston Woods Studios. 21 min, color. Illustrates the short story.

The Call of the Wild. 20th Century-Fox; Films, Inc. 78 min, b/w. Clark Gable and Loretta Young star in film based on book.

Jack London—To Build a Fire. Robert Stitzel; B F A Educational Media. 15 min, color. Adapted from the short story.

To Build a Fire. Montana State University. 20 min, b/w. Based on the short story.

G42

*Filmstrips (35mm)**

Call of the Wild. Brunswick; Educational Record Sales. Filmstrip with captions, 56 frames, color.

Call of the Wild. Listening Library; Educational Record Sales. 2 filmstrips, 60 frames each, color; 2 cassettes; study guide; illustrated manual.

Call of the Wild. Filmfax Productions; Current Affairs. 56 frames, color; cassette; teacher's guide; test. Reading incentive program provides open-ended story; reviews plot, setting, character, and themes. Audience level: slow, intermediate, and gifted, for junior high through senior high students.

Jack London: A Life of Adventure—Parts 1 and 2. Guidance Association A/V Subsidiary. Filmstrips with records/cassettes; Part 1, 93 frames; Part 2, 83 frames; color. Personal portrait of London, the man and his works.

* When two sources are listed, the first is the producer and the second is the distributor. To locate addresses of producers and distributors, use the *Index to 16mm Educational Films* and the *Index to 35mm Educational Filmstrips,* both published by the National Information Center of Educational Media at the University of Southern California. An alternate source of addresses is *Audiovisual Market Place,* published by R. R. Bowker Company. The *Educational Film Locator,* also published by Bowker, lists university libraries that are film rental centers. In addition, many of these audiovisual materials may be available through your local library.

2 3 4 5 6 7 8 9 10 11 12 13 14 15–KP–90 89 88 87 86 85 84 83 82